Cast of Characters

Clifford Flush. President of the Asterisk Club, aka the Balliol Butcher.

Mrs. Naomi Barratt. An elderly self-made widow, also an Asterisk.

Colonel Quincey. Treasurer of the Asterisk Club, a spruce, red-faced old man with a white mustache.

Lilli Cluj. An Hungarian temptress, also a self-created widow. Before she became an Asterisk she enjoyed playing bumper cars.

The Creaker. An enormous misshapen man of sixty, so called because of his squeaky wooden leg. He frightens even his fellow Ast

Benjamin "Benji" Cann. Newly acquitted of   ess, he's been invited to join the Asterisks.

Beecher. Jailed 14 times for houseb   butler to the Asterisks, who never hire murc

Squires. Beecher's assistant, too law-ab   t in with the Asterisks.

Fan Hilford. An artist who lives at 15 Flood Walk.

Peter Hilford. Fan's husband, a photographer and detective novelist.

Bertha Berko. A weaver.

Hugo Berko. Her husband. They share the house with the Hilfords.

Marleen. Their servant, of a perpetually amorous bent.

Rex. Fan's friend, a muscular and ebullient ballet dancer.

Bunny. Strong drink and cross-dressing are his undoing.

Alfred L. Beesum. A retired Rodent Officer who takes his work very seriously.

Sidney Crick. A man in a bowler hat.

Tom. The Creaker's enormous, molting, asthmatic ginger cat.

Croydon. Bertha's temperamental miniature poodle.

Books by Pamela Branch

The Wooden Overcoat (1951)
Published in the U.S. by
The Rue Morgue Press
January 2006

The Lion in the Cellar (1951)
To be published in the U.S. by
The Rue Morgue Press
February 2006

Murder Every Monday (1954)
To be published in the U.S. by
The Rue Morgue Press
April 2006

Murder's Little Sister (1958)
To be published in the U.S. by
The Rue Morgue Press
June 2006

The Wooden Overcoat

By Pamela Branch

Introduction by
Tom & Enid Schantz

The Rue Morgue Press
Lyons / Boulder

Introduction
Pamela Branch
"The funniest lady"

Pamela Branch was "the funniest lady you ever knew," according to fellow mystery writer Christianna Brand. Brand was referring not only to her books but to Branch herself, who delighted Brand by sending her countless "postcards with smears of pretence blood on them, purporting to be from her various characters," or "a dreadful squashed box of chocolates with very obvious pinholes into which poison had clearly been injected." That wicked sense of humor permeated Branch's four mysteries as well, leading contemporary reviewers to describe her first book, *The Wooden Overcoat*, as a "delightfully ghoulish souffle" (*The Spectator*) where "even the bodies manage to be ghoulishly diverting" (*The Sunday Times*) graced with "the gayest prose" and a "gloriously gruesome" touch (*The Queen*). *The Spectator* welcomed her second book, *The Lion in the Cellar*, as a "charnel-house frolic." Nancy Spain, to whom Branch was favorably compared, called it a "masterpiece," a blend of "the Marx Brothers, Crazy Gang and the Little Intimate Reviews." *The Times Literary Supplement* strayed from the mystery field to compare her third book, *Murder Every Monday*, to satirist Evelyn Waugh. Her fourth and final book, *Murder's Little Sister*, was published in 1958 and was the only title to see publication in the United States. American mystery writer Carolyn Hart listed it among her five favorite mysteries of all time. It was reissued in 1988 in England as part of Pandora's Classic Women Crime Writers series after twenty-five years of being out of print. In spite of these extravagant reviews, Branch is rarely mentioned in any of the standard reference books devoted to the mystery genre, perhaps because her career was cut short by cancer at the age of 47.

Nor does anyone have any idea what happened to her fifth book. In

1962, her paperback publisher reported that she had begun the book in the Scottish Highlands and was finishing it in Ghana, West Africa. She would not die for another five years, so either her illness prevented her from finishing the book or she encountered a major writer's block. Or maybe Branch or an editor didn't feel it was up to her earlier books. No one knows because she appears to have left no estate behind. Since she died so long ago, even the literary agency which holds her copyrights no longer knows what happened.

Why she isn't better known among the historians of mystery fiction is perhaps even stranger. She rates an entry in the third edition of *Twentieth Century Crime and Mystery Writers* but is dropped from the fourth edition, retitled *The St. James Guide to Crime and Mystery Writers*. Critic Gillian Rodgerson summed up Branch's writing by saying: "The humor in Branch's books lies in the situations, the outrageous characters and in the dialog which almost makes sense but not quite. This is life viewed through a fun-house distorting mirror where the ordinary suddenly becomes bizarre and then ordinary again." Rodgerson admits that the situations, as in *The Wooden Overcoat,* make for "a very silly book but the writing is seamless and witty and the denouement makes it all worthwhile." It's a fair judgment, though Branch's books are no more silly than those of P.G. Wodehouse or Sarah Caudwell.

Some critics were not enthralled with the idea of introducing humor into crime fiction. English critic Sutherland Scott admitted in his 1953 study of the genre, *Blood in Their Ink,* that writers such as Phoebe Atwood Taylor (aka Alice Tilton) and Constance and Gwenyth Little "serve up a sparkling cocktail" but he questioned if the idea of "mixing hectic humor and even more hectic homicide is entirely to be recommended." Taylor and the Littles were American writers who were very popular in Britain. He was somewhat alarmed that British writers might follow suit in turning chills to laughs. "It is interesting to note that the most recent addition to the mix-your-murder-with-plenty-of-fun brigade is also a lady, this time a home product. If you can digest this kind of hot-pot, Pamela Branch's T*he Wooden Overcoat* and *The Lion in the Cella*r should be to your taste. Some digestive systems may tend to rebel."

While Scott merely comes off as being more stuffy than perceptive, it has to be admitted that humor is subjective. Yet, other English writers were known to go for a laugh. There's more than a touch of the absurd in many of the books by Edmund Crispin (*The Moving Toyshop,* 1946) or Michael Innes (*Appleby's End,* 1945). Branch's humor, of course, was a bit blacker ("ghoulish" in an adjective often pops up in her reviews) that either of those two gentlemen. Though a bit more farcical and madcap,

Branch may also remind some readers of Richard Hull (1896-1973) who plumbed the darker side of humor in his crime novels, most notably in *The Murder of My Aunt* (1934), a book whose marvelous title can—and should—be read with two vastly different interpretations, or in *My Own Murderer* (1940) wherein a staid Londoner's lifestyle changes when he comes across a murderer in his apartment and decides to hold him captive rather than turn him over to the police. Anthony Rolls's homicidal minister in *The Vicar's Experiment* (aka *Clerical Error*, 1932) would be perfectly at home in Branch's world. Her brand of madcap black humor was also present in many of the British film comedies of the 1950s, especially in such Alec Guinness vehicles as *Kind Hearts and Coronets*.

While these British films fared well in the U.S. during this period, American publishers didn't believe that readers on this side of the Atlantic would embrace Branch's books. Of course, one has to remember that the early 1950s was seeing a change in direction among publishers, who were pulling away from the traditional mystery so popular before World War II and replacing it with action thrillers by the likes of Mickey Spillane and John D. MacDonald. The 1970s and 1980s saw a rebirth of the comic traditional mystery. The blackest of these were the biting satirical novels of English writer Robert Barnard, whose *Death of an Old Goat* (1974) and *Death by Sheer Torture* (1981) remind one of a less frenetic Branch. Even closer in tone to Branch are the recent "subversively funny" (*New York Times*) novels of another English writer, Ruth Dudley Edwards.

Biographical material on Branch is sketchy at best and is mainly derived from the short biographies found on the Robert Hale hardcover and Penguin paperback editions of her books. She was born in 1920 on her parent's isolated tea estate in Ceylon (now Sri Lanka). Her earliest memory is of helping her father attempt to persuade an elephant to swallow a homemade aspirin the size of a croquet ball. The elephant did not oblige.

She was educated at various schools along the south coast of England and then went to Paris to study art. She quickly tired of painting the traditional still lifes of "guitars, grapes and Chianti bottles" and returned to England where she studied at the Royal Academy of Dramatic Art for a year, once performing in a modern-dress version of *Hamlet* wearing a mackintosh and gumboots. This flirtation with an acting career led many researchers to confuse her with the actress Pamela Branch, best known for playing one of the nuns in the Sidney Poitier film *Lilies of the Field*.

After she left the RADA, she returned to Ceylon and then moved on to explore nearby India, starting in the north and gradually working her way south. For three years her home base was a houseboat in Kashmir. She trekked across the Himalayas by horse, living out of a tent during the summer months, and went skiing in the winter. She learned to hunt with guns and falcons, once shooting a black bear. During this period she also learned Urdu, with a special emphasis on the racier words in that language, painted several murals, and trained two racehorses.

Returning to England, she met and married barrister Newton Branch and moved to Cyprus where the two of them lived in a twelfth century Greek monastery poised precariously on the edge of a cliff overlooking the sea. Both tried their hand at writing, Pamela producing *The Wooden Overcoat*, Newton a number of boys' books. Pamela is said to have collaborated with him on film scripts but there is no record that any of them ever were filmed, although one biography listed Newton's profession at the time as that of a "film censor." Branch did collaborate with Philip Dale to produce a stage version of her third novel, *Murder Every Monday*, which was performed in Chelmsford in 1964. She and Newton continued to travel extensively. She wrote *The Lion in the Cellar* in a fisherman's cottage in Ireland, and *Murder Every Monday* in various parts of England, France and the Channel Islands. Her last published book, *Murder's Little Sister*, was written in a mews flat (converted stables much coveted by English bohemians of the period) in Kensington.

Friends described her as a very glamorous woman. "Beautiful, marvellous Pamela, with eyelashes like bent hairpins," is how Christianna Brand remembered her. Brand herself often had financial problems, which for a while forced her to set aside her writing career for more profitable endeavors. Pamela appeared to have had all the money she needed. "No, I can't come tomorrow, darling," she once said to Christianna. "We're flying to Geneva." Pamela paused, then added, "My husband wants to buy a watch." That was in 1967. Brand never spoke to her again. Shortly afterwards, Pamela died of cancer.

British mystery fiction authority Barry Pike, with whom Brand shared her memories of Branch, suggests that this exchange shows that Branch was quite well off. While that may be true, it also shows that Branch was still able to make a joke in what may well have been her darkest days. Her life may have been a short one but there is little doubt that it was a full one.

Tom & Enid Schantz
November 2005
Lyons, Colorado

CHAPTER 1

BENJAMIN CANN sat in the warm afternoon sunlight and basked. There had been no time, during the past months, for that sort of thing and no opportunity even to think about it. A pain in the neck had driven all other thoughts from his mind. It was a nervous pain which had started on the day of his arrest for wilful murder. It got worse as the trial approached and became acute when the judge made his first entrance.

The vision still made Benji shudder. The wizened little figure in scarlet carrying the regulation bouquet of flowers, the old, nightmare eyes peering at him from beneath the scrolled horsehair ... The jury was almost as bad – twelve closeups of ordinary men and women with a subtle, ghastly difference from all other human beings, enough to give anybody the hump. Benji gave each his most ingratiating schlapper smile, but with each his custom was rejected.

A woman passed. She glanced at him. She had a little paper bag in her purse with stale cake in it. She had come to feed the birds as usual, but her face instantly reminded Benji of the woman in the second row of the jury. He bristled and stuck out his lower lip. "Have a real *good* look!" he invited her aggressively and showed her both sides of his profile.

The woman did not recognize him. She hurried away, scattering the pigeons. They flew up in a great, wheeling circle. Some of them settled on Nelson's hat, high above Trafalgar Square.

Benji felt his hands shaking and buried them in his pockets. He wondered whether he had been thinking aloud again. That and his prison
pallor were dead giveaways. Not that it mattered, really. He had been
acquitted, hadn't he? *I got away with it!* he thought. *Cor! What a bit o'
fat! I got away with it!*

He was amazed. His legs still had a tendency to tremble.

The jury had been out for three hours. He had sat in the dock with a
slight sneer on his face. But when the foreman had said *Not Guilty,
Milord*, Benji breathed a great sigh which was audible all over the court.

"It's the cut that counts," he muttered. These words were an incanta-
tion, the boast and philosophy of his grandfather whose horsemeat kiosk
had once flourished in the Mile End Road. The words had turned the
tide of the family fortune. They were now limned in neon on the window of Benji's small but flourishing men's wear shop just off Shaftesbury Avenue.

He probed his left ear with a broken match. Counsel for the Prosecu-
tion had given him one very nasty moment. Benji had clenched his
hand in his pocket and felt the match snap. Afterwards, waiting fever-
ishly for the jury to return, he had found it again and promised himself
that, if he got out of this mess, he would light his first cigarette with that
match.

Odd, he remembered, the things he had thought of then. He had been
nervous, he had to admit it. His palms were sticky and he was unable to
keep his hands still. There had been a man in the well of the court who
was busy with a pencil. He was not writing but kept looking up at Benji,
screwing up his eyes and making minute additions to the paper. Finally
Benji had scrawled a note to his counsel. "Tell that steamer to stop
sketching me." The barrister looked at him with disapproval, scratched
the back of his wig, and took no notice.

During a half-hour of incomprehensible argument about the relevance
of some item of evidence, Benji had thought a good deal about the
black cap. Where did they keep it? he had wondered, and concluded
uneasily that the judge had it tucked away somewhere handy. Somebody had put it there that morning, ironed out freshly, just in case. Who
laundered it? Did they wear a different one every time? Who made
them and how much were they and who paid? Cut on the cross like that,
they would take quite a bit of stuff. Imagine Himself going along to
have it fitted! That would be a treat for a wet Monday! What did they
look like anyway? He still imagined a compromise between a jockey's

cap and a deerstalker, perhaps with a sort of wimple attached to add dignity. What were they made of? Satin? Watered silk? Or ponjee like the remnant with which he had strangled Rachel Bolger?

He took a photograph of Rachel from his pocket and smoothed the dog-eared corners. He had had to make quite a fuss to get it back from the custody of the court. Rachel gave him a trusting, melancholy smile. It was the only picture of her he would ever have now. He had taken it himself with his box Kodak. It was not a good picture. She was standing beneath the sign outside a One-Day Cleaners and it cast a heavy shadow across one of her eyes. They laughed about it afterwards – it looked like a black eye, a real shiner. Poor old Rachel! If she had not persisted in using the petty cash box as an auxiliary housekeeping account, he would not have lost his temper and, at this moment, she would be at home brewing up the afternoon tea for the girls in the workroom. He had spoken to her about it again and again, but she just laughed. "What d'you want it for?" he asked a dozen times. "I never keep you short." And she had smiled slyly and said, "Sundries, Ben. Sundries." He had intended to teach her a lesson, frighten her, so that she would not do it again, but, so help him God, he had not meant to kill her.

He lit a cigarette with the broken match. He felt that he ought to celebrate, but he did not know where to go and he did not want to be alone. Trafalgar Square seemed much larger than it used to be.

He knew that the man in the black homburg was going to speak to him some time before he actually did so. He turned away his head and studied the man from the corner of his eye. He had obviously been recognized, but it was too late to make a getaway. He thought fast. The man might be a reporter, and there was no reason why Benji should not make quite a tidy packet out of his life story in three installments. He had never, during the long weeks of his trial, actually made the front pages, but that was only because the Russians had been playing up again. He decided to be careful.

"Mr. Cann," said the man. It was not a question. "Good afternoon. I followed your taxi from the Old Bailey, but I lost you in that jam in the Strand. May I congratulate you?"

Benji nodded, not giving anything away. The man sat down beside him and smiled disarmingly.

"Had any offers from the dailies?" he asked, apparently reading Benji's thoughts. "Of course, you weren't exactly a *cause célèbre*, were you, although there seemed to be considerable feeling when you left the court?"

"They was shouting right out," said Benji quickly. He felt that it enhanced his news value. "Booing and I don't know what else! And somebody chucked a stone!"

The man raised one eyebrow and looked at him sideways. "Indeed?" he said.

Benji glanced at him furtively to see whether he was laughing. "Yes," he said uncertainly. "I ducked all right, though."

The man smiled. "Good for you! Personally, I should hold out. The Sundays are a far better proposition and you'll get a full-page spread. I imagine that you are reasonably photogenic. The only photographs to date were small and quite shockingly reproduced. Have you any immediate plans, or may I offer you a cup of tea at my club?"

"Daresay I could manage it," said Benji. He was pleased, but he was not going to admit that he was a man with no prospects.

The man hailed a taxi and it drew in beside them. He opened the door and smiled again with almost hypnotic charm. Benji warmed towards him. It was the first time he had been treated with civility for eleven weeks. Some people might think he was a bit – well, *off* now. He got into the taxi and looked surreptitiously at his companion. The man had a pleasant face. Although Benji was certain that he had never met him before, it was vaguely familiar. He looked about forty-five but was probably older. His skin had the healthy sheen of good living. *Takes his exercise in a car*, Benji thought, *but he's got a first-rate masseur on the side.* His suit had not come off the peg, either. *A lovely roll on the lapel – beautiful job, that!*

The man told the driver to go to No. 13 Flood Walk, Chelsea. Benji was slightly disappointed. He had expected it to be Mayfair, perhaps Park Lane, or somewhere off Piccadilly – but then you never knew with the press. Anyway, he did not want to go home. He wondered whether the police had taken Rachel's clothes.

"Of course, you can play it either way," said the man, offering a thin gold cigarette-case. "Suppose you carry on with the shop …"

"Establishment," corrected Benji. It was a mistake people made too often.

"Forgive me. Suppose you cash in on the – er – notoriety. What happens? A brisk but temporary increase in business, since people are incurably morbid. You will sell ties, handkerchiefs, braces, tric-trac of that kind, but suits, the backbone of your income – will you sell suits?"

Benji looked at him sharply. "Don't see why not."

The man raised his shoulders and spread his hands. "Imagine the fittings, my friend. We will not use harsh words, but consider yourself with a large, sharp pair of scissors in your hand! Would not the trimming of the collars assume a dubious aspect? Might not your clients, under the circumstances, find even a tape-measure stretched between your hands at least embarrassing? No, Mr. Cann! I think that you will sell no more suits."

"Oh yes, I will!" said Benji belligerently. "You're here, aren't you, alone in a cab with me and my hands? You're not scared."

The man fastidiously removed a shred of tobacco from the tip of his tongue. Again, Benji was not sure whether he was smiling. "My dear fellow!" he said. "I could give you at least six inches and roughly fifty pounds. I have an excellent physique and a useful smattering of medical knowledge. I know, for instance – excuse me – that a slight pressure applied simultaneously *here* and *here* makes it extremely difficult to breathe or even think."

Benji felt himself blacking out, but he could not move. Then the man released him, giving him an affable pat on the shoulder.

"Even if I were a little clumsy," he went on pleasantly, "and the post-mortem showed slight abrasions just *here*, the overwhelming symptoms would point to perfectly straightforward heart failure."

Benji adjusted his collar, stretched his neck, and coughed. "Look, Mister," he said, "who are you and what do you want?"

The man looked surprised. "My dear fellow, I do sincerely beg your pardon. I thought that you had recognized me. I am Clifford Flush and, as one who knows the ropes, I want to help you to avoid some of the pitfalls which lie before you."

Benji's eyes bulged. "Clifford Flush!" he repeated in a loud unnatural voice. "In 1936 ..."

"1937, actually. Bournemouth."

"And Folkestone ..."

"And just outside Bath. You may remember that the public ire was especially roused by the fact that I used the Southern Railway as my *abattoir*. And, of course, the old school tie aggravated things considerably. As you know, it led the gutter press to dub me the Balliol Butcher. Vulgar, I thought, and as it happened, premature. I sued the three worst offenders and invested in real estate in Bournemouth, Folkestone, and Bath."

Benji tried a laugh. "I'd never of known you!" he said with a show of bravado. "You looked quite different with a beard. Pushed 'em off trains, didn't you? Four of 'em."

"Three," said Flush without rancor. "The fourth survived. They brought her into court in plaster of Paris. Strangely enough, if it hadn't been for her evidence ..." He shrugged his shoulders and threw his cigarette out of the window. "Of course, when I was acquitted, I was obliged to marry the woman. Mercifully, it lasted a bare three months. She committed suicide. Don't look like that, old chap! I assure you that I was in Aix-les-Bains at the time – which was perhaps fortuitous, because, as a final disagreeable gesture, she jumped off the Flying Scotsman."

Suicide! thought Benji. *If he pushed me out of this cab, would it do me in? He might do that thing with the hands first ...* He did not comment. He stuffed his hands into his pockets and looked out of the window. The taxi was nosing out of King's Road into Flood Street. The driver turned right on the Embankment, and Benji had a glimpse of the gray river swirling around the foundations of Battersea Bridge. Then they turned right again, up Flood Walk.

It was a narrow street with elm and plane trees planted at intervals down its length. On one side was a row of semidetached cottages, newly renovated; on the other side, the one which never caught the sun, the houses remained untouched. They were three-storied, grimy, matted with debilitating creepers, set away from the road and each other by their walled courtyards and quasi gardens. Yet they had a certain hangdog charm, and most of them clung to their pre-Raphaelite memories, some being adorned with epitaphs to the famous who had frequented them.

The taxi drew up in front of one of the latter, behind a furious old Bugatti with chromium exhaust pipes on each side of the bonnet. In the garden wall there was an iron gate enwrought with an elaborate 13, and a blue faience plaque beside it saying that Tennyson had once stayed there.

Benji got out of the taxi. He did not want to go into that dark house with Flush. He was wondering whether to make a bolt for it or to brazen it out, when Flush made up his mind for him by taking his arm and leading him through the gate into the flagged courtyard. The house faced them, tall, slim, and covered in dusty ivy. Two Doric pillars, between which was the black-painted front door, supported a fragile balcony. Gravel paths and a hedge of unclipped privet ran down each side of the house, separating it from its neighbors.

Flush led the way through a dim hall with an ornate ceiling and into a room on the left. Benji registered a chandelier and four people sitting around the fire. It was a homely little group and he was immediately reassured.

An elderly woman rose from behind a silver teapot.

"Welcome!" she said warmly. "Welcome."

"Mrs. Barratt," Flush introduced her. "Mrs. Barratt – Mr. Cann."

Mrs. Barratt held out her hand at shoulder level, and Benji was obliged to kiss it. He looked over her shoulder at the girl by the hearth. She had long, red-blonde hair and she was smoking a black cigarette. She slanted her green eyes over him and breathed smoke in small puffs through her nostrils.

"Lilli Cluj," said Flush, patting her lightly on the head. "And this is our Treasurer, Colonel Quincey."

"Delighted, sir," said the Colonel. A spruce, red-faced old man with a white mustache, he used his prepositions with economy and spoke as if there were good food concealed in his mouth. "Always delighted welcome new blood."

The fourth member of the party was an enormous, misshapen man of some sixty years. He had coarse, collapsed features and a curiously flat head.

"And this gentleman," said Flush, "is affectionately known as the Creaker." He sounded a trifle apologetic.

The Creaker surged up from the sofa. There was a prolonged squeak on two descending notes. "Me leg," he explained, extending a vast hand. "Genuine article was broke in '29 on the Great North Road. Snapped like a ruddy twig. Began to creak '31 at West Wittering – sea air got at the joints. Always explain to people so's they don't take on. Pleased to meetcher."

"West Wittering?" said Benji. His eyelids dropped in sudden suspicion. Photographically, he remembered front-page pictures of a splintered and blood-spattered deck-chair, an irregular stain on a sand dune. His knees felt suddenly weak. He sat down hastily on a small gilt chair.

"Lilli," said Flush. "Pass me the Accommodation ledger."

Mrs. Barratt gave Benji a motherly smile. "You poor dear!" she said. "I'm sure you're tired out. I know *I* was! You take Naomi's advice and have some nice, strong tea. It'll make a new man of you." She passed a cup.

Benji took it. A little tea slopped into the saucer. He felt a light sweat break out on his forehead. *Naomi!* He thought frantically. When he was a nipper, there had been an old Brahma who had done her old man in with powdered glass because of a chauffeur called Barratt. Naomi

Barratt! *Come off it, Ben! You're thinking silly! Common enough name. Barratt died under what they called Questionable Circumstances. Flush is One, he said so. Clubfoot's One, too, I'd bet me last score!* The teaspoon was rattling in the saucer. He put his thumb on it. *Are they all* THEM? *Don't let on, Ben! Act natural – they think you're another. So you are, aren't you?* He rallied fiercely. *I am not. I didn't mean it. It doesn't count.* He saw Lilli Cluj watching him through her hair. She dropped her eyelids slightly and it was as if she had touched him. He gave her a glazed smile.

"I'm sorry, old chap," said Flush, looking up from the ledger, "but at the moment we've got a full house. We shall have to find you some quiet cloister in the neighborhood. Your expenses will, of course, be taken care of until you decide whether you want to become a member of our little club."

"Very kind, I'm sure," said Benji uncertainly. "Ought to get back, though." He had a sudden picture of the empty flat. When they had come to arrest him, he had been packing. The place was untidy and desolate enough then. Now that the bogies had finished with it, it would be even worse.

Flush lit a cigarette. "Well, my friend, you must please yourself. Personally, I advise against it. We have found from experience that a return to one's former environment always proves – disappointing."

Benji's heart lurched. There it was – the admission! They were all THEM! Aghast, his eyes flickered around the circle of faces. What had the Colonel done – who, how many? And the girl, what about her? It was difficult to associate her flowerlike features with violence. *May have been a mistake, like mine. That would make us companions in bad luck.* Pleased with this idea, he looked at Lilli more closely. *Either way, she's just my type! I could go for her!*

"S'pose I do join up," he asked warily, "how much'll it set me back?"

Flush smiled. "Not a penny. We stipulate that our members, in return for the amenities they receive here free of charge, make their wills unconditionally in favor of our organization." He stirred his tea, frowning. "I'm afraid that we find among our number a high percentage of – bunglers. Intoxicated with freedom, they are apt to repeat their previous mistakes. Naturally, a jury is prejudiced by knowledge of former indiscretions – and the Club – er – benefits."

"I expect some of 'em have died here, eh?" asked Benji before he could stop himself. "The older ones, I mean," he amended hastily.

"Naturally," said Flush.

"Naturally?"

"That is what I said. We are all friends here." Flush's tone was cool. "It's entirely up to you, Mr. Cann. You are under no obligation to join us."

Benji bridled. So they did not want him, eh? Well, he wanted no part of them, either, but he would have liked them to be disappointed and chagrined by his refusal to join. He felt Flush's eyes on him and wondered whether the man had read his thoughts.

"I leave you all me worldlies and live here free, right?"

Flush nodded. "There is no need for you to decide immediately. Suppose you sleep on it? There is a room to let next door. I will telephone and make the necessary arrangements and we will expect you back here – the Asterisk Club, we call ourselves – for dinner at seven-thirty. How's that?"

Benji floundered. He did not know what to think. He could walk out of their house and never come back. That was what he had a good mind to do ... But what about the girl? He did not want to lose track of her. He would like to know her better, a lot better. Everything free, too. On the house! He had always wanted to live in a classy joint like this ... But, he'd never know where he was. They might break out again any time! Sign over all your worldlies? Sign your own death warrant! ... That Clubfoot's case – oh, a dirty thing that was! It did not bear thinking about ... *I'm O.K. as long as I don't sign anything. I'd be sorry for the bleeder who tries to make a monkey out of me! ... Oh, I don't know, I don't know, I'm sure!*

Flush, watching him, laughed. It was a friendly, boyish chuckle. "If I didn't know your record, old chap, I should have said that you were *scared*!"

That clinched it. "Scared?" said Benji loudly. "Who, me?" He tried a laugh. It went better than he had expected and he held it, slapping his thigh. "One thing Ben's never been known to pass up – free grub!"

The laugh was getting out of control. He could not stop. They were all joining him. They were shaking with laughter, and the Creaker was wiping his eyes. Benji wondered why. Nobody had said anything comical. There was nothing to laugh at.

But they went on laughing, Benji the loudest of them all.

CHAPTER 2

THE house next door was an exact replica of the Asterisk Club except that, in the middle of the courtyard, there grew a large monkey-puzzle tree. There was a hump of dark granite at its base with a carved inscription which read – DANTE GABRIEL ROSSETTI PLANTED THIS TREE. There were also small firs in pots painted the same red as the front door.

Benjamin Cann rang the bell and stood wondering whether his future landlady would recognize him. Did she know about the gang next door? Was she One, too? If she did recognize him, would she turn him away? The picture of him in the *News* had been the best – but it was very small, it might have been anybody. *Go on, Ben! You going to turn milky now?* It did not occur to him that the woman might know him and believe him to be innocent.

The door was opened by a small blonde in a sweater and corduroy slacks. She had wide, clear eyes and a provocative figure.

"Damn!" she said with an engaging smile. "I thought it was Peter. But I expect you're the rat man."

"I beg your pardon?" said Benji. Whatever he had done, she had no right to call him that.

The girl pushed her hair over her shoulder. "Sorry," she said amiably. "I mean the Rodent Officer. Honestly, we've got rats the way some people have lice. We tracked down GHQ last night. It's in the coal cellar. Where's your box of tricks?" She broke off and looked at him doubtfully. "No, I don't believe you're him at all. He came this morning, but I was out. We couldn't understand how he *knew*, but he said he could smell a rat miles away. It's rather shaming, isn't it? Did *you* smell them?"

"I am Mr. Cann," Benji announced stiffly. He watched her closely, but the name made no impression on her. He breathed a tiny sigh of relief.

"Oh, you're *him*!" said the girl. She shook hands. "A Mr. Flush rang up about you. I'm Mrs. Hilford, one half of your landlady. The other half is Mrs. Berko. You see, Peter and I share the house with Bertha and Hugo, so we have half of you each. Come on in."

She disappeared into a room on the left, leaving Benji standing in the hall. It had a low ceiling and the floor was covered with rough

18

cobalt tiles. It was unfurnished except for a large studio easel, a pile of canvases stacked with their faces to the wall, and a jam-jar full of paint-brushes. At the far end, the stairs rose against the wall to a large window, then doubled back. To Benji's right was an open door through which he saw a refectory table with a half-eaten apple on it. The apple had been forgotten. It was turning brown around the bitten part. On the wall was a picture of an angular musical instrument, probably a guitar, and a bowl of red fruit, probably tomatoes. At the foot of the stairs was a green baize door which obviously led to the kitchen.

A handsome girl with red hair and colorless eyebrows put her head round the door on the left, studied him, and, not realizing that Benji was well versed in taking stock of customers while looking in an entirely different direction, withdrew. She did not close the door, and Benji, who had abnormally acute hearing, heard her whispering to the blonde.

"My dear, what a gaudy little chap! Do you think he'll pay?"

"Make him cross your palm before you give him a key. We can always lock him out and hock his clothes …"

That was the blonde. Benji remembered her candid eyes and shook his head. It just went to show that you never could tell.

There was a moment's silence, a smothered laugh, then the girl with the red hair reappeared. She was tall and built on generous lines. The placket of her skirt was undone and a pink ribbon hung out of it.

"How do you do," she said sociably. "I'm Mrs. Berko. I'm so sorry to keep you waiting. I had to have a business discussion with my colleague." Something in his expression made her look at him again, wondering whether he had heard the discussion. "You're our first lodger," she said brightly. "Haven't you got any luggage? A pity. But as you're by yourself, I'm sure it's all right. My father told me never to take *two* people with no luggage because they only stay for an hour and they usually steal the sheets."

Benji frowned. He did not comment. He and Rachel had once stolen a pillowcase from a hotel in Paddington.

The girl led him upstairs. Benji lagged behind her, watching her legs appreciatively. They were large but shapely. He liked that – something to get your claws into. Rachel's legs had never been the same since she had her appendix out. He remembered them oddly twisted, sprawled on the floor in the flat's dark little hall …

The girl stopped on a half-landing and opened a door painted an odd shade of green. Benji glanced inside. It was a nice room in green and yellow. There was a large window overlooking a mottled lawn. He produced the wallet recently filled by Clifford Flush.

"I'd like a key," he said sourly. "I'll cross your palm."

Mrs. Berko blushed. It made her eyebrows look white.

"*Please*," she said. "Really, there's no need for that. My colleague was only joking. Mr. Flush recommended you strongly, and after all he lives right next door. Here's the key. I'm sure we can trust you."

"Got rats, eh?" Either they had not recognized him or they did not mind. He could afford to get a little tough. He stared at her left leg. There was a ladder in her stocking with a blob of nail varnish at the end to prevent it running any farther. The girl edged her left leg behind her right.

"Just a few," she said. "They're quite small, almost babies."

Benji took the key. He put his hand on the door handle and stood looking at her, waiting for her to go. She backed on to the landing.

"Well," she said, with an uncertain smile.

Benji threw the key into the air and caught it. He suddenly bared his teeth in a dog's grin. The girl started. She felt for the banisters behind her.

"It's a postwar mattress," she said defensively.

Benji began to close the door. The girl nodded and made her escape downstairs. Benji shut the door and went to see whether she had told the truth about the mattress. It annoyed him slightly to find that she had. He took off his hat and opened the window. He had not opened a window for some time and he quite enjoyed it.

*

Bertha Berko went downstairs, planning to take away the potted chrysanthemum she had given him at the first possible opportunity. He had not even noticed it and anyway he did not deserve it. An unattractive little man. She hurried into the room by the front door. There was a rat sitting under the window. It was eating something. It looked at her indifferently and went behind a stack of plywood. Fan Hilford was standing at her easel with a paintbrush in her mouth. She was touching up a still life of square blue pears.

The room was used as a communal studio and was cluttered with the tools of each of their trades. Officially, the west half of it belonged to the Berkos, the east to the Hilfords, and a painted line on the floor marked the boundary. But the large loom on which Bertha Berko wove lengths of spongy tweed had a habit of sliding on to Hilford preserves.

The coffin-shaped chest in which Hugo Berko kept his clay and the boulders of basalt which he carved into images of his few patrons had been edged off his own territory during a party and were too heavy to be repatriated. Fan Hilford's easel and model throne led a nomadic life following the north light. Her husband's photographic apparati had infiltrated from the cupboard which was his darkroom on to every available flat surface.

Bertha moved a bust of Vansittart and sat down on the model throne.

"My dear," she said, "he *heard*!"

"Who?"

"Little Runty. He heard every word we said. He must have ears like a Seeing Eye. I could have died." She squinted at the blue fruit. "Don't you think that background's a mistake?"

"No, I think it's jolly tasty."

"Oh, well. Personally, I don't care if he did hear. He means less to me than a hole in the road. I hoped we'd get a madly attractive medical student or something. A real *dish*, if you know what I mean." She absently measured a skull with a pair of calipers.

The front doorbell rang.

"Peter!" said Fan. She dropped her paintbrush with an indigo splash and scuttled across the room.

It was not Peter. It was a small man with spectacles, wearing a Burberry and with his trousers neatly furled around his legs by steel bicycle clips. He had a bedraggled mustache and carried a cardboard attaché case. He took off his hat and disclosed a bony forehead and a lick of hair which drooped almost into his eyes. He handed her a card and watched with a watery stare while she turned it over. *Alfred L. Beesum*, it read. *Rodent Officer, retired.*

"Good afternoon," said Fan. "Retired?"

"Thet's right," said Mr. Beesum. He spoke with hardly any movement of the lips. It flattened his vowels and, as if to make up for this, he enunciated his consonants with great care. "I em now freelancing," he explained. "Hev you rets or mice?"

"Rats. Dozens of them."

"Good. I don't do mice."

"We killed eight this morning in no time at all."

"Oh? Mey I inquire by what method?"

"I'm afraid it was a tennis racquet."

The little man sucked his teeth. He looked pained.

"My campaign will be on a broader scele."

"What are you going to do?" asked Fan.

Mr. Beesum hesitated. He took off his spectacles, polished them, and replaced them.

"Em I essured thet it will go no farther?"

"I won't tell a soul."

"Well," said Mr. Beesum. He looked suspiciously at the house next door and lowered his voice. "I shell open the offensive with sticky boards. The secret glue thereon hardens almost instantaneously when in contact with anything cold. *Rets' feet are cold.*"

This surprising information made Fan glance at him quickly. He was quite serious. She swallowed a giggle and adjusted her expression. She wanted to ask him why he had chosen his esoteric profession, but she was sure that he would take umbrage.

"I see," she said carefully. "What do you use for bait?"

"Rets like cake."

He seemed indisposed for further discussion, so she led him along the gravel path to the right of the house. As they passed the dining-room window she saw Bertha inside, scratching her leg reflectively and eating a biscuit. Outside the back door, on the small brown lawn, lay eight dead rats, carefully graded in size. Some of them were quite young.

"That's this morning's bag," said Fan.

Mr. Beesum considered them with professional interest. He took eight paper bags from his attaché case and put one rat into each, writing something on every bag in pencil. He sealed the bags and put them into a paper carrier.

"Well, thet's *ret!*" he said. For a second his shoulders heaved but he made no sound. Fan looked at him blandly, then his face sagged into its former gloom and she realized that he had been laughing.

"What's thet?" he said sharply, looking over his shoulder.

Fan turned round. Croydon, Bertha's miniature poodle, stood in the back door glaring at Mr. Beesum.

"You will hev to lock thet enimal up when I commence to ley arsenic," he said coldly.

"Arsenic?" said Fan, startled. She associated arsenic with older-generation murder.

"I em probably the most experienced Rodent Officer in the United Kingdom. I hev always used arsenic es my first string end I do not propose to alter my methods for *thet* enimal."

Fan wondered whether she ought to apologize. She tried to push Croydon inside the back door, but the small, silvery bitch eluded her and dodged around Mr. Beesum's legs, sniffing at him. Mr. Beesum took no notice, but Fan knew that he was acutely conscious of the animal.

"This evening," he said, trying to concentrate, "I shell note the runs end launch en etteck upon a small front. I shell edvance two sticky boards to locate the enemy's main forces. *Time spent on reconnaissance is seldom wasted.*" He gave Croydon a surreptitious kick with his heel. Croydon rolled over on to her back and screamed. Fan and Mr. Beesum looked down at her. Both were embarrassed.

"She always does that," said Fan.

"I did not touch the enimal," said Mr. Beesum.

"It's perfectly all right. She always does it."

Mr. Beesum said nothing. He dug up a dandelion with the toe of his boot without looking down. Fan cleared her throat.

"How long do you think the rats will take?" she asked.

"Thet depends," said Mr. Beesum. He was still annoyed about Croydon.

"A week? It's quite awful, you know. We can't sleep and they keep taking the soap."

Mr. Beesum was interested against his will. "They like soap," he admitted. "I shell launch a further offensive tomorrow morning," he said more amiably. "Its nature will depend upon the night's casualties. With your permission, I shell leave my heavy artillery on the premises." He glanced at Croydon. "I edvise, if you value thet enimal, thet this is placed somewhere inaccessible. It contains certain dainties which would finish her off pronto. Kindly inform the other members of the household thet I prefer my beg to remain untouched."

Fan assured him that she would do so and, feeling that the interview was at an end, led him into the kitchen and introduced him to Marleen, the general help.

Marleen was of uncertain age, with a love life stranger than any fiction. Her head was bound up in a piece of orange cloth which bulged with unseen curlers. Like many of her type, she lived in a private world of chronic erotic reverie. She raked Mr. Beesum with her yellow eyes and smiled. She promised to show the Officer all over the house, scratched her armpit, and suggested archly that he might like a cup of tea first.

"Thenks," said Mr. Beesum noncommittally. He sat down at the kitchen table and clasped his hands on his attaché case.

Fan left them. She saw, as she passed the larder window, that Mr. Flush was in the next-door garden, spraying a rose bush. The poor old cripple was there too, sitting in a deck chair and absorbing the last of the doubtful sunlight. She stood watching Flush for a moment. Somewhere, back in her schooldays, she was sure she had seen him before. She studied the classic profile and the sweep of graying hair, but she could not remember. She forgot about him and went through the green baize door, across the hall, and into the studio. Bertha was halfheartedly setting up her loom with mustard-colored wool and Peter was sitting on Hugo's coffin of clay drinking Guinness.

"Hullo, love," said Fan.

Peter threw a ball of clay at his camera. It fell off a soapbox on to the floor. "The shutter on that bloody thing has stuck again," he said. He looked hot and tired.

Bertha caught Fan's eye. She raised her eyebrows and jerked her head backwards, implying that she was willing to leave the room in case of impending discord. Fan ignored her. She picked up the camera and kissed Peter.

"Break it up," said Bertha.

"What a day!" said Peter. "I want to take a routine picture of a murderer. It's not much to ask, is it? People do it every day. Everybody except old Jonah Hilford! With me, it's different. I get up at crack of dawn; I stumble around in the dark; I have no breakfast; I tote that bloody iron lung all the way to the Old Bailey; I fight and bribe my way to a good angle; my feet hurt; my stomach rumbles; I am out of cigarettes; I stay there until I am numb all over. Just as I am thinking I would rather be dead, my killer comes out of court. The man on my left with the box job gets his picture – *and my shutter sticks*!" He closed his eyes and breathed hard through his nose.

Fan poured him some more Guinness. "I'm here," she said. "You just bite my nails."

There was a knock at the door and Benjamin Cann inserted his head. "I want a reading-lamp," he said flatly. "I got ..."

Peter leapt to his feet, upsetting his Guinness and knocking the bottle out of Fan's hand.

"What the hell are *you* doing here?" he roared.

"I got as much right as you," said Benji, immediately aggressive.

"He's the lodger, my dear," said Bertha. She frowned at Peter.

Benji was badly shaken. He had been recognized. He turned at bay. "I didn't come here to be insulted either," he snarled. "Nor to stay in a house creeping with rats. Eaten half the soap already! I'll leave first thing tomorrow, I will."

"You're damn right you will!" shouted Peter.

Benjamin Cann had gone. The front door slammed. Fan stared at her husband.

"Now I wonder why you did that," she said with interest.

"Are you crazy?" asked Bertha. "Four guineas straight down the drain! Who do you think you are?"

Peter twisted a piece of clay into the shape of a head. He laid it on the chest and squashed it with his hand. He did not answer.

"What's the matter with Little Runty?" asked Bertha.

"There are eight million people in London," said Peter. "Why do you have to pick on him?"

"We could ask the same thing of you."

"You'd be wasting your time. I'm not going to tell you. You wouldn't sleep a wink." He got up and tramped out of the room.

Somewhere upstairs, Croydon began to bark.

CHAPTER 3

BLOODY ARTISTS! thought Benjamin Cann. Still ruffled, he rang the bell of the Asterisk Club. You would not catch *him* staying there much longer! What if that chap *had* recognized him? "I'm legal, aren't I?" he said to himself furiously. "I was let off, wasn't I?" He unwillingly considered the queasy thought that other landlords might react in the same manner. If he didn't go back to the flat it might be a bit difficult to find rooms. *What a ruddy sauce! Artists, too! I know all about artists! Living in squalor and mucking around with models! Taking lodgers, too! That gives the show away, doesn't it?* And the place was crawling with rats. He had not been there half an hour before a seedy little man in a fifty-shilling blue serge walks into the room, cool as you please, and starts mumbling about secret glue. He had laid a sticky board along by the bed and told Benji not to touch it. Benji, being a skeptical character, tested the glue gingerly with his toothbrush. It immediately stuck fast to the board and resisted all his efforts to pry it loose. *Better stay there tonight, though. Don't want to take a chance of being turned away anywhere, not again today. Tomorrow ought to be O.K. – just today, the day they know I'm out's a bit off. Wouldn't mind joining that club as a country member. Just so as I don't have to live in ...*

The door was opened by Lilli Cluj. Her long hair hung over her left eye and she had changed into a pair of gold-tissue pajamas. She smiled and produced a small bag of boiled sweets from her swathed bosom. She put one between Benji's lips and brazenly invited him to replace the bag.

Benji hesitated. There was something which he had to straighten out before his relationship with Lilli developed into anything less platonic. "Are you – um ..." He paused, considering the least offensive manner of asking a young lady whether or not she had committed homicide. "Are you one of THEM?"

"Pliss?"

Benji plunged. "You ever *bumped* anybody?"

For a moment Lilli looked puzzled, then her face cleared, and she clapped her hands. "In Budapest iss liddle autos call Dodgem. Iss *gemütlich*! I laugh."

"No, no," said Benji. "What I mean is – you wouldn't rub a person out, or would you?"

"Ah," said Lilli. "I comprehend. Bonk! Piff-paff! Go dead!"

"You wouldn't do a thing like that, would you? Not a nice little girl like you?"

Lilli shook her head violently. She seemed about to add something further, then changed her mind.

"Naw," she said simply.

Benji was satisfied. He was about to do something about the bag of sweets when Clifford Flush came out of the drawing room. He wore a velvet smoking jacket with corded froggings.

"Ah, there you are, old chap," he said warmly. "The Colonel owes me a fiver. He bet me that you would not come back."

"Why shouldn't I?" said Benji quickly, watching him.

"Exactly." This time there was no doubt about his smile. He had a gold tooth at the back on the right.

In the drawing room, the curtains were drawn and the chandelier blazed. There were bottles and glasses on a table against the wall. In front of the fire, Mrs. Barratt with a pale sherry was taking on the Colonel with a large whisky at Snakes and Ladders. They greeted Benji and returned to their game. The Creaker was partially hidden behind an old copy of the *News of the World*. He emerged for a moment, nodded, and ducked back again. Lilli sidled into the room and went across to the table where the drinks were. She stood gracefully on one leg, pouted at

Benji, and in two movements poured herself an outsize gin, then emptied it down her slender throat.

Flush gave Benji a sherry. Benji sipped it without a qualm. He was all right as long as he hadn't signed anything. His host waved a glass at Mrs. Barratt and the Colonel and explained that the Club rules allowed Ludo, Halma, draughts, and other such wholesome relaxations, but chess, dice, and cards, particularly bridge, were forbidden. Benji understood. Remembering the cold-blooded records of Mrs. Barratt and Flush and the extraordinary brutality of the Creaker's last brainstorm, he could well imagine that a simple checkmate might lead to a hideous atrocity.

Flush, watching him, laughed and said that in the event of any resident member entertaining uncharitable thoughts about another, he or she was expected to donate five shillings to the Benevolent Fund. It was to be inserted at the time of the incident in the papier-mache box which stood for that purpose on the mantelpiece. The proceeds were invested weekly in football pools on a permutation system devised by the Colonel, and the profits shared equally.

"Did you think over our proposition, old chap?" he asked casually.

"Might like to be a country member or something like," said Benji cautiously. He thought he caught a gleam of triumph in Flush's eye and added hastily, "Nothing permanent. I'll think it over."

"As you like, of course. It's merely a matter of affixing your signature to a single document. Sherry?"

He was about to pour it when the door was thrown open by a rough-looking man in a mess jacket. He glanced at Benji, stepped back one pace, and came smartly to attention.

"Grub," he announced.

A ginger cat walked into the room. It was the biggest cat that Benji had ever seen – a giant. It looked him up and down with its uncandid eyes then walked slowly out of the room with its tail stiffly in the air. As it passed Benji, he got a whiff of it. It smelt stale. He looked up and caught an odd expression on his host's face. One of his eyebrows was slightly raised and he was biting his underlip. He was watching the cat. Then he smiled and took Benji's arm.

"I don't like that cat," he said lightly.

The Creaker limped after the animal, clicking his hairy fingers. "Tom!" he called. "Come 'ere, Tom!"

"Molting," said the Colonel, pointing to a tuft of sandy fur on the carpet.

"'E's all right," said the Creaker tenderly.

Flush led the way across the hall and into the dining room. It was somberly paneled in dark wood and lit only with candles whose meager light did not reach the corners. Benji sat on his host's left, Mrs. Barratt on his right. The Creaker sat at the far end of the table with the monstrous ginger cat on his knee.

The rough-looking man and a pale youth similarly attired served soup. The youth was deft and neat with the plate, but the older man was distinctly clumsy. Flush confided in a low voice that Benji must overlook certain gaucheries on the part of these two. He preferred to have uncouth and predictable stewards rather than none at all. He had found that such institutions as Borstal, Holloway, and Wormwood Scrubs yielded a regular supply of men and women who were not above serving a tolerant employer in a wealthy district.

Benji did not answer. The older steward was hovering behind him, making him uneasy. As the man set down Benji's soup, he tilted the plate so that a small puddle drooled on to the table; Benji looked up quickly and caught a flicker of malice in the small eyes. He sat back in his chair, assuring himself that he had imagined it. The man bent over him on the other side, offering wine in a bottle wrapped in a napkin. He filled Benji's glass and, as he moved away, poured a few drops on to the back of Benji's hand. This time Benji knew that it was deliberate. His hands began to shake again. He caught Flush's eye and nodded towards the older steward.

"Who's he?" he murmured.

Flush touched his lips with a napkin. "That's Beecher. He passes for our butler. He has just – I believe the expression is *done a carpet* – in the Scrubs."

"For You-Know-What?"

"No, no. Beecher may look murderous, but I assure you that he wouldn't hurt a fly. He's our oldest retainer. He is invaluable. He has served sentences for everything from arson to petty forgery."

Forgery! thought Benji. He felt the goose-pimples rise on his arms. *If I don't sign their ruddy form, that's the steamer that'll do it for me! And he'll do it over my dead body.* He clasped his hands tightly together. He was now convinced that if he were suddenly to drop dead, the Club would benefit, quite apart from his small savings, to the tune of roughly six thousand pounds worth of men's wear, only a third of which was shop soiled. He watched the older steward drop a piece of grilled turbot on to the floor and flick it under the Creaker's chair with his foot. The ginger cat lolled off his master's knees and went after it. Benji could hear him under the chair, chewing and breathing asthmatically. Glancing covertly at his fellow members, he wondered whether they would try to pull anything tonight. Probably not – obviously a forgery was not as satisfactory as the real McCoy. But he was not going to take any chances. He knew as well as anyone else that most of the more easily obtainable poisons were colorless. But surely they would not try anything now, not in front of the ladies? *I'm thinking silly again. Go on, Ben, eat your fish. You like turbot.* He ate the turbot and found it tasteless and difficult to swallow. He toyed with the saddle of mutton. But when the dessert arrived he hesitated and studied his plate more closely. The ice cream was green. It was sprinkled with what might or might not be powdered sugar. It smelt faintly but unmistakably of bitter almonds. Benji laid down his spoon and studied his companions obliquely.

Flush, who had refused the sweet, was selecting a chocolate from a silver dish. The Colonel was snapping a rubber band between his fingers and gazing into the shadows behind Benji's chair. Mrs. Barratt was scooping up what might or might not be split salt and throwing it over her left shoulder. Lilli was either busily concealing something or doing up a suspender under cover of her napkin. The Creaker was fingering the tip of his cat's tail and looking everywhere except at Benji's ice cream. The two stewards were standing motionless at either end of the table, their shadows bent on the walls behind them.

Benji sat quite still. He could not look at his plate. It was cyanide that smelt of bitter almonds, wasn't it? It paralyzed your blood or something. It gave you just enough time to ring up the rabbi and that was all. He felt the hair rise on the back of his neck. He pushed the plate away from him.

The Creaker's cat made a sudden lunge at the butter. Flush looked up and saw it. He threw his napkin on to the table and stood up. There was a vein bulging on his forehead.

"Are we to be tyrannized by that brute?" he asked harshly. On his face was the strange expression which Benji had noticed before dinner. He was quite disproportionately angry.

Why? thought Benji frantically. *Because of the cat? Or could it be because I didn't eat that green thing?*

The ladies had left the room. The Colonel helped himself to port and passed the decanter to Benji.

"Interested in machinery, sir?" he asked. He did not wait for an answer but plunged immediately into a description of the ignition system of his first de Dion Bouton.

Benji considered the port. The Colonel had drunk it, hadn't he? It all came out of the same bottle, didn't it? It must be all right. This was the time, though, while the women were out of the way. He could do with a bit of port. It would buck him up. Cunningly, he poured a tot for the Creaker and watched to see whether he would drink it.

"Ta," said the Creaker, and threw the port down his throat.

"I believe our friend here is bedazzled by the fair Lilli," said Flush. He had recovered his temper and sounded amused.

Benji blushed. "What's she doing here, anyway?" he demanded, pouring port. "She told me herself that she hadn't – she hasn't got the proper qualifications."

"Don't be misled," said Flush. "I'm afraid that our Lilli is inclined to prevaricate about the rather ghoulish affair of her second husband. While disporting themselves upon some small, electrical cars ..."

"Dodgems," said Benji slowly. "In Budapest. She likes them, she said so. They make her laugh."

"I dare say. Spouse Two fell out of one and Lilli swerved off her course and rammed him against another. His skull split ..." He crushed a walnut between his fingers, "... just like *that!* She is not, bless her, as naive as she would have one think."

Benji digested this in silence. He was shocked and at the same time relieved. If, he comforted himself, he were going to see a lot of Lilli, it would probably be more satisfactory if she were unable to cast any one-way aspersions. He was still staring thoughtfully at a cruet when he heard the Creaker's leg squeak and looked up with a start, expecting violence. Flush was looking down at him with another of those missing smiles. Benji could have sworn that his host had read his thoughts.

"Shall we join the ladies?" said Flush. He turned away with a well-bred cough. Only Benji knew that it was not a cough. It was a laugh.

The Creaker's cat left the room first, dragging a piece of braised celery along the carpet.

"Beecher," said Flush. "Remove that animal."

Benji saw him exchange a glance with his murderous steward and his blood ran cold. *We're for it,* he thought. *Me and the cat.* The older steward stepped forward with unashamed eagerness and Benji instinctively shut his eyes.

"I'll take 'im," the Creaker volunteered quickly. "Come on, Tom." He hobbled out of the door and the cat stalked after him.

In the drawing room, Mrs. Barratt was pouring coffee. Benji accepted a cup, drank it quickly, and, too late, remembered where he was. Appalled, he cautiously tasted his mouth for any telltale bitterness. He found a grain of sugar lodged in a wisdom tooth and felt it frantically with his tongue. One side of it was sharp and for a minute he was convinced that it was powdered glass. Then it dissolved and he breathed an inaudible sigh of relief. He sank on to the sofa and immediately leapt to his feet. He had been pricked by something sharp. *I been stabbed!* was his first thought. Then, *I been pricked with a poisoned pin!* Overlapping this, another – *what's that untraceable one? Arrow poison, curare. I'm a goner!*

Mrs. Barratt glared at him. "You sat on my knitting," she said irritably. "You have broken one of the needles."

Benji controlled himself with an effort. "Sorry," he said weakly. He cleared his throat. "I didn't mean it," he added with more confidence.

"It's perfectly all right," said Mrs. Barratt. "Of course, it's completely ruined, but I'm sure it was an accident. Least said, soonest mended." She rose and dropped two half-crowns into the Benevolent Fund.

Benji's knees began to tremble again. He saw that Flush was standing over him with a liqueur glass in his hand.

"No," he said. He shook his head feebly. "No."

Flush put the glass into his hand. "Try it, old chap," he said. "It's something really special. It's made from the flowers of the Pyrenees."

Benji took it with the calm of despair. *I'm for it*, he thought. *I'll never get out of this house except feet first.* "I don't like liqueurs," he said piteously, rallying for the last time.

"Ah, but this one is different," said Flush. "You've never tasted this one before."

And I never will again, Benji grieved. *Not this nor any other.* Apathetically, he drank it. It was too sweet, but otherwise tasted quite normal. He handed back the glass to his host, searching his face for a reaction. Flush's expression did not change. He patted Benji's shoulder and begged to be excused, saying that he would send over to the house next door all Benji's requirements for the night. Benji followed him into the hall. He touched Flush's elbow. He had to know whether already there was some obscure, tasteless, untraceable poison corroding his insides.

"Will I come back to breakfast?" he asked faintly.

"It's up to you, old chap," said Flush amiably. Then, struck by something about his guest's sagging shoulders, he studied him more closely.

He raised his eyebrows and began to laugh. "Surely," he said, shaking, "*surely* you don't think …" He roared with laughter, wiping his eyes with a fingertip. "My dear old fellow, surely you don't think I would be so rash as to poison you on my own premises? Really! Come, come, old chap!" He produced a silk handkerchief and blew his nose. "Perhaps, after your sojourn in Wandsworth, you have become overimaginative. I suggest that you go home and have a good night's rest. I will say good night now."

"Good-bye," said Benji. He was not convinced.

He watched Flush pick up a brown-paper parcel and leave through the front door. Now he did not know what to think. Undecided, he stood fingering the fleshy leaves of a potted cactus, until it occurred to him that its spines, too, might be poisoned. He was staring at the bead of blood on his left index finger when the drawing room door opened and Lilli Cluj appeared. She took his arm and allowed her thigh to brush his. She escorted him to the front door; there she bit him tenderly in the ear and said that she wanted to know him much, much better.

"Nice Benji," she murmured, rubbing her nose softly against his cheek. The street-lamp turned her hair the color of freshly polished copper. She stood on tiptoe and kissed him on the lips, pushed something into his hand, and, with a whisper of gold tissue, melted back into the house.

Benji was left standing on the steps. He walked slowly across the courtyard. In the middle was a rococo pool in which a large carp lay motionless, apparently asleep. Outside the wrought-iron gate Benji stood on the pavement, sniffing the night air. He could hear the distant rumble of traffic on Battersea Bridge and the wash of a tug going up the river. He was thinking about Lilli. Tomorrow he would take her to have tea at Gunter's. Afterwards, perhaps they would go to the Rialto. The two-and-fourpennies would do. The dark was the same whatever you paid. He looked upwards at the pink night sky. It was the last day of the old moon. There was a thread of cloud sliding across it. He opened his hand to see what Lilli had given him. A large chocolate covered with silver foil lay in his palm. He unwrapped it absently and popped it into his mouth. At the bottom of the road, on the Embankment, he saw the Creaker. The old cripple was leaning over the parapet, gazing at the river. The massive ginger cat was beside him, leaning against his shoulder. Benji watched them for a moment. He never intended to see them again. He was quite determined to have no more to do with the Asterisk Club, free living or not. This evening had been one of the most unpleas-

ant he had ever spent, and he had no intention of repeating it. Nevertheless, he did not propose to let Lilli Cluj slip through his fingers. A real
smasher, she was.

He let himself into No. 15. He hung up his coat in the hall and noticed a cardboard attaché-case on the neighboring peg. A. L. BEESUM, it
had indifferently printed on it. DANGER, POISON. Benji stared at it. At
least in this house, they labelled it. He went upstairs to his room. The
artists were in the room on the landing just above him. He could see a
light under the door and hear a woman talking about Matisse. He waited
to see whether they would say anything about himself, but they did not.
They had settled down to Matisse. He went into his room and turned on
the light. The curtains had been drawn and somebody had put a thermos on the bedside table. He opened it and sniffed. It was cocoa. On
the bed was a brown-paper parcel. It contained a pair of Nile-green silk
pajamas, a Paisley dressing gown, a razor in a pigskin case, and a jar of
shaving-cream. *Suckers!* was Benji's immediate thought. *You'll never
see these again. Me and them's off first thing tomorrow and you know
what you can do with your uncanny old club!* He stroked the pajamas
with a professional touch. *Oi! Yoi! That didn't cost fifteen and eleven-
three.* He undressed and put on the pajamas and dressing gown. Admir-
ing himself in the mirror, he wished that Rachel could see him. He
changed his mind. He wished that Lilli Cluj could see him. So she had
been married twice, had she? Well, that was all right too. He liked them
experienced. Lilli Cann, he said to himself, savoring it. *I bet she can!*
he thought lewdly.

He put out his tongue and examined it for any traces of abnormality.
He was slowly persuading himself that he had not been tricked into
eating or drinking anything fatal, but there was no harm in checking up.
His heart leapt as he saw a dark brown smear around his gums. Then he
remembered Lilli's chocolate and smiled. He felt all right. He looked
all right. Almost certainly, he was all right.

He made another futile attempt to retrieve his toothbrush from the
sticky board, gave up, and got into bed. He stretched his toes. It was
some time since he had slept between linen sheets. He sighed with deep
enjoyment. He poured himself a cup of cocoa. Surely he was imagining
that it tasted slightly bitter? Of course he was! He was safe here. This
was a house where they labeled their poison.

CHAPTER 4

In the room above that of Benjamin Cann, Fan and Peter Hilford were undressing. That is, Fan was undressing and Peter was sitting on the floor in front of the gas fire in his underpants. He had a sheet of manuscript paper in his hand and he was preparing to read aloud the first page of his new novel. This was the fourth of a series, and Peter wrote them as fast as he could and rarely bothered to reread them. To the amazement of himself and his friends, they had found a niche. He cleared his throat.

" 'Detective-Inspector Carstairs,' " he began.

Fan sniffed.

"I know, I know," said Peter. "But I have to cater for my public. You want to go on eating, don't you? Everybody else loves Carstairs."

"I'd just like him to pull a terrible boner once in a while."

"Will you be quiet?"

"Certainly."

"Good. 'Detective-Inspector Carstairs was not himself. He walked morosely down Upper Thames Street, tugging at his grizzled mustache. It was a dirty night, a night on which anything might happen. The fog swirled about his broad shoulders. As he turned into the velvet darkness of the tunnel, some sixth sense told him that he was being followed. The footsteps were deliberate but stealthy. Carstairs walked faster and they increased their pace. He looked over his shoulder, but even his keen eyes could not pierce the gray veils of the fog. "May be trouble tonight," he mused, and ducked instinctively as the first shot rang out. With surprising agility for a man of his bulk, he wheeled on his toes and, in hot pursuit of his invisible antagonist, disappeared into a bank of putrid fog.' "

"Mm-hm," said Fan. She stood in front of the mirror, arched her back, and sprinkled talcum powder on to her stomach. She wore a coral necklace and nothing else.

"Aren't you rather overdressed?"

"Frankly, I'm fed up with Carstairs."

"Well, would you mind keeping it to yourself? Shall I do your back?"

"No. And don't you try to suck up to me, you – you *spy*! I'm not a complete moron. I know perfectly well that all you want is to get downstairs and lock antlers with that poor little man again." She sprang angrily into bed and turned her back. "Go on, for heaven sake! Go and beat him to a pulp and get it over with."

"All right," said Peter. "I'll do just that."

He pulled on his dressing gown and savagely tied the sash. Fan sat up in bed.

"Peter, come back! Don't be a donkey!"

She listened to him padding downstairs. It made her even angrier that he had gone barefoot. It was the first time she had ever had a lodger, and she wanted to do the thing properly. A serious landlord would never be seen in his dressing gown – and particularly not in that dressing gown, in which Peter frequently worked at Carstairs or in his darkroom. It was generously splashed with ink, and parts of it had been rotted away by developer. Anyway, why was he so allergic to Mr. Cann? It was the first time he had ever refused to tell her anything.

She got out of bed, wrapped herself in a shawl, and crept after her husband. The landing was in darkness. Croydon barked once from the Berkos' room opposite. Fan hovered at the top of the stairs, peering downwards. A few seconds later she heard Peter coming up. He growled something at her and pushed her into the bedroom. He shut the door behind him. He moved with difficulty because his right foot was attached to an eighteen-inch board. Fan stared and turned away. She was angry and she did not want to laugh, but her shoulders shook.

"*Do* something!" said Peter furiously. "*Help* me!"

"It's the rat man's secret glue."

"I trod on it in the bloody dark. It was by his bed. Don't just stand there! Get it off me."

"What's that toothbrush doing?"

"I don't know and I don't care. Will you kindly do something before I lose my temper?"

"But I shall get gummed up too."

"Hold it underneath. Try twisting it."

Fan twisted it. She pushed it and pulled it. The board did not budge. She began to laugh again.

"All right!" said Peter bitterly. "Laugh! *What am I going to do?*"

"It looks like a tiny ski."

Peter stood up and clumped out of the room. Fan followed him. He went into the bathroom and turned on the taps. He sat on the edge of the bath waiting for it to fill, then heaved the foot into the water.

"Fan," he said. "Promise me something."

"All right. What?"

"That you'll have that man out of here by tomorrow midday."

"Mr. Cann? But *why*?"

"I'll explain everything tomorrow when you've got rid of him."

"But why not *now*?"

"Because there's no point in – look, love, will you believe me just for tonight? I'll tell you all about it tomorrow. Right now, just believe me that he can't stay here. When you know what I know, you'll understand. I don't care how you do it, but you throw him out tomorrow. Promise?"

"No. I don't believe in Cloaks and Daggers."

"All right, don't!" shouted Peter, suddenly losing his temper. "I'll send Sylvia up from the office. I can always rely on her."

Sylvia was Peter's secretary. She had never actually said so, but she was fond of hinting that she was more indispensable to Peter than his wife.

"What a good idea," said Fan, making patterns in the soap with her nails. "Sylvia'll love that." After a moment, she said, "Whatever Sylvia can do, so can I."

Peter said nothing.

"I don't want Sylvia to come here. She seeks out dust and offers to mend your clothes, and it makes me hopping angry."

"There's a hole in my brown socks."

"Well, suppose there is? Take it to Sylvia and let her wave her magic wand at it." The soap broke in half.

"Are you going to do what I say?"

"Yes. I'll do anything rather than have that great brood mare stamping around."

"Would you mind lowering your voice?"

"Not at all."

"Thank you. Are you going to get rid of Cann?"

"Yes."

"You promise?"

"I've said so eight times."

"Well, come and give me a kiss. I'll send Sylvia out to buy you some flowers in her lunch hour."

"Will you? Will you, darling? And I'll get rid of Little Runty first thing in the morning. I'd like a potted bush better than flowers. In a tub."

"Something heavy, you mean?"

"She's very strong."

"I'm not making a drama, but really, sweet, as long as he's here, he's rather a menace."

"He hasn't done anything to me. Why didn't *you* tell him he'd got to go?"

"That's what I went down for. He wouldn't answer. He was pretending to have a nightmare. Most embarrassing. And I'd got this damned thing stuck on to my foot, and one can't behave with dignity under those sort of circumstances. Don't look now, but my big toe's loose."

He wriggled his toes experimentally. The board plunged and then popped out of the water, leaving a trail of bubbles. It fell on to the floor and claimed the bath mat.

Drying his foot, Peter said, "Fan, I'd rather you didn't mention this to Hugo or Bertha."

"My dear love, of course I won't! They'd dine out on it for weeks."

"What shall we do with this thing?"

"*I'm* not going to touch it."

"Nor am I. Let's go to bed."

"All right. I can't help feeling rather sorry for the rats, can you?"

"I don't believe it'll catch any. No self-respecting rat will be fooled by a thing that size."

"You were."

"That's got nothing whatever to do with it."

*

All night long, the rats ran about in the walls. They had only just taken over the house, and they were still busy consolidating their positions.

*

When Fan woke in the morning, Peter had gone. There was a note pinned to the front of her nightdress with a tie pin. *Dear Madam*, it read. *I may be late back. Get rid of Little Runty. If he's here when I get back, expect trouble. If you're a good girl, I'll make Sylvia buy you a cast-iron lawn dog. With love from Sir.*

Fan dressed quickly, combed her hair, and went into the bathroom to wash. She glanced out of the window. It was directly opposite to the bathroom of the Asterisk Club. She saw Mrs. Barratt peering into a mirror and inserting her dentures. Both stepped back hastily. Fan missed the sticky board by an inch. She pushed it carefully under the bath. In the far corner, where she could not reach it, was the soap. The rats had towed it up to their hole in the skirting, but it would not go in. It was covered with deep scratches where they had gnawed at it. Fan cleaned her teeth. She was experimenting with a new way of spitting toothpaste when she saw from under her eyelashes that the woman in the opposite window was still watching her. She had drawn the net curtains and apparently thought that Fan could no longer see her. She had butterfly clips in the front of her hair.

Fan went downstairs. As she passed the Berkos' door she heard Hugo gargling. He always did it in the autumn because if he got a cold it lasted the whole winter. Bertha was in the kitchen, frying sausages. Her hair hung down her back in a red mane and her face shone.

"My dear," she said without preamble. "I can't help agreeing with Peter. Little Runty's got to go. He kept me awake for hours. God knows what he was doing, but he was making a noise like a Koran reader."

She speared a piece of sausage and gave it to Croydon, who yelped and dropped it. Bertha snatched the animal into her arms.

"Izza poor-poor?" she said. "Did Muvver burnums?" She turned over the sausages with her free hand and sighed. "My dear, I do so want a child," she said. "I think one feels so *unfulfilllled*, don't you? But Hugo *will* go straight to sleep. There's absolutely no excuse for it, because, after all, it's years since he's been an active refugee. Is Peter like that?"

"No. Is there any bacon?"

"Not a bite. The rats took it. They seem to like it next best after cheese. I do wish they'd pick on things that weren't rationed."

She put Croydon down on the floor. Croydon ate the piece of sausage, heaved, and spat it back on to the linoleum. She stood there looking at it, waiting for it to grow cold.

Fan made some coffee. She drank a cup, thinking uneasily about her lodger. She poured another cup, put it on to a tray, and took it upstairs to Mr. Cann. She decided that she would let him drink it first and then tell him gently but firmly that he must go.

She knocked on his door three times, but there was no answer. Wondering whether he had already left, she opened the door and peeped in. The curtains were still drawn and the room was in semidarkness. She switched on the light and nearly dropped the cup of coffee. For a moment she stared, then she walked into the room, carefully shut the door, and sat down on the nearest chair.

Mr. Cann sprawled over the edge of the bed face down. His head hung just clear of the floor. One of his arms trailed on the carpet, and his knees were drawn up against his chest. She knew at once that he was dead.

Her heart began to pound. She sat on the chair with the tray on her knees and drank the cup of coffee she had brought for him. She put the cup neatly back on to the tray and the tray on to the table. She walked across the room and stood looking down at him. She had never before seen anybody dead.

His watch was still going. The secondhand was moving around its little dial and she could hear it ticking. Hooked on to the index finger of his right hand was one of Bertha's yellow cups.

Fan walked steadily downstairs to the telephone. She picked up the receiver and stood listening to it buzzing, trying to make up her mind who to call. Peter? A doctor? Or the police? Obviously, the police. But what did one say? *Can I speak to Detective-Inspector Carstairs? I think my lodger has committed suicide.* But had he? She shut her eyes and leaned against the wall. Peter's voice said to her clearly, "I don't care how you do it, but you've got to get rid of him." His foot was attached to the sticky board which had been beside this man's bed. He was saying, "He can't stay here. I don't care how you do it, but throw him out tomorrow." His face came closer until he was staring into her eyes through her eyelids. "Promise me," he said. "If you knew what I know, you'd understand."

She swallowed. She had never before thought of Peter as anything but the stubborn, casual, dear character she had married. She did not understand at all, but she knew what she must do. She replaced the receiver and went back upstairs to Mr. Cann. She looked at her watch. It was nearly half past eight. Mr. Cann's watch said twenty to nine, but she knew that it was fast. Marleen and the Rodent Officer would be arriving at any moment. The house would be full of people. She had about five minutes to get rid of Mr. Cann.

She locked the door and looked around doubtfully. For a wild second she considered throwing him out of the window. If she could get him downstairs she might be able to bury him in the back garden. No, you couldn't bury a corpse in broad daylight, overlooked by the windows of at least five other houses. *I'm just being silly. I'm sure it's perfectly easy if I think it out carefully.*

She dismissed the idea of taking Bertha into her confidence. Bertha would not be able to resist telling her greatest friends in the strictest confidence. Within a week everybody in Chelsea would know that, to put it mildly, Peter was not a reliable landlord. Rumors would reach the ears of the police, and Peter would be arrested and hanged by the neck until he was dead. No, this was a private matter between herself and her husband. She was not going to allow a simple little problem like this to break up her marriage. One false step now, and within a week she would be virtually a widow. She had got to be practical.

She looked resentfully at Mr. Cann. It would, she was sure, have been difficult enough to persuade him, in spite of his protestations, to leave the house alive. Dead, he was going to be far more trouble. If she had known how, she would have cut him up into pieces and distributed him around the house. But she did not, and anyway there was not time. She must hide him somewhere, that was it. Just temporarily, until she thought of something better.

Downstairs, the front door slammed. She heard Marleen singing tunelessly to herself in the hall. She began to panic. She rushed to the wardrobe and flung open the door. Running to the bed, seizing Mr. Cann, she gripped him around the waist and tried to lift him. He rolled over, his arm raised stiffly in a fascist salute. Levering him into an upright position and easing him on to the floor, she held him under the arms and dragged him halfway to the wardrobe before she dropped him.

The room shook. A flake of plaster fell from the ceiling.

Fan closed her eyes and counted up to fifty before she was satisfied that there was no reaction from downstairs. Then she grabbed Mr. Cann by the upraised hand and towed him along the floor. His head got wedged against the dressing table and she had to reverse. She dragged him up to the wardrobe, tensed her small muscles, and humped him in. Breathing heavily, she hoisted him into a corner, propped him up, and hurried around the room collecting his few personal effects. She wrapped them in his handkerchief and put them into his trouser pocket, then stood gazing at his ration book. It was in an imitation leather folder, and he had not drawn his rations for eleven weeks.

She washed out the thermos gingerly. It was not unreasonable to suppose that the cocoa had been laced with the Rodent Officer's arsenic. She took a last look at her first lodger. He had not even paid. He crouched in the wardrobe, his arm raised in farewell. She shut the door and locked him in, drew apart the curtains, and turned off the light. She put the wardrobe key in her pocket and took a final look around the room. There was a piece of brown paper on the floor and the bed was unmade. It looked as if somebody had left in a hurry.

She went shakily down to the hall and phoned up Peter.

"You-know-who is safely cached away," she said cautiously.

"*That's* my girl!" said Peter.

"I must say it gave me quite a shock."

She heard papers rustling.

"What?" said Peter.

"I said that I think it was jolly mean to go sleazing off to the office and leaving me to cope. I've only made a temporary arrangement, if you see what I mean. I think the least you can do is to come home and help."

She heard Sylvia say, "Here it is, Peter. It was in the blue file after all."

"I shall do no such thing," said Peter. "You can do it perfectly well by yourself. It's too easy for words. Just kick him out."

"You know very well it's not as simple as that. I'm scared stiff. And so is he, at the moment."

"Look," said Peter. He was trying not to be impatient. "I'm up to the neck in this stuff. There are three people waiting to see me. So be a good girl and get it over with, will you?"

"But, *Peter* ..."

"If you're scared, make Bertha do it. Or Hugo. Or Mr. Beesum." He was working himself up. "Or ring up the chap next door who sent him. Or call the Fire Brigade. Or ring up Scotland Yard. But, please, let me get on with my work now. I'll be home as early as I can and I'll bring you a nice potted bush, but I'm busy now and I'm going to sign off."

She heard Sylvia say in a low voice, "Be firm, Peter. Crawley's getting impatient. She'll get over it."

"Listen!" shouted Fan. "You tell that old seed catalogue ..."

"This evening," said Peter. "'Bye now."

"*Peter!*"

He hung up. Fan slammed the receiver on to its rest. She picked up the telephone directory and threw it on to the floor.

Marleen came out of the kitchen wheeling the Hoover and munching something. Croydon ran after her, snapping at a trailing loop of flex.

"Mornin', dear," said Marleen, giving Fan a sympathetic leer. "Don't take on. They're all the same." She went into the dining room, pushing Croydon ahead of her with the Hoover.

Fan stamped into the kitchen. Bertha was sitting on the table eating a piece of Ryvita and watching the sausages.

"Peter is an absolute beast," said Fan.

"Well, you're a very lucky girl," said Bertha. "Personally, I only attract eunuchs."

Fan pushed her hair back. Restively, she dipped a spoon into a jar of jam and licked it.

"Little Runty's gone," she said carefully.

"Well done! Did he take it quietly?"

"He didn't say a word."

"He's left his overcoat behind. It's on a peg in the hall. Let's hock it and go fifty-fifty. After all, he didn't pay." She turned over the sausages. "The moment I laid eyes on him, I knew he was a dead loss."

CHAPTER 5

MR. BEESUM arrived at nine o'clock. He wore his Burberry with the dignity of a general and looked at Marleen, who admitted him, as if he expected her to salute him. He dragged his bicycle into the hall and chained it to the studio door. He inquired whether there had been any night skirmishing on the part of the rats.

"I dunno," said Marleen. "I ain't done the upstairs yet." She pinched up her lanky hair and swung one leg provocatively.

Mr. Beesum dispatched her to fetch the sticky boards and marched into the kitchen. He found Mrs. Hilford and Mrs. Berko there. Mrs. Berko wore a faded cretonne housecoat. It had parted slightly in front, and he saw a triangle of pink knitted vest. Mrs. Hilford had on a pair of brown corduroy trousers and a red sweater. She looked, Mr. Beesum decided privately, Arty. Both greeted him eagerly, telling him how the rats had taken their bacon and molested their cold cream. Mr. Beesum listened attentively. He wondered whether Mrs. Hilford could be sickening for something. Her eyes were too bright.

A few minutes later Mr. Berko appeared, haggard in a dressing gown covered with smears of clay. He had combed the dark, dapper beard which was his one vanity and was holding a plate of congealed sausages. Being an enthusiastic sleeper, he was not at his best in the mornings. He had formed the habit, during his enforced treks across Europe, of being able to sleep profoundly for a few minutes at a time. He could do this standing up, floating in the sea, and even, Bertha claimed, while dancing certain slow waltzes. He was a Hungarian not yet naturalized. He had dark, enigmatic eyes and was a head shorter than Bertha.

"How do you do," he said to Mr. Beesum. He yawned widely. "Excuse me. I am delighted to see you. The rats are undermining my morale." He put the plate of sausages on the floor, offering it to Croydon, who sniffed at it and declined it. Hugo leaned against the dresser and went to sleep.

Marleen returned with the sticky boards, carrying them carefully by their outer edges. One bore the toothbrush and the bath-mat, and on the other was a large rat *couchant*. Marleen placed the boards on the table before Mr. Beesum with the air of an acolyte offering a sacrifice. She had attempted to curl her lank hair and doused herself with a racy perfume. She looked wistfully at the back of the Rodent Officer's head, but he was more interested in the rat.

"Yes," he said with a smack of the lips. "About eighteen months, I'd sey. Thet ret, if left to its own devices, could in three years have been responsible for three hundred and fifty million progeny. *Thet is a vital statistic.*"

The rat stared at him, swishing its tail. Hugo also had opened his eyes and was studying the Rodent Officer. His expression said clearly that, in his experience anyway, Mr. Beesum was unique. The little man, obviously enjoying his moment in the limelight, snapped the locks on his attaché-case.

"If you would not mind," he said gravely, "there are certain devices I hev in here which are strictly professional secrets. They are not for the eyes of leymen." He waited until all had looked decently away, then, with the swiftness of a conjurer, opened his case and whipped out a standard rat trap. "Right," he said. "You can look now. You are surprised, are you not? En ordinary beck-breaker, you say! But, say I, *hold hard!* I em fully aware thet every London ret hes seen a replica of this clumsy mechanism end knows it for what it is. Rets are not fools. With just such chicanery, we shell lure them into a sense of false security. Psychological warfare. Never fear, we hev meny tricks up our sleeves."

He slid a hand into his case and brought forth a cube of cheese. It was faintly iridescent. "Phenyl-thiourea!" he said proudly. "Some smell it, some don't. Like arsenic, if carefully disguised, some rets will tek it."

Fan poured herself some cold coffee. She felt slightly sick. So some rats would take it, would they? That was, if it was carefully disguised, with malice aforethought, in something pungent like cocoa. But Mr.

Cann was not a rat. He was, or had been, an unattractive but harmless little man. For the first time in her life, Fan thought of her husband without affection.

She slipped out of the room. Hugo was asleep, propped against the dresser and, except for the fact that he had his eyes shut, he looked quite intelligent.

She went upstairs to the drawing room and crouched in front of the fire. Shivering, she took the key of Mr. Cann's temporary coffin from her pocket and laid it on the floor. She was still gazing at it, trying to plan her ex-lodger's immediate future, when Marleen pushed open the door and wheeled in the Hoover. Fan snatched a book from the shelves and pretended to be reading. It was called *What To Do Before The Doctor Comes,* and she read a few lines about thrombosis.

"Don't take on, ducky," said Marleen cheerfully. "They're all the same. I tell you straight, I don't like men. But what I say is where would the yuman race be without?" She plugged in the Hoover. It whinnied and settled to a low drone. "Wonderful invention!" she yelled. "'S what I mean 'bout men. Regard 'em as 'ome comforts and you got to admit they're ingeenious."

Finding Fan uncommunicative, she made a few symbolic passes with a duster and retreated, dragging the Hoover behind her like a victim.

At half past eleven a car drew up outside. Fan, hoping that it was Peter and deciding in the same second that if it was she was not going to speak to him, ran to the window. It was Rex. He was arguing with a taxi driver. He was wearing a yellow beret and waving his hands about. Fan stood watching him, pleased that he had come. He rummaged in his pockets for his latch key and she heard him coming upstairs. She would have recognized his footsteps anywhere. She knew the way they all came upstairs after they had been out. Peter slammed the front door and whistled to her. Bertha shut the door carefully and then came up slowly, squeaking her hand on the banisters. Hugo gave the door a push but never quite shut it. Marleen banged the door and went slopping across the hall, singing to herself under her breath. And Rex, who lived in the next road, did not shut the door at all and he came upstairs lightly, three steps at a time.

"Olé!" he cried on the landing. He threw open the door and struck an attitude. "Angel!" he said. "I *bite* you. My teeth *meet*! The most vile taxi! I know it was naughty, but I put the money on the roof."

Fan tried to rouse herself. Rex was clearly in one of his loquacious moods. He threw himself into a chair and combed his hair.

"My dear," he said, "I've had another *barking* row with Bunny. Really, he is *quite* nauseating. He foams at the mouth, have you noticed? And *spots*! Neville says he means well, but in my opinion to foam at the mouth and grow spots and mean well is simply not *enough*. I'm still mad with rage. Let's go somewhere and do something quite outrageous."

Fan looked at him thoughtfully. Rex was a ballet dancer. Despite his superficial air of frailty, he had well-developed muscles. She had seen him lift a plump ballerina with one hand and walk about a stage smiling.

"What sort of thing had you in mind?" she asked.

Rex waved his hand. "I don't know, dear. Something gay and daring."

Fan considered him. She had known him almost all her life. They had played together as children. They had grown up together. They had been together to the Slade when Rex was in what he called his Purple Period. As long as she could remember, she had told Rex all her secrets.

"Make yourself at home," she said. "Put your feet up. I might know of something."

"But is it *gay*, dear?"

"Not very."

"Exciting?"

"Oh, yes."

"Illicit?"

"Definitely."

"Wrap it up. I'll take it."

Fan was still doubtful. She got up and poured two tots of gin. "I've got a rather awful secret," she said.

Rex choked. "*Give!*" he said.

"If I tell you, will you swear to keep it under your bonnet?"

"But darling, *of course!* You know me."

"All right. Come with me."

She led him down the short flight of stairs into her ex-lodger's room. She locked the door and drew the curtains. She handed him the wardrobe key.

"Look in there," she said.

Rex fitted the key into the lock and pulled open the door. He peered inside. "Well, *really!*" he said. "What ever next?"

"I didn't do it."

"Come off it, dear! Who is he? I've seen that nose before."

"No, you haven't. He's *dead*, you know."

"Well, I didn't think he was making that grotesque face for fun."

"You're taking it jolly calmly."

"Angel, when one's worked with a Russian ballet for any length of time, one loses one's capacity for surprise."

"Well, I call it downright indecent."

"If it'll make you any happier, ducky, just say the word and I'll scream my head off."

"Rex" – she shook his arm – "Rex, you've got to help me! You've *got* to! You're an accessory after the fact now."

Rex looked down at his feet. He arranged them carefully in the third position. "Not yet, I'm not," he said. "Tell me more. If you didn't do it, who did?"

Fan told him the events of the night before. He listened in silence. He wandered over to the dressing table and looked critically at himself in the mirror.

"Peter!" he said when she had finished. "It was Peter, the monster!"

"Will you be my accessory?"

"I'd do anything for Peter. He's a *steaming cup*."

"Well, how are we going to get rid of this character?"

"Isn't it customary to put them in trunks?"

"It's not very original."

"Well, he can't grumble, can he, dear, if you see what I mean?"

"Would he go into a suitcase?"

"Don't be disgusting. Let's do the thing decently."

Fan went upstairs to the attics at the top of the house. Here both families' luggage was stacked in pyramids. As she opened the door she heard a rat tearing up shavings in a tea-chest. She kicked the box, but the rat took no notice. She chose a large wardrobe trunk of Peter's. All the time she was unstacking and re-stacking the luggage, the rat ran about in the shavings.

She eased the trunk downstairs as quietly as possible. On the landing outside her bedroom door, with only a half-flight of stairs to go, she heard Bertha in the hall. She was trying to persuade Croydon to eat some whale meat. Croydon was not interested. Bertha bought whale meat for her every other day, but Croydon had never eaten it and never would.

Fan stood still, holding her breath until she heard Bertha say, as she did every day, "All right, *don't* eat it, you little cretin! *I* don't care!" and go through to the kitchen to prepare something else.

Croydon came frisking upstairs. She sniffed at the trunk. She ran beside it growling as Fan slid it down the last flight. Outside the door of the spare room, Fan tried to shoo her away. Croydon promptly threw herself on to her back and screamed.

"Croydon!" called Bertha from downstairs. Her heels came tapping out of the kitchen.

Rex jerked open the spare room door and snatched the trunk. He dragged it inside and kicked the door shut. Fan was left standing on the landing. Bertha started upstairs.

"What are you doing to Croydon?" she demanded.

"I didn't even touch her," snapped Fan. "She's just doing film star again."

Croydon squirmed along the floor to Bertha, looking beaten. Bertha picked her up.

"I do wish," she said frigidly, "that you'd be more tactful. You know perfectly well that she's terribly sensitive and she understands every word we say." She went downstairs, carrying Croydon, who lay over her shoulder and watched Fan with bright, malicious eyes.

Fan went into Mr. Cann's room and locked the door.

"Did she see?" asked Rex.

"No."

"Frankly, I spit on that dog."

"It's not a dog."

"Agree, agree."

Rex had taken Mr. Cann's body from the cupboard and, as it was still quite stiff, was having trouble in dressing it in its street clothes. Finally, he adjusted the tie, picked up the body as if it were a baby, and dropped it into the trunk. One arm stuck rigidly into the air, defying them to close the lid. They tried him in several different positions, but Mr. Cann was adamant. They shut the lid as far as it would go and draped the arm in a tablecloth. They sat on the edge of the bed and looked at each other.

"You don't know off hand how long rigor mortis takes, do you?" asked Fan.

"No."

"Do you think we could ring up a hospital and make discreet inquiries?"

"No. *Not.*"

"Well, really I suppose it doesn't make much difference. We can't very well take him out of the house until it's dark."

They discussed the main ways of disposing of bodies. First, there was cremation. This was the most honorable but also the most impractical. Fan reckoned that if it took twenty minutes to the pound to roast a leg of lamb, it would take two days and four hours to do Mr. Cann. Anyway, he would only be roasted, which obviously was not enough. Secondly, there was interment. This was all very well in the country but almost impossible in London. To dig a grave in their own garden was out of the question as it was overlooked on all sides. In the public parks, even in the dead of night, it would be asking for trouble, as there were unseen lovers in every bush and shadow. They decided against, thirdly, leaving him in a trunk at the cloakroom of a railway station. It had been done before, several times, and inevitably it attracted the attentions of Scotland Yard. For similar reasons they could not abandon the body in an empty house or deserted road.

Mr. Cann, they agreed, had got to disappear without a trace – or anyway be unidentifiable by the time he was discovered. Therefore there remained only disposal by acids, quicklime, or water. Acids and quicklime presented all sorts of difficulties, and the Thames was just around the corner.

"He'd float."

"We'd have to weight him."

"He'd bob up in the end and somebody would recognize him."

"You forget the fish, dear."

Fan shuddered. "I thought only lobsters did that sort of thing."

"Oh no. Rockfish ..."

"*Are* there fish in the Thames?"

"I suppose so. It must be a paradise for the mud kind."

It was at this moment that Mr. Cann's arm began to fall. Very gradually, it dropped until it was resting on the carpet, palm up. Inside the trunk, they heard a slow, slithering noise as Mr. Cann relaxed gently forever. Fan shut her eyes and dug her fingernails into the eiderdown.

"Rex," she said in a chocked voice, "let us ring up the police immediately and have them take him away. I've had enough."

Rex lit a cigarette and put it between her fingers. He said nothing for a moment. Before both of them rose Peter's reproachful face. Peter in handcuffs, looking abashed. Peter in court, looking scared. Peter in the condemned cell, looking desperate.

"You don't mean that, of course, do you, dear?" asked Rex with an effort.

Fan drew a deep breath. "No."

"You take it back?"

"Yes."

"Good. Let's lock this old zombie in and go upstairs and have a drink."

At half past one, Clifford Flush rang up from the Asterisk Club. Fan raced downstairs and beat Bertha to the telephone by a short head. Flush asked if Fan would very kindly tell Mr. Cann that luncheon and his fellow members were ready and that both were growing colder. Fan gripped the receiver tightly and told him that Mr. Cann had left with his few possessions shortly after eight o'clock. He had left no forwarding address. She agreed that it was most extraordinary and could think of no reason why he should have behaved in such a manner. She warmed to her task and added that she considered it extremely rude and that he had left in a hired Daimler. She rang off and found Bertha watching her suspiciously.

"I didn't see any Daimler," said Bertha.

"Didn't you?"

"No. I don't believe you did either. I think you're making it up."

"Do you?"

"What color was it?"

"Sort of silvery plum."

"Well, there aren't any silvery colors now. There haven't been since before the war."

"It looked quite old."

"Well, I didn't see it."

Bertha went into the kitchen looking dissatisfied. Croydon ran after her and leapt through the swing door just in time. Fan went upstairs. Rex had locked the door of the spare room. She went up to the drawing room and repeated the entire telephone conversation to him.

"There was once a murderer called Flush," she remarked. "He pushed old virgins off trains."

"Quite right too," said Rex.

"It couldn't possibly be the same one, could it? I'm just being silly, aren't I?"

"You said it, ducky, I didn't." He stood gazing out of the window. "Did Rossetti really plant that tree?"

"No."

"It says he did on the knob of granite."

"Hugo carved that. It's one of his sidelines."

"I should have had Diaghilev. That would really have been something."

"Bertha wanted Charles Boyer, but the tree was too old."

"It must have been thirty feet high when he was a little baby."

"Yes. Hugo said that if she insisted upon Charles Boyer, he'd put another rock right next door to it saying 'And Who Else?' "

"I wonder why they're called monkey *puzzle*. Isn't it odd? It's probably something to do with the Chinese. These things usually are."

Fan moved restlessly. "Dear Rex, I know you're trying to distract me. You've done very nicely. Now will you please let me worry in peace?"

"All right. Let's worry like mad. Shall we start on a worldwide basis and work down to ourselves, or start with ourselves and spread?"

"I'm going to do me-and-Peter and that dead man."

"All right. I'm just going to do a wee one about Bunny and then I'll join you. Always creeping around telling tales and stealing people's tights! How can anyone be that scrofulous and live? Now if somebody bumped *him* off, that would make sense."

"Ring him up and insult him."

"A weeze, dear!" "Go back to your wet cave," I'll cry. "I will personally roll the stone to its mouth."

"You can think of something worse than that. There's no hurry. We've got hours and hours to kill."

"Your tone, dear, is down-at-heel. Let's leave Himself to his siesta and go to a really murderous movie."

"No," said Fan. "No thank you. I couldn't eat the last one."

It was an old joke. For the first time, they did not laugh.

CHAPTER 6

LUNCHEON at the Asterisk Club was a silent affair. Flush's brooding calm was contagious. Shortly before, while the members were drinking an aperitif in the drawing room and waiting for Benjamin Cann with varying degrees of impatience, Flush had informed them of his telephonic conversation with Mrs. Hilford. Watching them closely, he had commented upon the inexplicable behavior of their newest recruit. All had appeared surprised though not unduly perturbed, but he himself was worried. Until summoned to luncheon by Beecher, he had sat with his chin on his chest, deep in thought. His taciturnity had infected the others one by one, and now, since entering the dining room, nobody had cared to break the silence.

Flush dissected his trout and wondered for the ninth time why the Hilford girl had lied about the Daimler. He had no doubt that she had lied. He had satisfied himself that Beecher, who was as usual on the morning lookout shift in his bedroom under the eaves, had not left his post. Beecher insisted that there had been no Daimler and that Mr. Cann had not left the house. Flush believed him. Although Beecher's record was mottled, he returned promptly to the Club after each of his sentences. Therefore Flush was forced to the conclusion that the wide-eyed girl next door had had the temerity to tell him a deliberate false-hood.

Beecher removed his plate and offered him a cheese souffle. Flush noticed that his steward's spatulate thumb was half submerged in the savory.

"Beecher," he asked slowly, "are you doing that on purpose?"

Beecher's small eyes flickered. He removed the plate. Flush began to peel a peach. He could do this without looking at it, so he turned his attention to his fellow members. Mrs. Barratt, he noticed, was eating with genteel relish. A portion of cheese souffle, in a test-tube, had played a prominent role in her trial. For years she had been allergic to the dish, but she was now apparently cured.

The Colonel was doodling on a table mat with the butter knife. Flush was not deceived by his listless manner. He knew that his Treasurer was trying to fathom out the pulley system, featured in a recent work by his favorite novelist, of shooting enemies in locked rooms. He was well aware that the Colonel could be made genuinely unhappy by any me-chanical device which he did not understand. Already that morning Flush had twice caught the Colonel experimenting. Once he had surprised him in the hall, weighting the pendulum of the grandfather clock with a large conical piece of plasticine. From this a long piece of wire led into the drawing room, disappearing under the carpet. This contraption had shown no results. But the second time, just before Mrs. Hilford's mad-dening lie, Flush had been sitting quietly alone in the library when an ancient blunderbuss hanging on the wall had swerved wildly and a cork had fallen out of its barrel. Flush investigated and found a thread of transparent nylon tied on to the trigger. He had followed this out of the room, across the hall, and into the butler's pantry. There he found the Colonel reeling it in on to an ordinary fishing rod. The Colonel turned the color of a ripe mulberry and said shortly that the pulley system was only feasible after years of practice. Flush, suppressing his irritation, agreed and they reached a tacit understanding that the Colonel should make no more disturbing experiments. But now, obviously, he was planning another stratagem and, quite apart from breaking his promise, he was ruining the table mats.

The Creaker was slapping his souffle with a spoon. His overgrown cat sat on his knee and watched. It was purring loudly and had smears of butter around its chops.

"Creaker, my friend," said Flush, frowning. "One eats souffle with a fork."

"Reelly?" said the Creaker unpleasantly. He inclined his large flat head towards Flush. "You want to make anythin' out of it?"

Flush did not answer. He knew better than to antagonize any of his companions, particularly the Creaker. Even now, memories of his oldest member's trial could cause him to glance nervously over his shoulder and, lately, the Creaker had shown signs of restiveness. If he were in for another bout … His thoughts changed the subject hastily. Lilli Cluj was the only one who had shown any real regret at Benjamin Cann's absence. Flush felt that she, like himself, was not satisfied with Mrs. Hilford's behavior. He had noticed her looking slyly around at her fellow members, as if wondering whether in any way one of them could be responsible. He wondered whether her interest in Mr. Cann, although purely erotic, was deep enough to cause her to lose her head. Once before, under very similar circumstances, he had had occasion to blackball a candidate for publicly commenting upon the unusual qualifications required to join the Asterisk Club. The man disappeared before he had done any real harm, but his observations, if unchecked, might well have proved disastrous. Although all the resident members had been legally acquitted, their proximity to each other, if advertised, would be, to say the least, intriguing to the police and the press. As Flush knew by experience, to arouse such interest in either of these bodies led to obtrusive activity of the type which he most resented.

"Lilli," he said. "Would you like to help me?" After the long silence, his voice was slightly louder than he had intended. The others looked up, startled.

"Yiss," said Lilli. If he had asked her to drink a pint of hemlock, her answer would have been the same. She was afraid of him. She knew that his questions, when accompanied by that courteous, fleeting smile, were not questions at all, but commands.

"Would you like to stay next door for a few days?"

"Yiss," said Lilli.

"You will report here for meals. I am rather curious about our neighbors. Do you understand me?"

Lilli nodded.

Beecher, unnoticed, scooped up a spoonful of souffle and flicked it at the Creaker's cat. It caught the animal on the side of the head and stopped its purring abruptly. The cat grunted and turned slowly to look at Beecher. It glared at him with extraordinary malevolence. Nobody else had seen. The episode was only one more manifestation of a bitter, atavistic feud.

CHAPTER 7

AT seven o'clock the light was fading fast.

At five minutes past, in his small office off Trafalgar Square, Peter Hilford dusted his enlarger, hung a row of prints to dry, and decided to go down to the Coach and Horses for a quick one before he went home.

At ten minutes past, the lamplighter zigzagged down Flood Walk on his bicycle, flicking on the street-lights with a long pole in passing. As he ignited the one outside the Asterisk Club the Colonel appeared, outward bound. He had an aster in his buttonhole and he climbed into his enormous Bugatti and revved the engine in friendly greeting.

At fifteen minutes past, Marleen made up her mind to forgo washing up the teacups and turning down the beds in order to walk halfway home with Mr. Beesum.

Five minutes later, the front-door bell rang and Bertha Berko, wearing a chintz apron and smelling strongly of fried onions, admitted Lilli Cluj. She showed her to the room recently vacated by Mr. Cann and accepted a week's rent in advance. She looked at Lilli's sheer, dark nylons and voluptuous figure and told her that linen was a guinea a week extra.

At half past seven, Croydon finished off a jar of Gentleman's Relish and lurched into the garden to be sick.

At twenty-five to eight, upstairs in the drawing room, Fan and Rex dressed Mr. Cann in his overcoat and hat and had another gin.

At quarter to eight, it was quite dark.

This was the hour that Fan and Rex had chosen. They reasoned that the people who were not at home having their dinner would probably be drinking in one of the area's numerous pubs. It was too late for those who took their dogs for an after-tea walk and too early for them to take the same dogs for a late-night final. The streets were as empty now as they would be that night.

Fan went on to the landing to see whether the coast was clear. She peered down into the hall and saw that the studio door was open. Hugo and Bertha were in there. The hall was in darkness, and for a second Bertha's huge shadow sprawled into the rectangle of light from the open door. She had her hands raised and her head bent forward and she was saying something in an angry monotone. Hugo answered clearly and without heat that he had never seen the woman before in his life and that if Bertha were going to make a scene, would she be kind enough to close the door. Bertha said something about strawberry blondes and the door slammed. A piece of Bertha's skirt caught in it and she had to open the door again to free herself. This time she closed it with elaborate care and without a sound.

Fan drew back. The drawing room door opened and the light clicked off. Rex appeared behind her. She could hear him breathing. She knew that he had Mr. Cann over his shoulder. He gave her a slight push with his free hand and she crept downstairs, across the hall, and opened the front door. She stood behind it and heard Bertha's voice saying from the studio that she knew all about White Russian cabaret artistes; and what her father would say, she simply did not dare to think.

Rex had started downstairs. Fan heard the second stair from the top creak, as it always did. She stood in the darkness, breathing carefully through her nose; then Rex slunk past her and Mr. Cann's cold, dangling hand brushed hers. She watched until Rex and his burden dissolved into the shadow of the monkey-puzzle tree, then slipped outside and closed the door behind her. It clicked loudly, but the voices in the studio did not stop.

It was very dark. The sky was overcast and it was too early for the moon. For a moment Fan hesitated. There was still time to turn back; to think of something else less venturesome. But at any second Peter would be home. If he found that she had not got rid of Mr. Cann, then he would enlist the aid of Sylvia – he had said so. But if Peter felt impelled to kill a man, then the disposal of the body was the duty of his wife, not his secretary.

She ran silently to the gate. She looked both ways, hurried back to the monkey-puzzle tree, and felt around for Rex. He reached out and touched her. She reported an empty street. He patted her hand. Each took an arm of Mr. Cann's around their necks. Fan shivered. Mr. Cann was cold and limp. He hung heavily between them, his head lolling.

"If we meet anybody, we're as drunk as owls," Rex reminded her in a breathless whisper. "Are you ready? *Now!*"

Fan nodded, unable to speak. She was trembling all over and did not want Rex to feel it. She took a firmer grip on Mr. Cann. They walked out of the shadow of the tree, through the gate, and across the road.

*

Beecher, who was doing his evening watch in the Asterisk Club, followed their progress with interest. He did not recognize Mr. Cann and, having not been informed of his disappearance, merely presumed that the nice little skirt next door was disposing of a drunken friend before her husband returned from the office. *Artists!* He thought. *Can't rely on 'em!*

*

His reactions were much as Fan and Rex would have hoped. Having reached the end of the road without incident, they gained courage. They had divided the journey into three laps, and the first was over. They turned the corner into Cheyne Row. An elderly woman bustled towards them along the pavement. She was holding a sprig of dead jasmine and turning it over between her fingers and she had a book under her arm.

Involuntarily, Fan stood still. "Rex …" she said weakly.

Rex broke into song. "… oh, bury me deep … on the lone prair-ee …"

Fan's small voice joined him valiantly. The woman looked up sharply. She stepped off the pavement and gave them a wide berth. She averted her eyes and dropped her book. A piece of pressed maidenhair fern fell out of it. The woman did not stop to pick it up. She scuttled round the corner as if she expected them to follow her.

Fan hitched up Mr. Cann and gave a little sigh. Rex gave an impatient tug at his half of the body. They hurried to the small public garden which formed an island in the middle of the road. An asphalt path ran down its length, edged with a narrow strip of grass and a screen of dusty shrubs and trees. They sank on to a wooden seat under an oleander bush. Mr. Cann drooped between them. They had completed the second lap of the journey.

They leaned across the dead man as a pair of quarrelling lovers approached. Rex took Mr. Cann by the scruff of the neck and held his head upright.

The woman looked at them without interest. "Well, all I got to say," she said to the man in the raglan coat, "is that there are some things you just don't *do*!"

"What about you?" said the man. "Two ports and I can't trust you! Nothing to do with you, was it? Oh, no!"

"Esme there and all!" said the woman. She was spoiling for a fight. "You see the way that bitch looked? I never been so ashamed."

"Your language," said the man.

They crossed the road and went down Cheyne Row.

Through the sparse trees, Rex was watching the far side of the road. His goal was the concrete walk which ran along the embankment and dipped to pass under Battersea Bridge. Here, the river would be just beneath them. There was a bench in the dip, a rockery, and a wire basket for refuse. It was hidden from the road by a semicircle of arbutus and thorn bushes, deep in the shadow of the bridge. Its very privacy made it a popular refuge for courting couples at a later hour. It was less than a hundred yards from where they sat, but it was also the far side of a broad and well-lit road with excellent visibility in both directions. This was the last and most hazardous lap of the journey. At the moment the road seemed to be deserted.

They had half-risen when a car passed. They sat down. A man on a bicycle passed in the opposite direction. They rose again and adjusted Mr. Cann. The elderly woman they had met across the road returned to retrieve her pressed maidenhair. She snatched it up and ran back around the corner holding on to her hat. An old man shuffled out of the pub on the corner by the bridge. They sat down. The old man crossed the road in slow motion. He leaned over the parapet, looking down at the river. He fumbled for a cigarette and put it into his mouth. He stayed looking at the river for eight minutes, then with a terrible rattle he hawked and spat. He broadcast an astonishing belch and shuffled back into the pub. He did not light the cigarette. He put it behind his ear as he went through the swing doors of the public bar.

"Now, dear," said Rex. "You stay here with the Loved One while I go and see whether we're going to be alone."

"Rex," said Fan in a despairing whisper, "if you leave me alone with him, I swear I'll never speak to you again!"

"Yes, you will, dear," said Rex. "Remember Pearl Harbor!"

He bounded into the bushes. He stopped to pluck a white flower and, putting it nonchalantly into his buttonhole, walked across the road.

Fan sat watching him with Mr. Cann leaning heavily against her. Now that Rex had gone, she was twice as frightened. *I'd make a rotten criminal*, she thought. *I shall never again be able to look a policeman between the eyes.* Rex, on the other hand, would be one of the mastermind type, the brain behind the brawn. *I hate brawn, it's made out of calves' faces.* Rex, she thought resentfully, was treating the whole thing as if it were a macabre, slow ballet. He seemed to be quite enjoying himself. But perhaps he was just being cunning … perhaps he had suddenly got cold feet and left her alone forever with Mr. Cann … perhaps he had gone to fetch the police! Panic began to swell inside her.

She was just about to leave Mr. Cann and run all the way home when she saw Rex hurrying down the path to her right. He must have crossed the road opposite to the pub and doubled back. She had been so intently watching the place where he had disappeared that she had not seen him. She jumped to her feet and clung to his arm. She was so pleased to see him that she could not stop smiling.

"Come on, ducky," said Rex. He was a little out of breath. "There's nobody there. Off we go! The curtain's up."

They picked up Mr. Cann, who had slithered on to the ground, and forced a way through the bushes. From behind a grimy laburnum tree, Rex looked up and down the road. There was nobody in sight.

"Are you ready?" He looked at her anxiously. "Don't try to hurry. We're overlooked by a million windows. Walk drunk. Sway. It's our only chance."

Fan nodded. She did not trust her voice. A twig was digging into the back of her neck, but she did not notice it.

"Allez oop!" said Rex.

They stepped out of the bushes into the road. They stumbled across beneath the bright strip lights. They were daylight lights; they made Fan's lipstick look purple and they cast no shadows.

On the far pavement, there was only twenty yards to go. Rex, against his own orders, walked faster. Mr. Cann began to slip. Fan ran a few steps to catch up, but she was too late. Mr. Cann slipped through their hands and fell in the road with a dull thud. Bending quickly to gather him up, Fan and Rex banged heads. Rex grabbed Mr. Cann, threw him over his shoulder and ran into the shadows. Fan walked after him. She tried to run, but her legs refused to obey her. Then she was inside the shelter of thorn and arbutus and she looked back across the wide road.

On the far side there was a woman leaning out of a lighted window. She was looking across the river.

"Rex," said Fan.

The woman had not seen them. She stretched and ducked back into the window, pulling the curtains.

"What?"

"Nothing."

"Well shush! Bags of hush!"

They propped Mr. Cann on the parapet and Fan supported him. She looked at him once and wondered whether to brush the gravel off his left cheek. The river made soft, slapping noises against the foundations of the dark bridge. Rex fetched two large stones from the rockery and unwound a length of rope from his waist. He tied the rope on to the stones, then attached one stone loosely to Mr. Cann's neck, the other to his feet. He balanced them on the parapet and took Mr. Cann by the small of the back.

"The Greeks," whispered Fan, "say that the souls of murdered men won't go away. They hang around and turn into werewolves."

"Really, dear," said Rex, "this is no time for fireside chat! I'm going to say one, two, three. Three's the cue. Don't throw him, *ease* him over. Now, are you ready? One … Two … *Three!*"

Mr. Cann crumpled. The stone tied to his ankles fell off the wall and jerked his feet downwards. He slipped, banged his head on the parapet, and disappeared. There was a dull smack, then silence.

"*You* look!" whispered Fan. Her eyes were round with horror. "I just *can't!*"

Rex leaned far over the wall. He stared downwards, then stood up slowly, and wiped his hands on a silk handkerchief.

"Of course, it's quite surrealist," he said, "but the tide's out!"

CHAPTER 8

AT twenty minutes past eight in the Asterisk Club, Beecher, whose evening watch had only ten minutes to go, noticed a party of three turn into Flood Walk. It was the girl from next door and her boyfriends and they were walking slowly as if they had been a long way. He was surprised to see the drunk was still with them, very dishevelled and covered with what looked like mud and green slime. *Something fishy 'ere!*

he thought, leaning out of the window to get a better view.

The drunk was no longer wearing a hat, and as the three passed under the street-light, Beecher stiffened. *Hul-lo!* he thought. *That's Benjamin Cann they've got there! He's drunk or doped or dead, but that is the old Tin Cann himself or my name is Agatha Christie!*

He watched them stumble into Number Fifteen before he hurried downstairs to make his report.

*

At half past eight, Mr. Cann had been sponged down and returned to his trunk in the drawing room. Rex was pacing restively and Fan, out of sheer relief to be home, had lost her temper and was lashing herself into a fury about Peter. He had not wanted to frighten her, she pointed out bitterly. Being a model of chivalry, he had not told her that he had foully murdered her first lodger. He wanted to break it to her gently, so he merely left her to cope with the corpse. And now, to crown all, he was late for dinner! She knew, as well as Rex did, that dinner was not ready, but it might have been, and if it had been Peter would have been late. Rex nodded sympathetically. As he passed the trunk for the fifth time, he suddenly bent down and gave Mr. Cann a savage push.

"I'll never speak to you again," he said. "Not you or any other of your tribe. I've crossed you right off my list."

"Leave him alone," said Fan crossly. "He's had enough for one day." She slammed the lid of the trunk on Mr. Cann and went downstairs to telephone. Hugo Berko was in the hall. He had just finished his dinner and was attending to his teeth with a gold toothpick.

"Hullo," he said. "Come and see my mustang. Not swanking, I think I've done some rather fascinating sketches."

Fan followed him into the studio. She was not going to telephone to Peter in anger with Hugo listening. Hugo pushed a large piece of cartridge paper into her hands.

"It's an understatement, of course," he said, "but, personally, I feel that underlines its strength. Have you seen Lilli Cluj?" he went on without a pause. "She's quite something! A strawberry blonde! I'd like to do a thoroughly sexy nude in terra cotta, but Bertha would have a fit. Dear girl, she's a jewel, but her father was a brigadier and it seems in some way to have *stunted* her. She has fixed ideas about things like nudity and adultery and garlic." He looked sideways at Fan and lifted his shoulders. "Myself, I think that, in moderation, any one of them has a certain charm, don't you? But not our Bertha! Has it occurred to you that the only other Big Bertha in existence, as far as I know, was designed to undermine the morale of Paris?" He laughed until it turned into a cough. He patted himself on the chest. "Honestly, he said, "I'm not being bitchy, but I swear to you that if Bertha got half a chance she'd wear red flannel knickers! Her gods are the hearth, the suet pudding, and the white cliffs of Dover. She couldn't understand in a million years that I regard Lilli Cluj, who I assure you undermined the morale of Budapest in no uncertain way, purely as ..."

"Purely as a lewd work of art?"

Hugo beamed. "We understand each other. Bertha, bless her, is jealous. She reasons that Lilli and I both have Balkan backgrounds, that the Balkans are rife with iniquity and that therefore Lilli and I have shared a clandestine couch."

"And have you?"

"Certainly not."

"You're lying, you fox!"

Hugo rolled a piece of clay into a ball and put it carefully on to the table. "Don't bully me," he said. "If you value your husband, go and rescue him. He is probably in peril. He is at this moment closeted with Lilli, who is about as affectionate as a giant squid and equally adhesive."

"I thought he was held up at the office."

Hugo laughed. "You're a very nice wife."

"I suppose you think I'm going to be jealous too."

Hugo crinkled his eyes at her. "Of course not! How absurd!"

"I'm never jealous."

"Of course you aren't!"

"I trust Peter implicitly."

"I'm sure you do."

"But perhaps I'd better go and fetch him. I expect he's hungry."

Hugo smiled after her as she left the studio. She had an enchanting little bottom. He would have liked to carve her in yellow sandstone, but he knew that Bertha would never allow that either.

*

Fan was about to knock on Lilli Cluj's door when, behind it, she heard Peter laugh. It was a low, intimate laugh, the kind that Peter had no business to share with other women – especially with Hungarian cabaret artistes who were Quite Something. And particularly not today, less than twenty-four hours after he had killed his previous tenant. She determined that Peter must be punished. She stifled an impulse to burst into the room and do it at once. It was just possible that Peter might think that she was jealous, which would be quite idiotic. She was merely indignant with good cause. If she flung open the door and confronted them, it might be misconstrued and give Peter a certain gratuitous satisfaction. She did not want him at the moment to have any sort of satisfaction whatever. Nor did she want to make a fool of herself. She had once seen Bertha furiously snatch open the studio door to find Hugo not, as she had expected, rolling around with a Burmese model but playing with the cat next door.

She compromised. She knocked and opened the door at the same time.

Lilli was lying on the bed in a coffee-colored negligee. Her spectacular hair hung over one eye. She had a cigarette in one hand and a drink in the other. Peter sat at the foot of the bed with one of her small, bare feet in his lap. He was tickling its sole. There was a potted bush in the middle of the room. It was a yew and it had been trimmed into the shape of a peacock. Askew on its head was Lilli's gay little feather hat.

"Which iss thiz whomarn?" asked Lilli. She raised her leg and sighted at Fan along it.

"Hullo, love," said Peter. He did not appear at all embarrassed. "This is Miss Cluj. She's Persian."

"Wronk," said Lilli. "I am Mede."

"How do you do," said Fan coldly. She tried not to look at the potted bush. "I hate to interrupt but I thought Peter might be hungry."

"I've eaten," said Peter calmly. "Lilli made me a rather weird pancake."

"I know mitwiz the charcoalz but the elektricks, no. Pieder laugh."

Peter winked at Fan. He made a slight movement with his head, implying that she was to leave. "Run along, sweet," he said. "Lilli and I are going to have a little talk."

Fan opened her mouth and shut it again. Peter began to stroke Lilli's instep again. Lilli gave Fan a feline smile over his shoulder. Fan turned abruptly and ran out of the room. Trembling with rage, she rushed upstairs and into the drawing room. Mr. Cann was propped up in his trunk with his chin on his chest and Rex was lying on the sofa cutting his nails.

"What's the matter, angel?" he asked. "You're as red as a rose."

"I'm so mad I could *spit*. Peter's been here all the time! He's down there horsing around with that dark White Russian."

"What Russian?"

"That Asterisk Russian. She only arrived this evening, and Peter's already scratching her feet."

"I thought she was a Croat."

"She's a foreign Hungarian and she's made him a joke dinner and she's got practically nothing on at all!"

"*Why* is he scratching her feet?"

"I don't know. She says she's a Mede. He's given her my potted bush. He didn't even come and ask about Mr. Cann! We might have been arrested! We might have been in jail! We might have been shot escaping – *we might have been lying there dead*!"

"Where?"

"What do you mean, where?"

"Lying *where* dead?"

"Anywhere. Just lying dead. What are Medes anyway?"

"God knows, dear. I thought they went out with the Old Testament."

"I would have liked that bush. It was rather gay. Why don't you put that man away? I'm fed up with him sitting there and staring."

"He's wet. I'm airing him."

"Yoo – hoo – oo!" called Bertha from halfway up the stairs.

Rex vaulted over the back of the sofa without a sound, pushed Mr. Cann roughly into his trunk, and slammed the lid. By the time Bertha appeared in the doorway, he was draped over the temporary coffin and casually smoking a cigarette.

"Hullo," said Bertha. She was carrying a plate of sandwiches, and she looked at Rex inquisitively. "Are you having a scene? What are you doing with that trunk? Are you going away?"

"Just tidying things up."

"Oh. I thought you might be leaving Peter or something. I don't mean leaving for good – I mean a sort of *token* leave. He made the most tremendous pass at that houri the moment she set foot. He's still shut up in there with her. If I were you, I'd be absolutely *livid*."

"I am."

"Are you going to speak to him if he comes out alive?"

"No."

"Good. Nor am I speaking to Hugo. I've made up a bed for myself in the dining room. Would you care to join me?"

"Thank you."

"Jugoslav my foot!" said Bertha. "Did she hand you that line too? She's a Levantine, that's what she is and I'm going to kick her out first thing tomorrow morning. Would you like a sandwich? They're anchovies."

"I can't touch anchovies," said Rex. "They make my nose bleed."

"Poor Rex! Are you going to sleep here?"

"Yes, dear," said Rex. He tapped his cigarette carefully over an ashtray. "I'm a sort of bodyguard."

*

At half past ten, Fan and Bertha went downstairs. They met Hugo on the landing. He had clay in his hair and was carrying a glass of milk. He had evidently forgotten that he was not on speaking terms with his wife, for he stopped and accused her of secreting a bottle of fixative. Bertha turned away her head and brushed past him.

"Oh yes, of course," said Hugo. He tapped himself on the forehead with his index finger and went on his way.

As Fan passed Lilli Cluj's door, she heard somebody inside talking in a rapid undertone. In the dining room, Bertha had pushed aside the refectory table and set up a camp bed. She obviously did not intend to be uncomfortable in her self-imposed exile. She had supplied herself with several pillows, two mattresses, and an eiderdown. She left Fan a heap of cushions and a moulting fur rug. Croydon, wrapped in a cashmere shawl, lay in her basket and watched with quick black eyes while they undressed in front of the fire.

Bertha undid her skirt with a sigh of relief, scratching herself voluptuously. She did not wear red flannel knickers but serviceable woolen ones with elastic just above the knee. She put on a pair of sensible blue pajamas and halfheartedly did her evening exercises. She did four kinds, six times each. The first two were to reduce her bust and hips, the third for her general poise, and the fourth to counteract the third, which was inclined to make her ankles muscular.

"Bitch!" she said breathlessly, twisting her trunk to the right and flinging out her arms. "I'd never have thought it of Peter, but I suppose they're all the same, the rats! Of course, I'd believe almost anything of Hugo. I've heard some *quite* extraordinary things used to go on in those D.P. camps, in spite of the barbed wire and everything." She began to slap herself viciously under the chin. "Double chins," she explained. "I know I haven't got one yet, but one has to look ahead." She spread a thick layer of Orange Skin Food over her face and neck. "It's really rather heavenly to be able to wallow in grease, isn't it? I adore doing all these rather humiliating things to myself, but when Hugo's there, just lying in bed and watching the way men do, somehow the whole thing turns to dust." She combed her hair, collected the biscuit tin off the sideboard, and got into bed. "Are you going to clean your teeth?"

"No, I don't believe I am."

"Well nor am I. Jugoslav! Who does she think she's fooling? She's not a woman, that one – she's an ice cream. Serve her up in a glass dish with a fid of cream and a couple of cherries and I'll eat her any day with a small, square spoon."

Fan sat on the heap of cushions, staring into the fire. "I wonder what Peter's up to," she said.

"My dear, he's probably looking for a small, square spoon. If I were you, I wouldn't speak to him for *days*."

Fan lay down and covered herself with the fur rug. "He's been very odd lately," she said. "You wouldn't believe the things he's done."

Bertha threw a biscuit into the dog basket and turned off the light. They lay in the darkness listening to the soft, liquid noise of Croydon eating. There was a faint belch, then silence.

"I'd forgotten how nice it is to sleep alone," said Bertha. "Men are all very well in bed, but you have to admit that they take up far too much room." A few minutes later she said, "My dear, this is pure heaven! I'm smothered in grease, the bed's full of crumbs, and I've got on my bed-socks." Ten minutes later she said, "I wonder what Hugo's doing, the oaf. I hope he can't sleep a wink. I hope the blankets come undone all around the bed and fall on to the floor over and over again."

"Shut up, Bertha. I want to go to sleep."

"I'm just going to eat two more biscuits, and then I shall doze off too. I wonder what that woman does to her hair. It must cost the earth. I expect, really, it's pitch black and terribly greasy. What an astounding little character our rat chap is, isn't he? I think he's rather sweet. He'd make a first-class leprechaun. Are you asleep?"

*

Fan woke with her heart banging in her throat. She pushed her hair out of her face and felt around for Peter. A sliver of flame shot up in the dying fire and she recognized the dining room. She sat up. Croydon's face rose out of her basket like a white chrysanthemum. The flame sank back into the embers.

Fan sat for a moment waiting for her eyes to get accustomed to the darkness. The rats were squeaking and scratching in the walls. Her heart began to bang again and she decided to wake Bertha. She crawled over to the camp bed and joggled it gently. She felt for Bertha's shoulder and found only a cool sheet. She ran her hand over the bed. Bertha was not there.

Fan sat back on her heels. *I'm not going to panic*, she thought. *The house is full of people and Peter is upstairs. I shall go up there and get into his bed and sleep till morning.* She wrapped the fur rug around her and crept into the hall. The house was in darkness. Except for the hammering of her heart and the scuffling of the rats there was not a sound. She tiptoed upstairs, dreading to wake the sleeping silence, afraid to advertise her presence by turning on the lights. Outside Lilli Cluj's door she paused. Inside, something was put down on wood, a match struck. Somebody whispered something. It had not the sibilance of Lilli's voice. Someone else was in there.

She crept on up the stairs. Her resentment against Peter flared again. He might not be in his room. He might still be with Lilli Cluj, to whom he had given her potted bush. He had been a stranger the whole day. He had killed a man ... She decided against waking him; she would wake Rex instead.

She opened the drawing-room door softly and stood blinking in the glare of the light. Rex was lying on the sofa fully dressed and eating an apple.

"Hullo, ducky," he said amiably. "Don't you believe in bye-byes?" His tone was normal but his face pale and there were shadows under his eyes.

Fan shut the door behind her. She sat on the back of the sofa, took the apple out of his hand, bit it, and gave it back.

"Quite tasteless, isn't it?" said Rex. "I've had four. It's two o'clock. Most girls and boys are in the Sandman's gondola."

"I had an awful dream."

"Well, me, I can't go to sleep at all. I'm beginning to get a bit testy. I'm fed up with sitting here eating these lousy apples. Gnaw, gnaw, gnaw, all night long. I don't see how *anybody* could sleep with that man in there not breathing." He threw the apple core, ostensibly out of the window, but the window was shut and it bounced back on to the floor. "All right, *don't* go out!" said Rex angrily. "Look, ducky, would you think I was an absolute monster if I put Dr. Watson outside in the air-raid shelter? He's just about to give me the screaming habdabs."

"I don't see why not. We could get him back first thing in the morning. It's rather damp, though."

"That's his funeral. I tell you frankly, dear, if Peter's going to make a habit of this sort of thing you can include me out."

"I'm sure he must have had a very good reason. He's never done it before."

Rex lifted Mr. Cann out of his trunk and tucked him under his arm. Mr. Cann slipped. His jacket came half off his shoulders and he slid out of it head first on to the floor. Rex picked him up again.

"Keep *still*!" he said. "Stop lolling around!"

Fan found a candle and turned off the lights. She opened the door and peered on to the landing. The rats were squeaking in the attics, and she could hear Hugo sleeping in the room next door. She knew that he was asleep because he was grinding his teeth. Rex followed her downstairs. In the heavy darkness of the hall she suddenly stood still. She blew out the candle and jerked at Rex's coat. Both stood listening. Somewhere upstairs, somebody had shut a door, shut it quietly and stealthily.

Fan and Rex backed silently against the wall. A rat squeaked quite near and skittered across the tiles. Fan strained her eyes upwards to the bend of the staircase. The window was just discernible, a patch of thinner darkness. Rex's watch ticked loudly.

The window went dark for a second. Somebody had passed it, somebody coming downstairs, walking carefully and making no noise. The second stair from the top creaked. Fan gave a small sigh. She heard Rex swallow. She groped for his hand and found Mr. Cann's icy fingers. It was too much for her. She gave a stifled gasp, stepped backwards, and knocked over a jar of paintbrushes.

Rex swore and there was an exclamation from the stairs. A torch was snapped on. Its beam raced across the floor. It found Rex's left foot, included Mr. Cann's dangling legs, hesitated, and glared straight into their eyes.

"Oh, *puke*!" said Rex in disgust.

"My God!" said Bertha's voice. "Who *have* you got there?"

Fan realized that she had been holding her breath. She expelled it noisily, fumbled for matches, and lit the candle. The flame shivered and settled. It shed its small radiance on the overturned jar of paintbrushes, on the half-open studio door, on Bertha, who stood at the foot of the stairs with Lilli Cluj hung over her shoulder like a stole. Bertha giggled nervously.

"I've got one as well," she said. "Is yours dead, too?"

CHAPTER 9

Rex led the way into the dining room. He turned on the light, propped Mr. Cann in a straight-backed chair, and wedged him against the table. Bertha followed, looking round vaguely for a place to deposit Lilli, finally spilling her into a winged chair by the fire. Lilli still wore the coffee-colored negligee. She had lipstick on her chin and she looked resentful. Croydon sat up in her basket and stared at Mr. Cann. She did not growl, but she made a tentative noise rather like a Primus stove.

Fan, without knowing what she was doing, put a minute piece of coal on the fire and then took it off again with the tongs. She found herself staring at Bertha and realized that Bertha was glaring back with equal hostility. Both looked away hastily. Fan put the piece of coal back on to the fire. Bertha took a broken biscuit out of her pocket and ate it. Rex produced a comb and attended to his hair.

"Bertha," he said with an effort. "One can only suppose that you did this foul thing. True or false?"

"False, you ape!" said Bertha with spirit. "Of course I didn't! I heard the oddest noises, and I thought it must be Peter up to fun and games with her and my blood absolutely *boiled*! I'll fix his hash, the skunk, I thought, so I padded off upstairs, hoping to catch him red-handed. But just as I got outside her door, the noises stopped. There was a sort of *swish* – I thought they were just lying low. By that time I was *livid*! I shouldn't wonder if it's brought me out in a rash." She studied herself in the mirror over the fireplace. "No. It hasn't. Well, it's a miracle, that's all. Where was I? Oh, yes – well, then I grabbed the door handle. I was sure that they would have locked the door. I was going to rattle it and say, 'The game's up,' or something, but it just opened! I went in and the light was on and there she was."

"I don't believe one word of it," said Rex.

"Well, what about you?" asked Bertha hotly. "Tell me about *your* adventures."

"There's no need to shout."

"I'm not shouting. I'm remarkably calm, considering what I've been through."

"Why didn't you scream?"

67

"Why didn't you?"

"Where were you going, prowling about like that?"

"Where were you?"

"You tell first."

"Why should I?"

"You're outnumbered."

"Oh, all right," said Bertha resentfully. "I should have thought that it was obvious to a child of four, but apparently not! I was prowling, you fool, because I didn't want to be heard. I didn't scream because I'm not the screaming type. And, as one can't leave bodies strewn around one's house, I was taking her down to the air-raid shelter until I thought what was best to do. Simple, isn't it?"

"No."

"Oh, for Heaven's sake, Rex! Are you *trying* to be stupid. Why *should* I kill her? I'd have spat in her eye and enjoyed it, but if I knocked off everybody I've ever wanted to insult, I shouldn't have a friend left in the world."

"Why didn't you send for the police?"

"Why didn't you?"

"Don't start that again!"

"Well, my dear," said Bertha kindly, as if speaking to a harmless lunatic, "when one finds a corpse in one's house, what does one think? First, one thinks, 'Dear, dear!' One takes another look and sees that it has not died in a normal way. 'Who did it?' one thinks. You follow me?"

"Go on."

"Right. Third thought – who knew her well enough to have a motive? There are five of us in this house, and four of us never set eyes on her until this evening. Four from five leaves one."

"Hugo," said Fan.

"Exactly. I don't want to be unpatriotic. I'm just telling you how I reacted. Hugo knew her in Budapest. He denied it, of course, but I know perfectly well when he's lying. We had quite a row. I knew he was upset, but I didn't think he'd go to these lengths. But, as I said to Fan only this evening, I wouldn't put *anything* past Hugo. All these mid-Europeans are hopelessly romantic. Haven't you noticed? Well, I took him for better or worse, and I'm not going to stand by and let him hang for that absurd little tart, so what do I do? I dispose of her. No body, no evidence, no murder." She sat down on the camp bed and began to eat a biscuit.

"I believe you, I think," said Fan. "Actually, ours is very much the same sort of thing."

She had got halfway through her story when the door opened and Peter looked in. Croydon woke up and barked at him.

"What the hell *are* you doing?" asked Peter irritably. "What's the matter with you all today?" He saw Mr. Cann. "What are *you* doing here? Fan, I told you distinctly to get rid of him."

Fan looked at him without affection.

Hugo slopped into the room in bedroom slippers. He rubbed his eyes, trying to focus.

"Oh dear, oh dear, oh *dear*!" he said peevishly. "Am I to get no sleep at all? Who's that man? What's going on? Why are you all staring?"

Peter was looking at Lilli. He made a stifled noise. He walked across the room and bent over her. He stretched out his hand and touched her cheek.

"Good God!" he said. "She's dead!"

"Don't be silly," said Hugo, yawning. He looked more closely at Mr. Cann and shut his mouth with a snap. He shook the body gently. Mr. Cann fell forward, cracking his head on the table. Hugo turned pale. "So's this one," he said weakly.

"I don't believe it!"

"He is, I tell you!"

"Oh, come off it!" said Bertha inelegantly.

Peter straightened up. He looked at Mr. Cann and back to Lilli.

"It's simply not true," he said. He went to the sideboard and found a decanter of Cyprus brandy. He poured some into a glass and drank it.

Hugo wiped his forehead with the sash of his dressing gown. He pulled back Mr. Cann's eyelid.

"It *is* true, you know. He's all clammy. He's been dead for quite a long time."

"Oh, stop it!" Bertha was getting cross. "You're just wasting time. The one each of you didn't do, the other did."

Peter poured himself out some more brandy and forgot to drink it. He looked at Hugo.

"Did you hear what she said?"

"Yes. I don't know what she's talking about. Have they all suddenly gone mad?"

"Is she trying to say *we* did it? I mean them. They're nothing to do with me. Did you do it? Do what? What am I saying? Does she mean they've been *murdered*?"

"Arsenic, dear," said Bertha patiently. "At least, I suppose it was arsenic. It was in the thermos. I tasted it and it was all burning and bitter. I spat it out at once and gargled. There isn't any other poison in the house and, as we all know, Mr. Beesum's little suitcase is still hanging in the hall, and inside it is masses of rat poison which he told Fan was mostly arsenic."

"And you think Hugo and I administered it? Why? Why should we? Which one am I supposed to have done?" He caught Fan's eye. "Don't look at me like that! Do *you* suspect me, too?" Fan was silent. "Answer me! Fan!"

"You might just as well come clean," said Bertha. "Then we can decide what we're going to do."

"I'm going to hit that woman soon," said Peter. "Do you mind, Hugo?"

"Help yourself."

"If somebody will condescend to explain … Hugo, if you *have* done anything rash …"

"Certainly not! Neither of them. Did you?"

"Of course I didn't!"

"All right, dears," said Rex. "It was little fairies with silver wings."

"Assuming that they *have* been poisoned," said Hugo, "how do you know that they didn't commit suicide?"

"Lilli was hardly in a suicidal mood when I last saw her," said Peter after a slight pause. "And, considering that Mr. Cann had been fighting for his life for the last couple of months, I think it's hardly like that, as soon as he's safely cheated the gallows, he'd take a dose of arsenic."

"Gallows?" said Bertha. "*Who is that man?*"

"He walked out of the Old Bailey the day before yesterday and I didn't get a picture of him because my shutter stuck. That's Benjamin Cann."

"*Benjamin Cann?*"

"Benjamin Cann!"

"But he's a murderer!" said Fan stupidly. "He …"

"Garrotted that woman in …"

"In the *News of the World*!"

"Oh, my God!"

"I don't believe it!"

"I shall have to burn those sheets," said Bertha.

"Why *us*?" said Hugo. "Why do they pick on us?" He sat down and put his head on his hands. "Lilli Cluj was one, too!" he murmured.

"One what?"

"Killer. Don't look at me like that. It's not my fault. She bumped off her second husband in Budapest."

"How do you know?" demanded Bertha, glaring at him. "You said you'd never seen her before in your life."

"I've never spoken to her," said Hugo. "When I was reporting in Budapest, I covered her trial. It was my first big assignment."

Bertha sniffed. Her frown said that she would inquire farther into the matter when she and Hugo were alone.

"It was a long time ago," said Hugo quickly. "Before the war."

"Which war?" Bertha asked unpleasantly.

"The large war. She was much younger and a brunette. I've passed her quite often on the street, but until I met her face to face on the stairs I didn't recognize her. She looks – looked entirely different."

"I see, dear," said Bertha in a ragged voice. "You'd never spoken to her, I think you said? That was why, as soon as my back was turned, you rushed upstairs into her room? Just to introduce yourself?"

Hugo became slightly confused. He got up and poured himself a drink. "It wasn't like that at all," he said.

"Like what, dear?"

"Oh, I don't know. Like whatever you're thinking."

"I'm not thinking anything, dear. I don't know what you mean. I'm most interested."

"I'd like a drink," said Rex faintly, undoing his tie.

Nobody took any notice of him.

"Well," said Hugo, "I went to tell her that she'd got to leave. She told me in vile French to *fiche* the camp. She is no lady, that one. I tried to reason with her, but she was extraordinarily offensive. So I left."

"Did you, dear? How disappointing for you!"

"Oh, be quiet! You brought her here, I didn't. A fine brace of lodgers you've chosen, I must say! Thousands of homeless people milling around, and you have to get *them*!"

"They both had references. How was I to know? That nice Mr. Flush next door said that they were the right type."

Fan glanced at Rex. She remarked that it was quite a coincidence because there had once been a triple murderer by the name of Flush. He had pushed his victims off trains. She remembered it distinctly. She had been at school at the time and as, due to Mr. Flush's second coup, none of the girls had been allowed to travel singly, she had been forced to escort a disgusting girl called Squib Cox from Eastbourne to Burnham Beeches. But, she said hastily, she was sure it was only a coincidence, because the Flush of the Southern Railways had a rather nice blond beard, whereas the one next door was clean-shaven. She was well aware that people shaved off their beards every day, but this had not been that type of beard. It was small but curly – a source of pride and personality to its owner and obviously a joy for ever. Anyway, the Flush next door had a delightful smile and two cars. Moreover, he was President of the Asterisk Club, which he himself had laughingly admitted to Bertha was one of the most exclusive in London.

"Asterisk is an odd name for a club," said Bertha thoughtfully. "I wonder whether they've read their Tennyson."

"Probably," said Hugo. "He once stayed there – unless one of my rivals carved that plaque. Why?"

"*Morituri Salutamus*, stanza ten," said Bertha. She ate a biscuit, looking intelligent, enjoying her moment of triumph.

"Well?" said Hugo impatiently. "What about it?"

"Oh, don't you know?" said Bertha. She looked surprised. "I thought everybody knew that. '… we against whose familiar names not yet the fatal asterisk of death is set.' Odd, isn't it? Three of them had horribly familiar names. One might even say notorious."

"Really, Bertha!" said Fan indignantly. "You can't be suggesting that those respectable old bodies next door are nothing more than a bunch of retired murderers!"

"They can't be, dear," said Rex reasonably. "One of them is a colonel."

"What of it?"

"No, no, dear. It's pure fantasy!"

"No," said Fan. "It's just a coincidence."

"I believe," said Bertha, "that after the first two, coincidences become very suspect. I think they degenerate into vulgar design."

"Well, dear," said Rex. "You're entitled to your opinion. Personally, I think you're wrong."

"She's not wrong," said Peter slowly. He got up and lit a cigarette. "You'll have to know it sooner or later. I had a long chat with Lilli before she – when I last saw her. She became quite talkative under the influence of four outsize gins. She told me all I wanted to know about the mob next door."

"Well?"

"Bertha's right. They're acquitted killers."

"I don't believe it for a moment," said Fan. "They're the staidest people in Chelsea. Murderers have glaring eyes."

"How many have you known?"

"Well, it's hard to say, isn't it? I always suspected that major you had in the army."

"He had a glass eye."

"Of course we shall have to move," said Bertha.

"Why? They haven't done anything so far except get themselves murdered."

"How do you know they haven't?" muttered Hugo. "Somebody bumped off these two."

Fan looked at Peter and away again. "Are you going to try to palm it off on the Asterisks?" she asked.

Peter pushed a hand through his hair. "I've got to think," he said.

"Do you really think they did it?" persisted Fan.

"What else can I suppose? The alternative isn't very attractive."

"No," said Fan. "No, it's not. What are you going to do?"

"I don't know," said Peter. He threw his cigarette into the fire. "We've got to be very, very careful. We might as well face it, chums." He managed a shadow of a ghostly grin. *"We're up against professionals!"*

CHAPTER 10

At half past six the same morning, Beecher, the ungainly steward, woke abruptly, snatched up his alarm clock, and hurled it against the wall. It exploded into several pieces, but its clamor persisted. Beecher lurched out of bed and went after it. He put on one boot and with the heel ground the clock into the carpet. It continued to ring. He found his housebreaking outfit, paralyzed the clock with a jemmy, and threw it out of the window.

He sat on the bed and began to clip his toenails with an instrument intended for the removal of wire-mesh windows. It was a sloppy job. He finished it off with a heavy rasp, stood up, and scratched his stomach. He was wearing his green nightshirt today. Tomorrow, he thought with regret, he would have to wear the blue one. He only had two, and he liked the green by far the best. He believed that baths disturbed the natural oils of the body; so, once a week, he put on a clean nightshirt and wore it for one hundred and sixty-eight hours until its fellow returned from the laundry.

He padded over to the window and began to do his breathing exercises. He did these regularly night and morning. It was essential, in his profession, to be able to breathe quietly. He had got to eighty-three when he heard a car pull up outside No. 15.

Still moving his arms spasmodically, he inclined his head in order to see. The photographer-writer got out of the car and hurried into the house. Beecher made an obscene gesture at him. He had never met Peter, but he disliked him thoroughly. He had once stolen three of Peter's books from a public library and had followed the exploits of Inspector Carstairs with a deep revulsion. The one in which Carstairs caught a burglar red-handed had made him so angry that he had returned it to the library.

He leaned out of the window and examined the car in which his enemy had arrived. It was an old Rolls-Royce with an open landau roof. Its body was painted to resemble wickerwork, and its upholstery was a faded blue whipcord. It was a car in which minor royalties might have made an incognito appearance. Beecher peered to see whether there was a crest on the door, but there was not.

The wife of the sculptor, whom Beecher privately called Epstein, came out of No. 15. She wore a baggy skirt of homemade tweed and a red jacket which clashed violently with it. She skirted the monkey-puzzle tree and leaned over the gate. She looked idly up and down the road. Her elaborate calm made Beecher glance at her again. His small eyes narrowed as he recognized the Regard Casual.

He watched her critically as she scanned the windows of the houses opposite. She was doing it much too obviously. Beecher smacked his lips disapprovingly. *A first offender, eh?* he thought. The woman fingered a leaf on the monkey-puzzle tree. Beecher shook his head. *Go on,* he thought. *Now make an itsy-bitsy signal nobody can see.* The woman made an almost imperceptible gesture with her head. She twisted her leg, wet her finger, and massaged a point above her knee. With her head down, she mouthed at somebody inside the house. Beecher sucked his teeth. He lost interest. He still watched, but he was no longer even intrigued. It was merely a matter for the records. He looked on, yawning, as Peter and Hugo between them carried Mr. Cann across the courtyard. He realized without surprise that Mr. Cann was dead. In his time he had seen many stiffs, and he knew at a glance that the Old Tin Cann had passed on.

He was jerked out of his complacency by Rex, who ran from the house with Lilli Cluj in his arms. *Cor!* thought Beecher. *Two! An' both life members! The Boss won't like that!* Lilli, he noticed, still wore the yellow suit in which she had left the Club. He wondered whether the amiable-looking quarter next door had creased her immediately she arrived.

His enemy, the creator of the insufferable Carstairs, was supervising the arrangement of the bodies in the back of the car. He was being quick and efficient. Beecher decided to call him Sunny Jim. La Cluj was clearly suffering from rigor mortis. Sunny Jim was having difficulty in persuading her to sit down. He was also having an argument with the dancing sissy, who was insisting with many gestures, but successfully, that he did not want to sit next to the Old Tin Cann. Mrs. Epstein walked briskly out of the house with a picnic basket and got into the car next to the two bodies. Sunny Jim's wife followed her with a thermos and a bottle of gin. Beecher abandoned his exercises. "So it's a ruddy *picnic*, is it?" he asked himself softly.

Sunny Jim was going to drive. His wife sat beside him, and the other two men sat on folding seats facing the back of the car. Sunny Jim had just released the brake when a small white dog galloped out of No. 15, barking hysterically. Mrs. Epstein leapt out and picked it up. Mr. Cann, relieved of his support, fell over sideways on to the seat. Mrs. Epstein tried to get back into the car with the dog, but Epstein would not let her. She carried it sulkily back into the house, her face pink with anger. Then she came back and got into the car, pushing Mr. Cann roughly so that he rolled on to Lilli. She was still grumbling as the car started forward. The left front wheel ran over the remains of Beecher's alarm clock.

He watched them until they turned into Cheyne Row, then he sat down and pulled on his socks. "Well, I dunno," he muttered. "Why di'n't they bring a brass band? Couldn't of bin much more conspicuous if they'd all bin riding giraffes! They'll get about 'alf a mile an' twenty years."

He pinned a dickey on to the front of his nightshirt, struggled into his mess jacket and trousers, and stepped into his boots. He was considering the most acceptable manner in which to report this new development to the Boss. He was intimidated by Clifford Flush. He knew that his master reacted erratically to sudden shocks. Beecher decided that he would take the early-morning tea, his first task for the day, to his other charges first, giving himself time to prepare his report in the least provocative manner.

He went thoughtfully downstairs. The Creaker's cat had made a mess in the middle of the hall. Beecher swore. He had expected something of the sort. He marched through into the kitchen.

The new maid handed him Mrs. Barratt's pot of weak China tea on a tray. He accepted it in silence. The woman had hair on her lip and was still defiant after her ninth sentence for shoplifting. Beecher considered her beneath his notice.

He climbed the stairs to Mrs. Barratt's room and tapped twice with his index finger, making a hideous face at the closed door. There were two vases of flowers and a pair of old pumps with steel buckles arranged against the wall.

"Enter," called Mrs. Barratt, who was apt to be regal in the mornings.

Beecher entered. She was, as usual, propped upright upon a pyramid of lace-trimmed pillows. She wore a serviceable woolen bedjacket as if it were ermine and, over it, her inevitable locket hung like an order. She had taken the butterfly clips out of the front of her hair and was pinching the stiff ridges with obvious satisfaction. On her bedside table were two photographs in a heavy silver double frame. On the left was an elderly man wearing pince-nez; on the right a swarthy youth with a leer and moist black eyes. The former, in a neat script, had signed himself "And may the days that are to be be perfumed and divine, Your affct. husband, Arthur Wottling." The latter, more simply, said Always, Bert." Both these comments had proved to be optimistic, as Mrs. Barratt, without regret, had arranged the demise of their writers within a year of each other.

Beecher laid the tray on her knees.

"Miss Cluj was creased last night."

"How extraordinary," said Mrs. Barratt, pouring tea. She did not appear at all surprised, and Beecher glanced at her with sudden suspicion. She picked up one of the sugar-sprinkled biscuits provided for her and eyed it with disfavor. "If I've told you once, Beecher, I've told you a hundred times, that I like *plain* biscuits in the mornings."

"Looks a bit like glass, dun it?" asked Beecher, watching her closely. "Powdered," he added softly.

Mrs. Barratt swung the locket between her fingers.

"Beecher," she snapped. "We both know the saying about sleeping dogs. You may go."

Beecher returned, grinning, to the kitchen. The new maid was placing a plate of buttered toast on the Colonel's tray. Beecher took it from her roughly.

"You need a shave," he remarked.

The woman blushed.

"Aren't you funny!" she said feebly.

Beecher went upstairs and beat a jolly tattoo on the Colonel's door. He knew that the Club's Treasurer would be up and dressed, and he went straight in.

The Colonel was poring over his latest invention. It was an outlandish contraption made of springs, rubber, a sawn-off petrol can full of some dark fluid, a Primus stove, and an expanding canvas arm to which was attached an enormous magnet. It was clamped to a trestle table and was emitting small puffs of steam. The Colonel pumped the Primus stove and covered the petrol can with a broken skillet. The canvas arm slowly inflated and moved uncertainly across the room at shoulder level. It approached Beecher and hovered over the tea tray. A teaspoon rose out of its saucer and clinked against the magnet. Beecher pushed the arm impatiently out of his way and cleared his throat. The Colonel straightened up.

"Ah ha!" he said, rubbing his hands. "*Chota hazri!*"

Beecher resented almost everything about the Colonel, but particularly he hated his frequent lapses into Hindustani. He showed his disapproval by tilting the tray so that the tea poured gently on to the buttered toast. He waited until it was absorbed before he laid the tray on a chair.

"La Cluj got hers last night," he said.

The Colonel turned to stare. His azure eyes widened.

"Pukka?" he asked. "By jove! Good riddance, I say! Any idea who did it? One of us?"

"Wouldn't amaze me," said Beecher, watching him.

"What method was used?" The Colonel always appreciated technical details.

"Dunno. Din see no blood."

The Colonel seemed about to say something further, then changed his mind. He brushed up the ends of his white mustache and stood gazing in a preoccupied manner at his farcical machine. He idly pressed a lever and it came away in his hand. He cursed mildly. Then he met Beecher's small, dull eyes and lost his temper.

"Get out, sir!" he roared.

Beecher went downstairs. Squires, the sallow youth who helped him to wait at table, was in the hall cleaning up the mess that the Creaker's cat had made. He had already attended to the affected part of the carpet. He was now sweeping lovingly the whole length of it. This was not his job, but he did it every day. Beecher had once heard him telling Mrs.

Barratt, his principal confidant, that he loved beautiful things.

He found the Creaker's mug of black tea and jug of condensed milk on the kitchen table. The new maid had shut herself into the scullery, but Beecher knew that she was listening.

"Ever try Blue Gillette?" he asked in a penetrating whisper.

"Aouw, go *away!*" The woman turned on the taps and began to splash about in the sink.

Beecher smiled. He reclimbed the stairs to where, on the second floor, the Creaker's one boot stood sentinel in the corridor. He slapped the door with an open hand. He knew that there would be no answer and he turned the faulty handle and went in.

The Creaker was sleeping profoundly and, as usual, Beecher was astonished at the variety of noises he managed to make while so innocently engaged. Tom, his unnatural cat, lay beside him, rolled up in an old pair of combinations. The Creaker had gathered the bedclothes around his shoulders and his one overdeveloped leg protruded from the sheets. His artificial one lay on a chair, wearing the pair to the solitary boot in the corridor.

Beecher moved a half-eaten slab of milk chocolate and banged down the tray on the bedside table. Tom opened one eye, saw Beecher, and leapt out of range on to the top of the wardrobe. The Creaker inhaled, making a series of sticky noises with his lips and tongue. The blankets rose, remained motionless for several seconds, then fell as he exhaled with a low snarl.

Beecher watched him with mixed feelings. He did not like the Creaker, but he was obliged to admit that, having committed one of the most brutal atrocities of the century, the old cripple was worthy of a certain grudging respect. But, as far as Beecher was concerned, it was indeed a grudging respect. The Creaker had won his evil reputation overnight, whereas Beecher had earned his the hard way, starting at the top and working steadily down. The Creaker, in a moment of fury, had made himself headline news for over a week. It had taken Beecher a lifetime of practice to win three half-inch paragraphs on page six of a county newspaper. Both kept scrapbooks, but whereas Beecher's had only three meager entries, the Creaker's was in two volumes.

*

Clifford Flush had founded the Asterisk Club nearly ten years ago. After his acquittal, he had been driven by his tormentors to a secluded villa outside Aix-les-Bains. There, in constant fear of recognition, he had lived for three horrible months. He hated the sunshine, the friendly inquisitive peasants, and the long grass, which gave him hay fever. But it was there that he met Mrs. Barratt, whose trial had recently drawn to its unpopular conclusion. She confided that she, too, was finding life increasingly complicated. There had been a wide selection of pictures of her in the English newspapers, and the hotels which subscribed to the continental editions had been suavely unable to provide accommodation. Shops refused credit, and nobody seemed anxious to make her acquaintance. She was already bored with Barratt, who spent the whole day swimming up and down the dirty lake and blowing spouts of water into the air. She sat on the banks, a prey to gnats and flies, watching him, wondering already how long she must endure him. She took her troubles to Flush, who smiled faintly and gave her the name of a reliable insurance company.

On the day that Barratt was found drowned, they decided between them that the founding of a pleasant cloister for their fellow unfortunates would fulfill a real social need. Together, they returned to England and sponsored this specialized sanctuary. A year later, in response to an increasing demand, they admitted as temporary country members those who had been accused of all capital as well as the more heinous indictable offenses. Now the Club's strength, although fluctuating, usually stood at around fifty. Flush, like the leaders of all underprivileged minorities, had recurrent spasms of jubilation about the success of his undertaking. Nothing, nobody, must endanger it.

This morning he woke in a vile temper. Beecher's bulletin of the previous evening was still nagging him. To be unable to understand anything maddened him. He prided himself upon his judgment of character and, having made his analysis, it infuriated him if its subject did not conform to type. He had summed up Mrs. Hilford as a pleasant, conventionally unconventional girl without a thought in her head beside her husband and her Art. Now she was behaving in an entirely unpredictable manner and it made Flush extremely angry. He was thinking graphically about what he would like to do to her when Beecher knocked discreetly and brought him his early morning tea. He noticed at once that his steward was ill at ease.

"Well, Beecher," he said sharply. "What is it now? I see by the delicate manner in which you are handling my china that you are not yourself."

Beecher shot him a glance from half-closed eyes. "It's like this, Boss," he began unhappily.

"Beecher, I have slept only casually I am extremely worried, and I have a slight headache. If you have anything to say, kindly say it."

"Yus, Boss. Might be a bit of a shock."

"Beecher!"

"Yus, Boss." Beecher drew a deep breath. "The Cann an' the Cluj has been ironed."

Flush's nostrils flared, but his expression did not change. "Go on," he said evenly.

Beecher stuck his tongue in his cheek and regarded his master obliquely. He considered that Flush had taken his news too calmly. Had he already known? Had the whole uncanny bunch of them already known? Had, in fact, one or all of them bumped off their two latest acquisitions? What did they stand to gain? Under the Club rules, the answer to that was easy. A men's wear shop off Shaftesbury Avenue and a large but dilapidated estate in Hungary, probably quite a tidy haul. That was the one disadvantage of working in a joint like this. You were never quite certain what they would do next, and they never told you anything.

"I said go on, Beecher," repeated Flush. "Have you lost your tongue?"

"No, Boss. They was ironed an' those birds next door has taken 'em away in a ruddy great car for a picnic."

"A *picnic*?"

"Yus, Boss. Sat 'em up in the back o' this car an' fussed around like they was still alive."

Flush lit a cigarette. His hands shook slightly. "A picnic!" he said under his breath. He poured himself a cup of tea and slid a slice of lemon into it. He stirred it slowly.

"There may be trouble, Beecher," he said at last. "Do not think me callous, but obviously the first consideration is our own security. See that the usual notice is posted on the board. Inform all resident members to provide themselves with alibis for an indefinite period." He sipped his tea, frowning out of the window. "You, I presume, have already done so?"

Beecher grinned broadly. He knew that Flush did not expect him to answer. It was common knowledge that he had several permanent alibis.

"I want no mistakes," said Flush. "Circularize the country members to take the usual precautions – avoid photographers, lie low, and expect impertinent inquiries. From members on the premises I shall expect sound watertight alibis all round. I want no nonsense about concerts, cinemas, or music halls. You remember the fiasco over Goonatilika! I repeat, we must be prepared for serious trouble."

You slippery! thought Beecher. *Have you been at it again? You're a nark and no mistake!* Aloud, he said, "Go on, Boss! Won't be the first time we laughed off a coupla stiffs, nor the last."

Flush gnawed his underlip. "I confess that I am uneasy," he said, and then, with apparent irrelevance, "Mr. Cann forgot to join our Club, Beecher."

Oh-ho! thought Beecher. Noncommittally, he said, "Well, well!"

"Yes," said Flush. "He omitted to sign either the membership form or his last will and testament. A matter of merely two signatures."

Beecher clicked his tongue.

"Wherever he is," said Flush piously, "it may be worrying him. We don't want him to be unhappy, do we, Beecher?"

"Don't know as I care much either way," said Beecher craftily.

"I am disappointed in you, Beecher. To speak so harshly about a man who I know would have wanted me to give you a bonus!"

"Perhaps I was a bit hasty," Beecher admitted.

"Do you think his oversight can be rectified?"

"Well, if 'e was really lavish with me, I'd feel under an obligation, wouldn't I? I'd just 'ave to accommodate 'im."

"I'm sure he would have wanted me to be generous."

"Well," said Beecher, grinning. "I expect we can set 'is mind at rest."

"He would not have liked an indifferent facsimile."

"'E gave a beauty to the *News of the World.* I don't think 'e need worry. I'll do 'im proud."

Flush allowed himself a faint smile. "Good. Now go and attend to the notice for the board. There is no time to be lost."

"Should I do it in your writin', Boss?"

"I think perhaps it would carry more authority."

Beecher nodded. He looked curiously at his master. He knew him perhaps better than anyone else in the world. "You're worried, ain't you, Boss?" he asked.

"Yes," confessed Flush. "Yes, I am. This situation is more hazardous than any we have faced before. It is impossible to predict what may happen next." He gazed at the slice of lemon floating in his tea. Then he raised his eyes and stared at Beecher's left shoulder. *"It appears that we have become involved with the insufferable amateur!"*

CHAPTER 11

WITH the suburbs of London safely behind him, Peter Hilford began to breathe more naturally. He took each hand in turn from the wheel of the archaic Rolls-Royce and rubbed it on his trousers. He mopped his forehead. He had expected, almost hoped, that they would be stopped by every policeman they passed. He had braced himself for it, thought out what he was going to say, waited for it – and nothing had happened. Now he had to reorient himself. He had not looked this far ahead, because it had never occurred to him that they would get out of London unchallenged.

He looked sideways at his wife. He wanted to ask her whether she still believed that he had killed Mr. Cann. She probably did. Otherwise why, back in Chelsea in a queasy dawn, when he had suggested sending for the police, had she looked so stricken? Why had she taken his hand and dug her nails into its palm? Why had she said that if he loved her at all he would think of some other way out? She had been so fervent that he had wondered for a nightmare second whether she herself had done away with her first lodger. In that second he hesitated and was lost. Each of the others, it appeared, also had indirect reasons for wishing to avoid the attentions of the police.

Hugo said that he had already waited two years for his naturalization papers. He was sick and tired of being an alien. If now, on the very eve of becoming a British subject, he were involved in a double murder he would have to undergo a further interminable probationary period.

Bertha said that she had only recently ingratiated herself with the local tradesmen. It had taken her two years to win her way into their hearts and under their counters, and a scandal involving Scotland Yard and the Old Bailey would set her right back where she had come in. Peter thought this reason was not good enough. He had said as much before he realized that Bertha still suspected Hugo of the death of Lilli.

Rex claimed that he had a chance of getting a principal role in a new ballet. His reputation in the dancing world was as clean as a whistle and, no matter what Caryl Brahms might say, a bullet or any other form

82

of violent death in the ballet was frowned upon by the management. It was crude, rude, and lewd. He looked shifty, and Peter wondered whether he could possibly suspect Fan. He was convinced that nobody had given his real reason. He wondered whether any of them were capable of cold-blooded murder; whether all of them except himself knew and were attempting to shield the culprit; whether there might even have been a quadruple conspiracy. He wondered still at the alacrity with which they acclaimed Hugo's suggestion that the bodies be taken into the country and buried in some quiet little wood. Did Hugo suspect Bertha? He had become so confused that he wondered whether one or all of them were in the pay of the Asterisk Club. He realized that he was fighting a losing battle. He knew that they were determined not to send for the police; that, with or without his cooperation, they would adopt Hugo's precarious plan. Either he would have had to stay at home, wondering every other minute whether his wife had been detained on a murder charge, or he would go with them to a mass arrest.

Just before dawn, he rang up a friend called Martin and asked for the loan of his car. Martin spoke roughly about being woken at such an hour, but eventually agreed to leave the key to his garage tied on a string inside his front door. He said that there was plenty of petrol in the tank. He asked no questions. He never did, which was why Peter had chosen him.

He glanced into the driving mirror and saw that Bertha's large, usually amiable face was grim. She was hunched in the corner of the back seat absently sucking a sweet and staring at Hugo. Mr. Cann sat beside her. His overcoat collar was turned up, his hat brim down. He sat low on the seat, his head against the cushions like a very tired man. Propped against him, and still stiff, was Lilli Cluj. Bertha had balanced a pair of smoked glasses on her nose and tied a scarf over her distinctive hair. Peter felt slightly better. Neither of them looked obviously dead.

He began to wonder for the first time whether they were going to pull it off. Then he noticed that the black sedan was behind them again. He had seen it first on Battersea Bridge and immediately thought that it was a police car; but the driver made no attempt to overtake him and had disappeared into a petrol station in Hammersmith. He reappeared in Roehampton. Peter had shaken him off after a mile or two, and since then he had been watching for him. With each mile, he felt safer. Now that he had finally persuaded himself that he was being unnecessarily suspicious, the sedan was back again, right on his tail. The driver was not wearing a helmet, but a bowler hat. If he was a policeman, he was in plain clothes. So was his car. It had no siren and no aerial. Peter knew that Hugo had seen it too and, without looking at it directly, was assessing it.

He glanced at Fan. She sat beside him with her hands folded in her lap. She had not spoken since they left Chelsea. Peter patted her knee and she jumped.

"Don't gloom, love," he said. For the first time in his life he found it difficult to speak to her naturally. "It may still be all right."

Fan moved restlessly.

"Peter," she said, and stopped.

Peter waited. He did not want to encourage her. There were only two things she could say. Either she would ask him whether he had killed Mr. Cann or she would say that she had. Peter did not want her to do either.

"Peter," she said again.

"What?"

"You didn't do it, did you?"

"Do you think I did?"

"I don't know," she said. "I'm all muddled up."

"I've been wanting to ask you the same thing."

"Me?" Her face was blank with surprise.

"I got a bit confused too."

"Then you didn't ...?"

"Of course I didn't!"

"Oh, darling! I didn't know. I wasn't sure. I thought ..."

"Do you believe me?"

"Yes, I'm almost sure I do. But if you didn't do it, him, I mean, who did?"

"I don't know. And at the rate we're destroying evidence we shall probably never find out. It may have been one of the pros next door keeping their hand in."

"Do you think there can have been *two* killers?"

"Doubtful. Both victims are Asterisk members, and they were both killed with the same weapon."

"Can they hear us in the back?" she asked.

"I don't think so."

"Bertha still thinks Hugo did it – Lilli Cluj, I mean."

"I know. I think Rex thinks you accounted for Mr. Cann."

"He *can't*, darling! I've known him since I was wee."

"One of my uncles went to school with Crippen."

They drove for a mile in silence. The black sedan was about two hundred yards behind them.

"Peter, why were you scratching that woman's feet?"

"I wanted to gain her confidence. I've suspected the Asterisk Club for some time. I recognized the old man with the gammy leg. I had to know. When I met her on the stairs, it seemed like a heaven-sent opportunity."

"I see," she said. She sounded dissatisfied. "She was quite pretty really, wasn't she?"

"If you like that type."

"Was she pleased with that bush you gave her?"

Peter looked at her sideways. She was industriously polishing her dark glasses.

Rex put his head through the glass partition.

"Turn left by that nasty old tree," he said.

Peter swung the car off the tarmac and down a pot-holed lane flanked with untidy hedges. The black sedan kept straight on. Peter breathed a sigh of relief. The lane twisted wildly. He slowed down to five miles an hour. Rex had insisted that he knew exactly the spot for dirty work. He said that it was secluded, sheltered, and surrounded by weeping willows. It was miles from anywhere, and they could dig away like sandboys.

"Peter," said Fan. "When you went in to see Mr. Cann yesterday night, how was he lying?"

"He was right on the edge of the bed. He was making a sort of puffing noise. I thought he was pretending to have a nightmare, but I suppose actually he was in a coma."

"Didn't you suspect anything?"

"No. Why should I? I couldn't see very well. Only the small light was on. And then I trod on that damned board and my one idea was to get out before he saw me looking like a bloody fool."

Fan ducked as a trailing bramble flicked into the car. The hedge stopped abruptly on the right side of the lane. Peter turned a corner and drew up with a jerk at a wooden barrier.

"No," said Rex's voice from the back. "No, no, no, *not!*"

Nobody else said anything.

Before them, stretching in a rough rectangle, were about fifty prefabricated houses. They crouched in rows with trenches between them destined for their plumbing. Their more perishable parts were draped with the silver remains of barrage balloons. Their drains, their sinks, their intimate entrails were stacked outside each doorless porch. In the middle of the colony grew a single willow tree.

Peter put the car into reverse and backed towards a coil of rubber flex. A man in dungarees staggered from the nearest house. He had an oddly-shaped piece of wood on his back and the guts of a geyser in one hand. He eyed the Rolls-Royce, cleared his throat, and spat into a jumble of lavatory bowls. Peter turned back into the lane. A bramble left a deep scratch on the front mudguard. He drove faster and the car lurched over the pot-holes. At the end of the lane he turned left.

He saw the black sedan immediately. It was parked at the roadside just beyond the turning. The man in the bowler hat was sitting sideways in the front seat, the door open, his feet in the road. It was too late to pull the heavy car around; Peter trod on the accelerator and shot past. He saw in the driving mirror the man in the bowler hat lean out of his car and wave his hand up and down. Peter drove on. The man withdrew into his car and started after them.

"Darling …?" said Fan, looking over her shoulder.

"Yes," said Peter. "He's following us. We've got to give him the slip."

Fan looked at him briefly and was silent.

The man in the bowler hat followed them for three miles, sounding his horn almost continuously. He was a few hundred yards behind them when they reached the crossroads. Peter saw his chance. Through the threadbare hedges he saw a large green removal van with its accompanying trailer. It was heading for the crossroads on the intersecting road at about thirty miles an hour. It did not slow down. It had the right of way. Peter's foot went down to the floor. The Rolls shuddered. The van sounded its ponderous horn. Somebody in the back of the Rolls squealed. Fan threw her arms up over her face and the windscreen was filled with a slewing close-up of an enormous mudguard. The hedge scratched past the Rolls on the wrong side of the road and with a scream of tires the giant radiator of the van swung clear of the back mudguard. Peter drove straight on. Fan lowered her arms and sat back looking white and shaken. The van pulled up across the road. The black sedan tried to nose past and was held up by the ditch. The driver of the van climbed out of his cabin and stood in the road shouting after the Rolls and shaking his fist. The man in the bowler hat got out of the sedan and ran up to him, pointing after the Rolls.

Peter realized that he had bitten his tongue. He found his handkerchief and dabbed at it. He noticed that his hands were shaking slightly and took a firmer hold of the wheel. Rex leaned through the glass partition and tapped him on the shoulder.

"Don't you do that again!" he said hoarsely. "We might *all* have been killed!"

"Brava!" said Hugo calmly. "I couldn't have done better myself!"

"Suppose I'd been crippled," said Rex shrilly, "where would I have been then?"

"Well, I'm going to have a sandwich," said Bertha. She adjusted Mr. Cann, who had fallen across her knees. "When I'm nervous I always get terribly hungry."

"I'm sure I'm making adrenalin," said Rex. "And it's all Peter's fault. You can sit by the telephone for six weeks, but nobody calls if you've got adrenalin. It's *known*."

Peter suddenly lost his temper.

"For God's sake!" he snapped. "Will you please stop chattering? Lot of bloody monkeys! Can't you understand that if we muff this we shall all get five years – that is, those of us who aren't actually hanged? You're behaving as if this is a bloody picnic."

"Very apt, dear," said Rex. "Only there isn't any blood." He giggled.

Peter looked over his shoulder. He met Rex's speckled eyes.

"Shut up!" he said with authority.

There was silence in the back of the car. Hugo puffed a black cigarette. Rex sulked. Bertha wadded a coat between herself and Mr. Cann, and munched a sandwich. Peter looked sideways at Fan. She had put on her dark glasses and looked frail and earnest. He decided that, if they got away with it, he would be nicer to her than ever before.

He overtook a small gray car and a single-decker bus. From the corner of his eye he saw several people in the bus look down into the back of the landau. He drove faster. He could see the beginning of a wood on his left. The tips of the beech trees were turning golden. He stopped at the side of the road and allowed the bus to pass him. There was a little boy inside it, standing on the seat with his face squashed against the glass. He pointed at the car and began to jump up and down. Peter kept the engine running. The bus changed gear, and for a moment he thought it was going to stop, but it did not. He waited until it had turned the corner. He looked into the driving mirror and saw that the road was clear behind. He started slowly after the bus.

He passed a whitewashed cottage with a child swinging on the gate. She waved. He turned the corner. The bus was out of sight. A quarter of a mile farther on he saw what he was looking for. There was a turning into the woods on the left. The road was clear ahead. He slowed down and the Rolls bounced as it jolted off the tarmac. It was a dirt track with a ribbon of grass down the middle. There were pines and beeches on the right and a field of cropped grass on the left. The trunks of the trees were well spaced out, and there was a carpet of fallen pine needles.

Peter saw his opening and dragged the wheel over. The Rolls took the dried-up bed of a stream in its stride. They were among the trees. There were rhododendrons. Grey moss and lichen grew on the trunks of the trees. Nobody spoke. A small nut tree scraped past the bonnet and pushed through the window. It scratched Fan's hand, but she did not appear to notice it. Peter maneuverd the car through the thickening tree trunks until he judged that they were roughly in the middle of the wood. He pulled up and looked over his shoulder. The trees had closed behind them. He turned off the engine.

He issued his instructions briskly. He, Rex, and Bertha were to make for the thickest patch of rhododendrons. He and Bertha were to begin digging immediately. Rex was to collect moss and ferns to lay over the new grave. He was not to break the roots, as it was essential that the plants should thrive after their transplantation. Hugo and Fan were to remain in the car. They were to remove all identifying labels from the two bodies. They were then to place the two deceased under a certain larch tree, return to the car, and be prepared, in an emergency, to sound an alarm on the horn. Hugo was to turn the car and be ready if necessary to make a fast-moving exit. Finally, there was to be absolutely no talking.

He eyed his team. He knew that he could rely upon Fan and Hugo. Bertha was pale, but she had a determined glint in her eye. Rex was the weakest link. He was obviously enjoying himself. He looked at Peter and smiled disarmingly.

"I don't often get out into the country," he said.

Peter looked at his watch. It was just after ten.

"All right," he said. "Let's go."

Bertha, armed with the trowel, got out of the car and bustled away into the bushes. Her large, sensible brogues crunched through the undergrowth. Rex laid a finger on his lips and tiptoed after her, making nearly as much noise. Peter took the shovel and followed them. As he pushed past a young fir-tree he turned to see whether Fan and Hugo were obeying their instructions. Hugo had already turned the car. It looked as alien as a block of flats among the delicate branches of the larch trees which drooped over it. Hugo and Fan were in the back, bending over Lilli and Mr. Cann. Peter turned and plunged into the trail of broken bracken left by Rex and Bertha. He passed Rex squatting under a beech tree prising up a slab of viridian moss. A large-leafed plant with an insignificant flower bloomed from the pocket of his jacket and he was singing to himself. Peter tapped him on the shoulder.

"Be quiet," he said sternly.

A few yards away he saw Bertha's feet, soles up, sticking out from under the trailing branches of a pine tree. He bent double and forced a way to the center of the tree and found himself in a dim cavern with almost enough room to stand upright. Bertha had prospected well. She had scraped aside the leaf mold and arranged the fallen fir-cones in a neat pile. She was now stabbing at the dark earth with the trowel. She nodded briefly to Peter. He began to dig. The soil was soft and light and he realized with relief that the grave was going to be an easier task than he had anticipated. After ten minutes he had made an appreciable hole. Rex appeared with an armful of moss and a large plant which he insisted in a shrill whisper was a mandrake. It had screamed, he said, as he pulled it up.

In the car, Fan and Hugo decided against undressing their ex-lodgers. They tossed as to who should remove Mr. Cann's dentures and Hugo lost. Fan saw them lying on the blue upholstery like an advertisement and stifled a nervous giggle. She began to collect the fallen jewelry, laundry marks, and labels. Hugo pulled the limp Mr. Cann across his back and got out of the car. He had just stepped into the bracken when he stiffened like a pointer and stared at Fan.

"Did you hear anything?"

Fan held a ration book and a wallet between her teeth. She shook her head mutely.

"You didn't whistle? I thought I heard somebody whistle."

Both were still, straining their ears. Two branches rasped together in the slight breeze. A fir-cone fell. The trees made their own soft noises. Then a shrill whistle rang out from the far side of the clearing.

Hugo moved like a lizard. He was back in the car in a single bound. He jerked Lilli on to the floor, hurled Mr. Cann on top of her, twitched the rug over both, and in the space of a breath was sitting over them unruffled with Fan in his arms. A second later there burst from the bushes opposite two small girls in navy-blue gym tunics. They wore satchels on their backs from which they were scattering small pieces of paper. They stopped short and looked curiously at the car. The one with straight hair and freckles skipped over, still dripping shreds of paper through her fingers. She wore a navy-blue beret with a gold and purple crest in front.

"Corks!" she said. "What an asinine place to park your car!"

"Not at all," said Hugo coldly. "We want to be alone."

"Come *on*, Biscuit," called the other child anxiously.

Biscuit grinned. "You won't be alone for long," she said. "Miss Hemming wouldn't let us play Lax 'cos the field's all mucky, so we've been made to play Hares and Hounds. We two are Hares, and the Hounds'll be along any moment now. There are twenty-three not counting Miss Hemming."

"Biscuit, do come *on*!"

"Well," said Biscuit. "I s'pose we ought to bunk. If you get caught too early you get wigged something fierce." She grinned. "We have an arrangement, of course. We shake off the Hemming fairly early and the decent bugs meet somewhere, but Porker's got a crush on Miss Hemming and she *tells*. What have you got under that rug?"

"Picnic."

"Have you got anything decent to eat?"

"No."

Biscuit stuck out her stomach and patted it. "Void," she said. "We have to give our Break buns to Porker just because she happened to see us stoning Honour Parkin. Honour wouldn't blab 'cos I'm the only one who can get cobbler's wax, but Porker would, just to suck up to Miss Hemming. Have you got any spare ball-bearings?"

"No."

"Pity! They're wizard for catapults."

The child hopped away in the direction taken by the grave-diggers. The other child ran after, trying to catch up. With one hand she was tugging at her suspender. There was a gap of pink flesh between her stockings and her knickers.

Hugo leaned through the glass partition and sounded an urgent tattoo on the horn. Fan climbed into the front of the car and started the engine. Bertha appeared first. She blundered through the rhododendrons looking frightened. Peter was behind her, holding the shovel shoulder-high to keep it clear of the undergrowth.

"Get in," said Hugo brusquely. "Paper chase. Twenty-three coming up, not counting Miss Hemming."

Peter slid under the wheel, slammed the door, and put the car in gear. Rex sprang through the bushes and hurled himself into the back. As it jolted forward, he was catapulted on to the floor. He extricated himself from Mr. Cann and sat back looking surprised.

"He *bit* me!"

"Wishful thinking," said Hugo nastily. "His teeth are in Fan's bag."

"Shut up, shut up!" said Peter. He was so angry that he drove carelessly. He grazed the front mudguard on a beech-tree. As he recrossed the bed of the stream he saw four small girls walking slowly along the track, deep in conversation. One held up her hand. Peter waved her out of the way, but she refused to move. He swore softly and pulled up.

"Hullo," said the girl. "Are you lost?"

"No. Would you mind getting out of the way?"

"Have you seen a stuck-up-looking girl running about?"

"Yes," said Hugo. He waved a hand at the field of cropped grass. "They went across there."

"*Did* they? Miss Hemming'll have kittens! It's not what they arranged either, the stinkers. Have you got any spare ball-bearings?"

"No."

"Could you spare a drop of petrol?"

"Would you mind getting out of the way?"

The child looked at Peter with interest. "You're in a bate," she said.

Peter released the clutch. The child sprang backwards and sat down in the ditch. The others stood around her, looking after the car. Peter ground his teeth.

"Well, they ought to remember us," he said furiously. "We'll all have a happy reunion at the trial."

He trod savagely on the accelerator and shot past several other girls in navy-blue blazers. A long bramble whipped into the car and pulled loose a strand of Bertha's hair. It hung over her shoulder with a kirbigrip attached to the end. At the end of the lane stood a buxom woman in a brown tussore tunic. Her muscular legs were encased in brown stockings and she wore a green sash loosely on her hips. Peter slowed down to turn on to the main road.

"Excuse me," she shouted.

Peter waved an arm backwards.

"*That* way," he said.

"Thanks awfully," said the woman. "They're so naughty, you know. They don't throw the paper, they just hide in the woods and talk." She smoothed her hair with a square hand. "Well, I'll go and extricate the little fiends. Thanks terribly."

Peter bowed and drove on.

"See you at the Old Bailey," murmured Hugo over his shoulder.

Peter turned right on to the tarmac. He began to feel defeated. He knew that the success of the funeral depended entirely upon himself. Rex and Fan had proved by their astounding escapade of the previous evening that, whereas they had the necessary courage, they lacked executive talent. Bertha was a sturdy lieutenant, but, outside the kitchen, had little imagination. Hugo, on the other hand, had too much. He was unable, after his years in Europe as a long-range refugee, to adjust his ideas to an overpopulated island at peace. Peter slowed down for a corner and when he was halfway around it saw that thirty yards beyond it was the black sedan.

The man in the bowler hat ran into the middle of the road and flung up his hand. Peter stamped on the brake and the car skidded to a standstill. The man moved around to the window. Peter released the clutch and trod on the accelerator. The engine stalled.

All right, he thought. *It's a fair cop!* It had been ludicrous ever to think that they would get away with it. He heard Hugo clear his throat and Rex whistling nervously between his teeth. Fan sat rigidly beside him. Her eyes followed the man in the bowler hat like a mesmerized bird. In the driving mirror he saw Hugo fumbling under the seat in the tool chest. Now he was sitting up straighter, looking secretive and cunning. Peter turned round.

"Put it down," he said in a hard whisper.

Hugo's black eyes looked over his shoulder at the man in the bowler hat. He took no notice. He had something in his hand under the rug.

The man in the bowler hat came closer to the window. He raised his hat half an inch and replaced it.

"Mornin'," he said heavily. "I been followin' you for a long, long way."

Peter said nothing. He looked at the man's feet. He wore boots.

"Thought I'd lost you," the man went on. He pulled his nose. "But after I'd gone that far, I was goin' to catch up with you no matter what. When I do a thing, I *do* a thing. Pure fluke you 'aven't been stopped before."

"What exactly do you want?" Peter asked. He heard Hugo sliding forward on the seat behind him.

The man in the bowler hat laughed.

"What do *I* want, eh? That's a good one, that is!" He wiped a fleck of foam from the corner of his mouth. "*I* don't want anything, chum – least of all to chase you all over the ruddy county. But I tell you what *you* want an' yours truly's got it." He whipped a hand from behind his back and waved a license plate. "Yours, that is!" he said triumphantly. "Noticed it was a bit wonky comin' through Battersea. Fell off soon after. So what do I do? I am goin' your way an' I like young people" – he leered at Fan – "so I picks it up an' gives chase. Rate you was travelling, anybody'd of thought the Russians was after you." He laughed again and smacked the car.

Rex laughed too, uproariously. Then he stopped as suddenly as he had started and looked embarrassed. Peter stretched out his hand for the license plate, but the man held on to it. He would attach it for them, he said. It would take only a brace of shakes. He could turn his hand to anything. He hurried around to the back of the car.

Peter leaned over the partition and gripped Hugo's wrist. He gave it a violent twist. Hugo did not say anything, but he looked resentful and there was a heavy, metallic clang as he dropped something on the floor. The man reappeared, wiping his hands together, beaming. He leaned against the car. He obviously wanted to enjoy their company for as long as possible. He sensed their mounting impatience and accepted it as a challenge to linger.

"There you are!" he said. "Everythin' 'unkey-dory an' shipshape now. Goin' far?"

"Yes," said Peter. He reached for the self-starter. "Thank you."

"That's all right," said the man. "I 'ad to go to Farnham anyway. Nice bus you got there. I always say you can't beat a Rolls."

"Yes," said Peter. "Well, thanks again."

As the car started forward the man's elbow was jerked off the door. He spun in a half-circle and they left him standing in the road, holding his hat in both hands. As they turned the corner he was still watching them dubiously.

"He'll be there, too," said Hugo.

"Where?"

"At the trial."

They passed a wood on the left. It would have suited their purpose admirably, but Peter did not stop. He ignored two more copses. He was sure that the man in the bowler hat would be after them soon. But when they approached the fourth wood and there was still no sign of him Peter slowed down. It was not a large wood. The trees were not more than twelve feet high, but there was bracken and a dense undergrowth. Fan sprang out of the car and unlatched a gate. It sagged on its hinges as she tried to lift it. Hugo got out to help her. They dragged it open. The Rolls shot past them and disappeared around a bend in the track. Fan and Hugo ducked as a lorry raced along the road. The shrub behind which they were taking cover was very small and the driver of the lorry leaned out of the side window and waved to them.

They left the gate open. Fan led the way up the path. It curled away into the thicket of young birch and nut trees and old brambles. The Rolls was about two hundred yards from the road. It was empty except for Lilli, who lay in the back covered with the rug. Her small body was limp now. She was folded up neatly like a hibernating animal. Only the closest observer would have noticed her. The other three were already at their appointed tasks. Peter was behind a blackberry bush. He drove the shovel into the ground. There was a dull clank and he stood up and massaged his wrists. Rex was towing Mr. Cann through the brambles by the legs. Bertha had found a rabbit hole and was worrying it with the trowel, trying to enlarge it. They looked grim and dishevelled.

Hugo plunged into the thicket to join them. Fan turned away, looking for a camouflage of moss. There was none on the ground, it was not that sort of wood, but there was a thin film of it on the trunks and roots of a young oak tree. She made for it and was trying to lever it off unbroken when she had the feeling that she was being watched. Her heart began to beat thickly. She did not turn around. She went on working on the moss and she began to sing carelessly to herself. When she had scraped loose the last tendril she rolled the moss into a neat ball and stepped back on to the path.

There was a square, stocky man watching her from less than fifty yards away. His gaitered legs were planted firmly apart and he had a shotgun under his arm. He watched her without moving and his expression was unfriendly. Fan shot a glance at the grave site. She saw nobody but Rex, who was bending over something on the ground.

"Rex," she called out clearly. "Here's a kind man with a gun come to help us."

Rex stood up. His mouth fell open. The man approached slowly. His eyes never left Fan's face. She saw from the corner of her eye Rex's nimble feet frantically working Mr. Cann deeper into a blackberry cane. There was no sign of the other three. Rex gave Mr. Cann a brutal kick, there was a series of crashes and the body slithered downwards dragging the canes with it. The bush sagged and slowly assumed an entirely different shape.

"'Ere!" shouted the man, and started to run towards them. "Wot you think you're doin'? Leavin' gates open an' breakin' up the coverts!"

Rex stepped out of the bush.

"Now look …" he said.

His voice was even more mannered than usual, and Fan's heart sank. She looked distractedly at his yellow beret, his bright hair, his Paisley shirt. As she had anticipated, the sight of him enraged the gaitered man still further.

"Oh, so it's 'look', is it?" he sneered. "If it isn't Peter Pan 'isself! Well, these ain't the Never-Never woods an' never, never will be! Yore trespassin'! Where's yore eyes?" He pointed his 12-bore obliquely behind him at a post topped with two large bent nails. "See that notice? Trespassers will be prosecuted, it says. Go on, read it!"

Rex looked down at his folded hands, raised his eyebrows, and said nothing. The man glanced over his shoulder, darted a venomous glance at Rex, and swung back slowly to the post. His jaw sagged.

"It's gone!" he said. "'Oo took it? 'Oo took it, I say?" His face was hideous with rage. "Trippers!" he roared. "Ruddy trippers! Stealin' my notices, muckin' up the coverts, breakin' the foliages, leavin' dirty things everywhere! Get out! Get out afore I *shoots* you out! *'Oo took my notice?*"

Fan got hastily into the car. She heard a twig snap in the thicket and caught a brief glimpse of Bertha's skirt crawling cautiously deeper into the wood. Rex stood his ground. His eyes were snapping with anger.

"You can't talk to me like that, you silly little man!" he said, trembling with passion. "Stomping around in those idiotic gaiters and playing at *l'après-midi d'un ogre!* You can't prosecute trespassers anyway. It's *known*. Trespass is a civil offense and prosecute is a police word, so there! And you know what you can do with your silly old notice!"

The man's hand curled around his gun. He cocked the hammer with a stubby thumb.

"I'll give you ten seconds to clear off," he said.

"Don't be such a nonsense! You wouldn't dare."

Without taking his eyes off them, the man discharged his gun into the blackberry canes. Rex winced and clapped his hands to his ears. He was in such a hurry to get into the car that he fell across the seat. He scrabbled at the dashboard, chattering to himself like a chipmunk. He ground the gear into reverse and the car leaped backwards. Fan saw Hugo flattened behind a tree-trunk, half-hidden by the leaves. He looked up and shrugged his shoulders.

"… six … seven … eight …"

Swerving wildly, the Rolls flattened two small fir trees and a giant fennel.

"… *nine* … I'll show yer! Breakin' my trees! I'll show yer! TEN!"
The man was beside himself with rage. He ran after them, levelling his
gun.

The car rocketed backwards through the gate, across the road, into
the ditch on the far side. Rex fought frantically with the gears. The
wheels skidded, gripped, and bounced on to the tarmac with a spray of
flints ricocheting inside the mudguards.

Half a mile farther on, Rex drew in to the side of the road and stopped.
He clasped his hands in his lap and breathed heavily.

"I'm not a terribly good driver," he said tonelessly. He reached into
the back of the car, rolled Lilli over, and found the gin. He drank and
passed the bottle to Fan.

"I'm not going to worry," he said. "Hugo'll get them out. He's been
playing Cops and Robbers for years." He took off his beret and combed
his hair.

"Rex," said Fan suddenly. "You didn't kill them, did you? I mean,
I'm sure you didn't, but I want to hear you say it."

"But how could I, angel?" asked Rex lazily. He leaned back against
the seat and gazed up at the sky. "What a monster you are!"

"You've got a key. You could have got in any time and made free
with the arsenic."

"Well, I didn't. I hadn't got any motives."

"People do odd things for sudden reasons."

"If I were going to kill anybody, ducky, it would be far more spectacular than this drab little business. I'd have bombs, blunt instruments,
krisses, and masses of blood."

Fan nodded. She was satisfied. A little later she said, "Rex, has it
occurred to you that people get sick after arsenic? Our two weren't
sick."

"I should hope not! Don't be disgusting."

Twenty minutes later they drove slowly back past the wood. A rabbit
flirted its tail and hopped into a bank, but otherwise nothing stirred.
Rex turned the car and cruised past again. Just before the gate he sounded
the horn. Hugo bobbed up in the hedge. His face was dirty and he had
leaves in his hair. He looked up and down the road and spoke to somebody over his shoulder. He sprang lightly over the bank and held out his
arms. Peter handed him Mr. Cann. Bertha tripped in the bracken and
slid down the bank ungracefully. Hugo threw Mr. Cann into the car and
plucked Bertha out of the ditch. Peter jumped into the back of the car
and slammed the door. Rex drove on.

"Darling," said Fan, twisting anxiously round in the front seat, "are you all right? That pig fired straight into your site."

"We're all right," said Peter somberly. "But Mr. Cann has had it again."

Bertha, who was pale and had a long scratch on one cheek, began to grumble about her stockings. Peter mopped his forehead and drank some gin. Hugo lit one of the small black cheroots which his wife allowed him to smoke only in the open air. Bertha had peeled off one ruined stocking when the engine coughed.

Peter leaned over Rex and looked at the petrol gauge. It stood at five gallons. It had stood at five gallons when they left Chelsea. Fan pulled out the choke. She knew nothing about cars, but she wanted to help. Two hundred yards farther on, the engine coughed twice. Rex pushed in the choke.

"I expect it's me," he said. "Cars never like me."

They passed a cottage with a corrugated iron roof, and half a mile beyond it the car began to move in convulsive jerks. It continued nobly for a mile, then the gallant old engine belched and died.

Peter dived under the seat and found a measuring rod. He got out and went round to the back of the car. When he came back his face was grim.

"We're out of gas, chaps," he said with a ghastly gaiety. He looked around. The old aristocrat had elected to stop on a straight stretch of road between flat green fields which offered no cover. There was not even a ditch.

Hugo got out of the car and rolled up his sleeves.

"Push," he said crisply. "Push to a hideout, then beg, borrow, or steal."

Rex vaulted into the road. Bertha sighed and followed him more staidly. With Fan steering, they started to push. As soon as they heard a car approaching they sprang into nonchalant attitudes, waving aside all offers of assistance. They covered about two miles. The car had reached the top of a slight incline and was moving grudgingly of its own accord when a hatefully familiar klaxon made them turn, flushed and panting, to face the man in a bowler hat.

He waved cheerily, shouted something, drew up in front of the Rolls, and hurried back, beaming. Hugo sighed loudly through his nose.

"Ulloulloullo!" said the man. "Troub again, eh? Old Lady outer gas?" He was delighted.

"We're perfectly all right, thank you," said Fan breathlessly. "We're – we're doing this for a bet."

"Now, now, now," said the man in the bowler hat. "Sid Crick 'as always been one to reckernize a damsel in distress. An' if I ever saw distress written all over a lovely face, I'm looking at it now." He bowed gallantly.

Hugo opened the rear door of the car and reached under the seat. He said something to himself in a guttural language. Peter caught him by the shoulder and shut the door. The man in the bowler hat leaned over the bonnet, beaming at Fan.

"Where was you 'eadin' for? Back for good old Lunnon? That's my guess. Am I right, eh? Goin' that way meself. We'll 'itch you up in no time and I'll give you a free ride back right to yer very doorstep. 'Ow's that? Okey-doke?"

"Look, sir," said Peter sternly. "We like it here. We are already in-debted to you, but we wish to be left alone."

"Well," said the man reluctantly, "wouldn't be my cuppa tea. Okay, it's your funeral. Cherrie bye, then."

He half-turned away. A new thought struck him visibly. He came closer, nodding slowly, his tongue in his cheek.

"Oh, so *that's* it, is it? I *bet* I know what's under all them rugs. Well, well, well! New to the game, eh? Well, I'm tellin' you in confidence that I do a bit o' fiddlin' meself. I got a rug in the back o' my bus, too. An' underneath it, just between ourselves, I got twelve turkeys, fifteen geese, and two 'undred and forty eggs!" He smiled at them proudly. "An' because I don't like to see young people get into troub, I'm telling you something else. There's a bobby comin' down this road, nearer an' nearer every second. Country rozzers are very, very *nosy*."

Peter turned quickly. It was a long straight road. Coming over the rise at the end was a large policeman, approaching them sedately on a bicycle.

"Sir," said Hugo, "please forgive my friend his discourtesy. He some-times speaks hastily. We shall be very much obliged to you if you will tow us back to town."

"Well, then!" said the man in the bowler hat. "That's more like it. Would one o' you young ladies like to keep me company up front, eh?"

CHAPTER 12

At one o'clock at the Asterisk Club, Beecher relieved Squires of the noon watch. As usual, he entered the attic room quietly, partly because he liked to practice moving silently and partly because he disliked Squires and wished to startle him. The youth, his fuzzy chin in his hand, was avidly reading a book propped on the window ledge. His lips were moving. He was whispering to himself. He had been convicted at fourteen for stealing a colander and two packets of steel wool and he had never forgotten it. He insisted that his mother had made him do it and that he was a *good* boy. Beecher had once heard him telling Mrs. Barratt that he had ideals.

Beecher crept up to him and kicked him in the ankle. Squires jumped. He looked at Beecher with loathing. He tried to hide a tattered copy of *Beau Geste*. Then he ducked under Beecher's arm and ran out of the room.

Beecher forgot about him. He sat down on the window-seat and moodily lit a cigarette. He disliked doing lookout duty. He considered that he could have employed his time during his brief stretches of freedom in a hundred better ways. Particularly today, for it was one of the pleasant, clear-skied days of early September which always filled him with a vague nostalgia. The old longing was upon him. His fingers itched for the chisel, the mica, the jemmy. He watched the birds wheeling high above the river and wondered why he had never cracked a bank. He stared sullenly down into the road. He was getting no younger and he was determined to retire at fifty. He had seventeen hundred iron men invested in National Savings under a false name. He would retire when he had five thousand and not before. That was the day he dreamed of, the day he had worked for. His profession would then become his hobby. He would take only the smaller jobs. The big stuff with the long sentences he could afford to leave alone.

He would, for instance, take one or two of the tobacconists who had refused to sell him cigarettes. He would attend to their plate glass and congeal the mechanisms of their cash registers with a blowtorch. He would visit the butchers whose offal was for registered customers only. He would leave the tills alone, but he would knock off the kidneys and make the meat smell funny. He would not go short of eggs either. He would lift them right under the noses of his various grocer enemies. His hands still moved faster than the eye. He chuckled to himself. With his left hand he took the cigarette out of his right so fast that he did not see himself do it. It would be just like the good old days. He had not swiped an egg since he was eight.

He was still smiling when he saw the Rolls-Royce turn the corner. It was right behind a small black sedan, and Sunny Jim's wife was sitting in the front car next to a man in a bowler hat. *A pinch!* thought Beecher. He was delighted. Then he saw that the Rolls was being towed. Sunny Jim was steering and there was no sign of the two stiffs.

The sedan nosed around the Colonel's Bugatti and drew up in front of No. 15 with the landau behind it. The two in the front car got out and Sunny Jim climbed out of the Rolls. They all stood talking on the pavement. Epstein, his wife, and the bally-boy sat in a silent, watching row in the back of the landau, a rug over their knees. The man in the bowler hat had his arm around the shoulders of Mrs. Sunny Jim. She was looking at him sideways and trying to edge away. The man slapped Sunny Jim on the back, laughing fit to kill himself. Sunny Jim stumbled, then linked arms with him, and marched down the road in the direction of the Ten Bells. The man obviously did not want to leave the blonde, but Sunny Jim had him firmly by the arm and was hurrying him along.

The three in the landau were looking idly up and down the road. The Regard Casual again! *My Gawd!* thought Beecher. *What's it goin' to be this time?* The blonde opened the gate of No. 15 and propped it wide with a stone. Beecher ducked back as Epstein glanced up at his window. He himself gave the road the professional onceover. Except for himself, there seemed to be no witnesses. There was a yew bush in the garden of No. 18 which he did not like the look of; it was the shape of somebody crouching down, but it did not appear to worry the amateurs. They were whispering together and pulling at something under the rug. When eventually Epstein moved, he moved with the most incredible speed. He snatched the Old Tin Cann from under the rug and was inside the courtyard of No. 15 in the space of a breath. The dancer moved more slowly with La Cluj wrapped in a rug as if she were an invalid, and the two women crowded round him with thermoses and picnic baskets.

Beecher scratched the back of his head. *Well, I dunno!* he thought. *I am mystified. I give up.* He admitted to himself that if he had been removing two stiffs from a car in broad daylight he could not have done much better. But then he would not have been doing it, not under any circumstances. He could not understand why anybody else should be doing it either. He stopped thinking about it. It only worried him. He would go and tell the Boss and let him sort it out.

When he went downstairs, the front door was open and he saw Tom in the courtyard. He was crouching on the edge of the rococo pool and reaching into the water after the carp. Beecher crept up behind him, hoping to be able to push him in. Just as he got within range Tom, without looking round, walked out into the road and ran up an elm tree. He sat on the lowest branch with his tail hanging down and looked at Beecher through half-shut eyes.

Beecher went back into the hall. Squires was standing at the bottom of the stairs, watching.

"Har har," he said.

Beecher took no notice. He found the four remaining resident members in the morning-room, drinking an aperitif and waiting for their lunch. Beecher fixed his eyes upon the clock on the mantelpiece and told his story in a weary monotone. The four listened without interruption and with incredulous faces.

"You're making it up, you bad man!" said Mrs. Barratt finally.

"Be quiet, Naomi," said Flush. "Let me think." He sat drumming his fingers on the arm of his chair.

Beecher shifted his weight to the other foot and watched him uneasily.

"Must be pukka rogues!" said the Colonel. "No respect for the dead!" He was playing with a small spring, an elastic band and a rusty magnet.

"Amazing!" said Flush, almost to himself. "It is impossible to know what madness these amateurs will perpetrate next! They seem to have – quite literally – got away with murder!"

"Sir," said the Colonel, "in the present company, I consider that remark is distinctly off color."

Flush's pale eyes turned upon him.

"I was not speaking personally, my dear Colonel. If you had not interrupted me, I was about to qualify my observation. I was about to remark that, by pure clumsiness, an amateur may get away with murder *once*!" He paused and stared down at his suede shoes. "Of course," he murmured, "with the exception of yourself, each of us can claim, even if only unofficially, at last *two* feathers in his cap."

The Colonel rose. His face was magenta.

"I resent your implication, sir!"

"It is a fact," said Flush coldly. "But perhaps you would like to deny it? Perhaps you have a further claim to make? *Where were you last night, Colonel Quincey?*"

The Colonel was about to lose his temper completely when he saw Beecher watching him with transparent pleasure.

"How dare you, sir!" he said with an attempt at dignity. "You insinuate that I would lay a finger on a fellow member! How dare you, I say."

"I asked you where you were, Colonel."

"I was playing Halma with Mrs. Barratt and two of the temporaries."

"That's a wicked fib," said Mrs. Barratt spitefully. "That's only our alibi."

"I'm waiting, Colonel."

"I refuse to be cross-examined."

The Colonel poured himself another pink gin and stood gazing sulkily out of the window. Flush smiled maliciously. He caught Beecher's eye.

"Stop smiling, Beecher," he said sharply. Beecher's face sagged. "Thank you. This is no smiling matter. The ludicrous activities of these fools must cease forthwith. We must seize the bodies and bring them here for disposal."

"'Ear, 'ear!" said the Creaker. He was sunk into the settee, eating fondants.

"Beecher," said Flush briskly, "you will take the necessary action tonight. I expect both bodies to be on the premises by dawn tomorrow. You will prepare your schedule and report here this evening at seven-thirty. Is that understood?"

"Yus," said Beecher. The thought of illicit enterprise filled him with exaltation, but he gave no sign of it.

"Good. As for the rest of you, I forbid you to discuss this even among yourselves. No alcohol is to be drunk after seven-thirty this evening. There is one of us who, when in his cups, is apt to offer gratuitous advice which always annoys me. There is a bottle of Cockburn '08 on the top shelf of his wardrobe. It is mine. It is concealed beneath a pile of underclothes. It will be handed to me in its present condition after luncheon."

"I protest, sir!" shouted the Colonel from the window.

"Oh?" said Flush. He was about to join the issue with his Treasurer when he saw Beecher's face. "You may go, Beecher," he said coldly.

Beecher went into the hall. Tom was there. He tried to dodge into the dining room, but this time Beecher was too quick for him. He did not exactly kick the cat. He merely raised it into the air with his foot. He smiled as the Creaker's pet thudded off the ceiling.

"See?" he whispered.

CHAPTER 13

PETER HILFORD steered the man in the bowler hat towards the Ten Bells. The man, who had reintroduced himself as Sidney Crick, was not altogether pleased by this display of friendliness. He had, he protested, taken quite a fancy to the young lady whose name was Fan. She was, he considered, a real peach and it was not polite of a chap to just push off and leave her with all those turkeys to lug into the house unaided.

Peter assured him that the hard labor would be done by Rex and Hugo, but Mr. Crick was not satisfied. He announced that he had half a mind to go back because what Fan must think of him, he hated to think. Peter, his nerves already jangled by the morning's fiasco, resisted the impulse to club him down in cold blood. He promised himself that he would knock Mr. Crick about only if the situation became out of hand. He forced himself to smile. He took the man by the arm and piloted him towards the swing doors of the saloon bar.

"No," said Mr. Crick. He stopped in his tracks. "First and last, I'm a gent. I can't 'elp it. I'm goin' back to give an 'and."

Peter took a firmer grip on him.

"Well, old man," he said carelessly, "of course, if you insist, I can't stop you. But she won't appreciate it. She can't bear helpful chaps. She likes lazy, brutish men who treat her like dirt. Odd, but there it is. Some women do."

Mr. Crick hesitated.

"Straight?" he asked.

"Fact."

"Well, well!" said Mr. Crick with quiet wonder. "You do surprise me! I've 'eard stories about foreign women as would make your 'air curl, but I didn't know English women was like that. Live an' learn, eh? I'm not 'itched, see. I've 'ad one or two near misses though, if you see what I mean!" He slapped Peter's shoulder and shook with laughter.

"Yes," said Peter. He knew Mr. Crick expected him to laugh. "Congratulations," he added heartily.

"Well," said Mr. Crick, mopping his eyes. "Well, if they want rough stuff, the little dears, 'ere's the boy what's goin' to change 'is technique. Won't come natural at first, I expect, but Sid Crick'll soon get the 'ang of it. Deceptive, though, aren't they? She seemed so quiet. You'd almost of thought she was scared."

He allowed Peter to steer him through the swing doors. The saloon bar was deserted except for a Chelsea pensioner who sat in a corner dreamily contemplating his beer. The barmaid was an improbable blonde. She welcomed Peter boisterously. Mr. Crick followed their amiable exchange of near-insults carefully. He was living and learning. When he thought he had got the hang of it, he asserted himself.

"Now then, you two!" he said experimentally. He slapped the counter. "Pint o' the best, gorgeous, an' shake a leg."

The barmaid stared.

"An 'oo d'you think you are?" she asked.

Mr. Crick blushed. He had shot his bolt. It was not as easy as it looked, this rough stuff.

"Thirsty, see?" he said. He smiled ingratiatingly. "Bring us a pint o' bitter, miss, there's a good girl. And a firkin for my friend 'ere, if you please."

"That's more like," said the barmaid. She smoothed her hips. "Caveman!" she added.

Mr. Crick brightened. He beamed at her.

"I am, at that," he said, winking. "'Airs on me chest like bars o' soap."

"Well, I'm not goin' to give up no points," said the barmaid.

"Double scotch," said Peter. He sat down. He was tired.

"No scotch, dear. You can 'ave gin or rum or me."

"Just now, I'll take gin."

The barmaid looked at him more closely.

"What's the matter with you today?" she asked. "Properly down in the mouth, you are. What you been up to, as if I didn't know?"

"Top secret."

"Wouldn't I love you no more?"

"Oh, no."

"I'd probably call the police."

"I wouldn't be at all surprised."

"Well, aren't you *dirty*?"

"No," said Peter. He was tired of this game. "Clean as a whistle. Just a little involved."

The barmaid laughed.

"I can guess," she said.

Peter watched her curiously as she moved away to draw Mr. Crick's bitter. He wondered down what primitive labyrinths her mind was wandering. His reverie was interrupted by Mr. Crick, who announced that he was going to ring up Fan and suggest that she came along for a snifter. He demanded Peter's telephone number and hurried away, selecting coppers from a palmful of loose change.

Peter leaned on the bar and lit a cigarette. He sat watching the smoke curling out of it. He was unable to shake off his depression. The spectacle of the large, distinctive landau being towed by a small and dusty saloon had excited derisive comment from what he gloomily estimated at half a million people. Some, if not all of them, would undoubtedly appear at the trial. For a second he clearly saw Fan's small, pointed face behind bars. He wondered whether they made women break stones and whether Fan would ever become reconciled to porridge. He wondered whether they would all go into the dock together. It would be quite a crowd. The Asterisk mob would be dragged in too and, presumably, a few of Mr. Beesum's dead rats, who had been cheated of their arsenic. It would be a ludicrous case. Too many prisoners, too many witnesses, too many killers, too many dead ...

It was anyway now too late to turn back. They had burned their boats. The police were now irreconcilably on the other side of the fence.

He looked instinctively over his shoulder. He half-expected to meet the relentless eyes of Inspector Carstairs. He would be in plain clothes, of course, a brown trilby and a no-colored trench-coat, but the boots and the set of the burly shoulders would be a dead giveaway. There was also something indefinable about the eyelids and the lower lip peculiar to policemen and established criminals. He decided that, in his next book, Inspector Carstairs would get discredited, tortured, and killed.

Mr. Crick came out of the phone box. He planted one foot on the brass rail and quaffed half his bitter in one draught.

"Ar," he said, wiping his mouth with the back of his hand. "Poor little squaw's in troub."

Peter's glass was halfway to his mouth. His heart plummeted into his stomach.

"Oh?" he said carefully.

"Made a shockin' mess in the back o' the car, she said! All over the upholstery an' all."

"What did? What are you talking about?"

"Keep your shirt on! Might of been worse. The thermos broke. Coffee all over the shop. Never comes out, either. I 'ad planned to treat 'er roughish, but honest I 'adn't the 'eart."

Peter drank his gin. As he motioned to the barmaid to bring the same again, Rex came in. Peter noticed that, as usual, he made an entrance. He flung open the door with an outstretched hand and looked around the saloon bar as if he were on a hilltop overlooking seven counties. Then he drooped and drifted over to the bar. He propped himself on the counter.

"Tired now," he said plaintively. He roused himself and lit a small cigarette. He turned to Mr. Crick. "Are you a policeman?" he asked.

"No," said Mr. Crick. He looked uneasily at Peter and back at Rex's yellow beret, which clearly fascinated him. "Bring the gent a noggin, miss," he called.

"Ordering me around!" said the barmaid, trying to make something of it.

"I adore 'gent'," said Rex. "The man means me!"

"Jump to it, gorgeous," said Mr. Crick.

"Don't boss, you," said the barmaid, delighted.

"I want my own secret thing," said Rex. "I want a Pernod and a slosh of gin and a piece of Drambuie the size of a walnut."

"Cor!" said Mr. Crick.

"Of course I shall be barking drunk," said Rex. "But after this morning I do feel I'm entitled to it."

Peter frowned heavily and kicked him on the ankle. Rex shut his eyes.

The barmaid poured a tot of gin into a double measure of Pernod. She held it at arm's length as if it might explode.

"And again, dear," said Rex. "Make with the wrist. You're a great strong girl. Heaven! Woof! Woof!"

"Eleven shillings," said the barmaid.

"Remind me never to take you out before payday," said Mr. Crick, paying. He looked at Rex resentfully.

"'Alf o' mild," said the Chelsea pensioner.

Rex tugged at Peter's lapel.

"Now don't you worry about anything at all," he said significantly. "Everything is back in its proper place and everybody's happy. And I've got a wonderful plan about how we can shake off those two bores who've been worrying us hairless. It suddenly came to me as I was under the monkey-puzzle tree. I can't imagine why we never thought of it before."

"Not here, Rex. We'll talk about it later."

"No, *now*." He raised his glass to Mr. Crick. "Whither away!"

The barmaid adjusted her bosom on the counter and eyed Mr. Crick. Rex drew Peter out of earshot.

"You *see*," he whispered, "we've all decided that we're up against pro., haven't we? There they are skulking around next door and bumping off chaps. Now what *I* say is that if they think they can palm off their bods on us, well, they're playing at wishful thinking. Why should *we* bear the brunt?"

"Last orders," called the barmaid, ringing the bell.

"Render unto Caesar?" said Peter.

"Exactly." Rex nodded several times. "I mean, they ought to know the ropes, oughtn't they? They'll get rid of the Loved Ones in no time at all. It was probably just pure laziness finishing them off in our house. So we render them right back where they belong. We merely have to hump them over the wall. Hugo'll do it. Then we'll pull up the drawbridge, and, if you see what I mean, our headache is next door."

"You may have something there," said Peter.

"Of course I have! If I drink this I shall be swinging from tree to tree."

"Time!" called the barmaid. "Time, *please!*"

"Flaxman eight four oh double two," said Mr. Crick, writing.

"That's right," said the barmaid archly. "Give us a tinkle."

CHAPTER 14

It took time to get rid of Mr. Crick. It was only after addresses and telephone numbers had been exchanged and a tentative date made for the following Thursday that he climbed unwillingly into his car and drove away, looking upwards over his shoulder at the first-floor windows.

Rex found his key and opened the door. Peter followed him into the hall. The rug which had camouflaged the two corpses was spilt into a corner and Rex's large-leafed plant was drooping in a jam-jar, otherwise everything was much as usual.

Marleen looked through the green baize doors and slapped a plate of sandwiches on to the bottom stair. She scowled at them.

"What's the matter, dear?" asked Rex.

"Oh, nothin' at all," said Marleen airily. She turned to go and changed her mind. She appealed to Peter, flinging out her hand in an enraged gesture. "Sandwiches!" she said, quivering. "I spent 'alf the mornin' makin' curry and two vedge an' what 'appens? They aren't 'ungry! They want sandwiches. Well, I don't care if they cripple their insides, but for the last two days I done nothin' 'cept make sandwiches. *Why* does everybody keep wantin' sandwiches? If you want to live on sandwiches for evermore, then *say* so – but don't make me cook an 'ot meal an' two vedge an' *then* ask! I am not an unreasonable woman, but I *don't like makin' sandwiches!* I got two blisters and I am never goin' to make them no more no matter what, an' that's flat!" She flounced back into the kitchen. She tried to slam the swing door, but it only flapped behind her.

Rex and Peter looked at each other. Rex grinned. Neither commented upon Marleen's outburst, because they could hear her breathing heavily behind the door waiting for them to do so. Rex went upstairs. Peter sat down on the stairs and waited for Marleen to go away. Presently, she tiptoed back to the kitchen. Peter heard her light the gas and drop the kettle. He stole to the telephone and softly dialed Martin's number.

"Martin?"

"In person. Who's that?"

"Peter."

"Hullo, cock."

"Martin, listen. I'm going to whisper."

"All right." He did not ask why, he accepted it at once. "Go ahead."

"Your car's hot!"

"What?"

"Hot."

"Hot?"

"Yes." Peter suddenly had a wild impulse to roar with laughter. He imagined Martin in his telephone alcove and his Irish tweeds, standing under the stained-glass window.

"Oh, well," said Martin philosophically. "I suppose it can't be helped, but I do loathe taxis."

"Hire a Bentley. Don't take it lying down."

"Where's the Heap?"

"Here. Out of gas."

"I'll pick her up."

"I suggest you have her painted."

"As bad as that? Dear boy! How long will it take her to cool down?"

"I don't know. I'll give you a ring."

"Right. Watch yourself, cock. 'Bye now."

"'Bye. And thanks."

Peter went upstairs. As soon as he opened the drawing-room door, he smelt burning. There was a pall of acrid smoke against the ceiling. As he shut the door, it swirled and curled downwards. Fan was crouching over the fire, stirring it with a poker.

"It's all right," said Hugo. "We're burning the labels."

"Did Marleen see you?" asked Peter.

"I don't think so."

"We thought we ought to have a sort of postmortem, darling," said Fan. "We've collected everything which might be a clue."

"Where are the Loved Ones?"

"In their trunks in the attic."

Peter moved Croydon off a chair and sat down. Croydon arched her back, stretched each of her hind legs in turn, fell over on to the hearthrug, and went to sleep.

"I found this," said Fan eagerly. She held up a wedge of dried mud. It was curved on one side. "It was by the wardrobe in the death chamber."

Peter took it and turned it over.

"Now," said Rex maliciously, "what would old On the Spot make of that?"

Peter did not look at him. "If you mean Inspector Carstairs," he said coldly, "he is dead. I've rewritten the last chapter. He gets shot."

"Oh, darling, what a *shame!*" said Fan. "*Must* he? He was almost one of the family. Who shoots him?"

"I don't know yet, but he gets shot."

"Couldn't he be dangerously wounded and recover for the next one?"

"No. He gets killed." Peter touched the piece of mud gently. "This is off somebody's shoe. A man's shoe. It came from under the instep of a shoe with a curved heel." He handed the mud to Hugo, who took it in silence and tried it against the sole of his shoe. It did not fit. It crumbled on one side and a piece fell off. Hugo passed it to Rex, whose expensive brogues had curved rubber heels. The mud slipped into place like a piece of a jigsaw puzzle. Rex clapped his hands.

"Cinderella!" he cried. "Bring on my prince!"

Fan was annoyed. She had been pleased with her clue.

"Other people wear shoes like that too," she said quickly.

"Be your age, ducks," said Rex. "This mud came off me. It probably let go while I was dressing Dr. Watson."

Peter took the mud and threw it into the fire.

Fan looked shocked. "You ought not to have done that. We ought to keep the clues."

"It's not a clue."

"It might be. Carstairs never threw anything away."

"This is nothing whatever to do with Carstairs, who is dead."

"This was under the bed," said Bertha. She handed over a burned out cigarette. "It's an Egyptian one. Lilli smoked them. I don't suppose it's a clue, but I couldn't find anything else."

Peter threw it in the fire. Fan clicked her tongue. She had brought an old cigar-box to put the clues into, but Peter kept throwing them away.

"They insisted that I kept this," said Hugo. He shook a small piece of white substance out of an envelope on to the palm of his hand. "It's a piece of clay. A red-hot clue! It proves conclusively that one of us, some time during the last three days, went into the studio and then into that room. Here you are. It's all yours."

Fan took the clay, put it into the cigar-box, and shut the lid. Bertha selected a sandwich.

"They're curry," she said, eating. "Marleen wins through!" She peeled two apart and handed the plate to Hugo. "Have a sandwich, dear. That one is brussels sprouts and that one mashed potato."

"Now we'll do the contents of their pockets," said Fan. "I was very careful, when I remembered, to touch them only with my hanky in case of fingerprints. This lot is Mr. Cann's."

There was a cheap fountain pen with B.C. engraved on it in gold, a ration book, a booklet of matches, a crumpled cigarette packet containing one Craven A, a handkerchief smeared with lipstick, a cigarette lighter, a latch key, and an expensive wallet holding twenty new one-pound notes, and a photograph of a dark woman whom Carstairs would have shrewdly recognized as Mr. Cann's recent victim.

Peter looked at this haul in silence. He was conscious of the other four watching him. He knew that Fan wanted him to deduce something. He picked up the cigarette-lighter and wondered what they expected him to do. He breathed on the lighter. It was tooled steel. It would never have shown any fingerprints. Fan leaned over him, gazing at it intently.

"I expect you've found something, haven't you?" she asked.

"Yes," said Peter irritably. "It needs a new wick."

"He hasn't drawn his rations for *weeks*," said Bertha, examining Mr. Cann's ration book.

Peter looked up sharply. "That won't make any difference to *you*," he said sternly.

"Oh, no," said Bertha. "Isn't it a waste, though? All that bacon and everything!" She met Peter's eyes, flushed, and laid the book back on the carpet. "Anyway," she said defiantly, "he's going to pay his rent." She peeled off five pounds from the roll of notes and put them into her pocket.

Fan took another five pounds without a word.

"I'm ashamed of you both," said Hugo. "The rent was only four guineas. Give the dead lady and gentleman their change."

"Four guineas a *week*," said Peter. "They were only here a few hours."

"No, they weren't," said Bertha. "They're still here, aren't they? And at this rate it looks as if they may be here for years."

Rex picked up the remaining ten pounds. "I'll take this," he said. "I'm his bodyguard. It's a retainer."

Peter was examining Lilli's effects. There was a gold compact, a bag of boiled sweets, two elastic bands, a lipstick which matched the smears on Mr. Cann's handkerchief, an enamel cigarette case containing four Egyptian cigarettes, a mascara brush wrapped in a dirty face tissue, some loose tea coupons, a teaspoon with Mecca Café stamped on the handle, and a screw of paper with a telephone number written on it.

"I rang up that number," said Fan. "It's a hairdresser. She was supposed to be having her hair done just about now. I cancelled the appointment."

Peter closed his eyes briefly. "That's fine," he said. "Just fine! When it's discovered that she's missing, there's going to be a checkup. They'll trace the call."

"It's all right, darling. I thought of that too. I pretended I was Lilli. I spoke all Balkan. I'm sure they fell for it. They'll think she was still alive. I thought it was rather cunning."

"Want to see a killer?" asked Hugo, who was standing by the window. His voice was full of suppressed excitement, and the other four quickly gathered round him, peering down into the road.

Mrs. Barratt walked briskly past their gate. She wore a shabby musquash coat and a felt toque. She had a string bag of groceries in one hand and a bunch of lilies in the other, and she looked kindly and respectable.

"Why *lilies?*" asked Rex nervously. "What would she want lilies for? Don't answer me."

"That's Naomi Barratt," said Peter in a hushed voice. "She bumped off her husband with cumulative doses of powdered glass. He left her nearly thirty thousand. The will said she was the best wife a man ever had."

Mrs. Barratt did not look up, but she knew that she was being watched. She held up her head higher and walked a little faster. She rang the bell of the Asterisk Club and stood tapping her foot. She waited several minutes, then, losing patience, seized the door knocker and banged it crisply. She looked up and saw that the watchers were still there, five of them and a dog, watching her every movement. She began to get flustered. She pressed the bell again and thumped on the door with a closed fist; lifted the letterbox and called through it; glanced back at No. 15 and saw to her relief that the watchers had vanished. She placed her parcels carefully on the step and raised her hands to her head. She fumbled with her knob of feathery hair and produced a hairpin. She shot a comprehensive glance up and down the road, inserted the hairpin in the lock, jiggled it, twisted it, and pushed open the door. She gathered her parcels and walked sedately into the house.

"*Well!*" said Rex from behind his curtain. "She picked the lock!"

"Of course," said Hugo calmly, drifting back to the fire, "this means that when she decides to go visiting she doesn't need to wait for an invitation."

"I wonder whether she's been in here?" said Fan faintly.

"Well, it just *shows!*" said Bertha, straightening a cushion. "You can't keep a room too tidy. You never know who's going to drop in."

"It's your nest, dears," said Rex. "But if I were you, I'd get me a couple of dozen great big bolts and a life-sized dog. That is unless you *like* your house overrun by murderers."

"They can all pick locks," said Peter gloomily. "Lilli told me so. That tough-looking yegg who wears a cloth cap taught them. He's meant to be the butler. He's been in jail fourteen times for housebreaking."

"Has he killed anybody?"

"No. The Asterisk mob are choosy. They won't have killers in the kitchen."

"But it's *terrible!*" said Bertha, who had just realized the implications of what she had seen. "They may wander in any time! We shall all be murdered in our beds!"

"What did that Colonel do?" asked Rex suddenly.

Backed over his wife in a Dusenberg.

"Backed over his wife in a Dusenberg."

"What about the cripple?"

Peter looked away. He moved restively. "Rather revolting," he said. "I don't want to discuss it."

"Well, thank God they seem to confine themselves to their own members!" said Hugo. "Unless they go berserk, there's no reason to think that they are after us."

Fan was sitting on the floor wrapping up the clues in tissue-paper and tying labels on them. Peter looked over her shoulder and saw her write "Bit of Suspicious Substance from Death Chamber" on an envelope. She put the piece of clay into it. Then she picked up the thermos which had held Mr. Cann's last nightcap.

"Bertha," she said, "is this yours?"

"No. I thought it was yours."

"You found it beside Lilli's bed?"

"No. That was a yellow one. I washed it out and put it in the pantry. Why?"

"Because they don't belong to any of us. I asked Marleen and Mr. Beesum, and they'd never seen them before. They don't belong to anybody in this house. They're *clues*!" She held on to the thermos with both hands, defying Peter to take it away from her.

"You know all this is very irregular," said Rex shakily. "The house is loused right up with corpses. The Loved Ones upstairs, eight dead rats downstairs. I suppose you'd call the little rat chap a sort of assassin and we've got four more next door. Seven killers and ten dead. Whichever way you look at it, we're outnumbered!" He ground out his cigarette and stood up. "My dears, I'm sure you'll understand. After all, they're your corpses. They're nothing to do with me, so, if you'll excuse me, I think I'll run along. They've taken about twenty years off my life already." He sauntered over to the door looking uncomfortable.

"Rex!" said Fan reproachfully. "You stay right here. You low skunk!" she added furiously.

Peter was leaning against the door, his arms folded, a cigarette in the corner of his mouth. He shook his head slowly at Rex. "Sorry, chum," he said.

"Now don't be a pig," said Rex. "It's no good playing Hemingway with me. They're not my bodies, and I'm going to run along."

"Nix. You stay. You're a material witness and an accessory after the fact, and if you attempt to leave this house I'll set the police on you even if we all hang for it. And don't think I'm bluffing."

There was a long silence.

"Well," said Rex eventually, "if you put it like that I don't seem to have any alternative, do I?" He walked moodily around in a small circle. He saw Fan's scowl and took refuge in sarcasm. "I suppose you'll club me down if I go and ring up Bunny? Why don't you lock me up in a trunk too?"

"You're not dead," said Fan nastily. "Yet."

Rex picked up a sandwich and wandered unhappily out of the room. As he reached the hall the phone rang. It was Sylvia.

"Isn't Mr. Hilford coming to the office today?" she asked with asperity.

"No," said Rex. "He's got mumps. He said to tell you to go at once to the Royal Hotel in Edinburgh. You're to sit in the foyer until a bearded man in a kilt gives you a large flat package."

"Are you crazy?"

"No. Peter says it's very important."

"Let me speak to him."

"You can't. He can't even whisper."

"Are you drunk?"

"No, no. This man's beard is long and rather matted. You'll know him at once."

"Well, really!" said Sylvia. "Of all the inconsiderate ... Really, Peter gets more impossible every day. Really!" She rang off.

Rex sat down on the stairs feeling much better. He peeled open the sandwich he was still holding and looked at it with interest. It was spread with chocolate blancmange. He tasted it gingerly and found it quite nice.

CHAPTER 15

DARKNESS fell at seven o'clock. A slight wind sprang up. It rustled the leaves of the plane trees and whipped up small ruffles on the dark river. It blew a piece of newspaper down Flood Walk and wrapped it around Rex's left leg as he walked back from the embankment. Rex folded the newspaper into a winged dart and looked around for a target. He saw an overgrown cat sitting on the wall of the Asterisk Club. He waited until he was nearer and then he let the cat have it. Tom fell off the wall. He fell clumsily, an abnormal cat, on his back in the flowerbed. Rex crept through the wrought-iron gate and retrieved the dart. He threw it at the cat again and left. He had been down to the river to check up on the tide. Peter had reluctantly agreed to consider the original plan of disposal by water. The tide was in, but there was a string of barges moored by the bridge, so he would have to think again.

The wind snatched the paper dart and blew it into the air. It blew it over the wall and against the kitchen window of No. 15. Marleen and the Rodent Officer, who were sitting at the table drinking an evening cup of tea, started. Marleen went outside and found the dart. She decided instantly that it had been thrown by somebody in the Asterisk Club, so she threw it right back. It bounced off the scullery window and caused Squires to plunge backwards on to an electric iron, giving himself a slight burn. He looked out of the window and saw Marleen going back into the next-door kitchen. *Mad!* he thought with a stab of panic. *What am I doing here, among all these mad people? I'm a good boy.*

Marleen shut the door and bolted it. She looked at the back of the Rodent Officer's head with a twinge of resentment. He had not yet succumbed to her charms, nor did he show any signs of doing so, but she had not abandoned him as hopeless. At this very moment, she had in her handbag a phial of perfume named *Hullo Brighton*, which she hoped might do the trick. She went into the pantry and put a dab behind each ear and then came back to the kitchen table and sat down, waiting.

Alfred Beesum was examining his sticky boards. He had two before him, and to each was attached a large rat. He did not notice the *Hullo Brighton*, but the smaller rat looked at Marleen and blinked.

"Nasty brute," said Marleen, tentatively opening the conversation.

"Check," said Mr. Beesum. "I do not like rodents. The danger of them is frequently underestimated. I do not expect you know," he added, "thet, for instance, in 1822, Alsace was completely in the power of continental field voles."

"Go on!"

"Fect. *Microtis arvalis.* Now this specimen" – he poked the smaller rat with a glass rod – "is a *rattus rattus fugivorus* – the bleck or ship ret. Notice the large, translucent ears, the long, thin tail. A lightly built enimal." He paused to see whether Marleen was assimilating this data. Marleen quickly looked intelligent. Mr. Beesum was satisfied. He tapped his larger captive on the head. The rat shut its eyes. "Now this fellow is a *rattus norvegicus.* Note the small furry ears, the thick, comperitively short tail. A burrower, he is. Nest underground. A neat swimmer, but not so nippy et climbing es the *rattus fugivorus*."

He was enjoying himself. He liked imparting technical information, and Marleen was an excellent listener. He looked up with unconcealed annoyance as Mrs. Hilford put her head around the door. She looked white and tired and her nose was shining.

"Marleen," she said, "I want you always to keep the back door locked. It's a dark night, and there've been a lot of burglaries lately."

"Trust me!" said Marleen. Mrs. Hilford had a green hat in her hand; she sometimes gave cast-off clothing to Marleen, and Marleen now hoped that if she played her cards properly she would get that hat. It would go very nicely with her Rust. She was displeased that Mrs. Hilford had interrupted her tête-à-tête, but she decided to be helpful. "If I 'as visitors, dear," she added, eyeing the hat, "they 'as been asked. I keeps the door locked, the mortise on, an' the bolt shot. Don't you worry, dear! Take a bloomin' spook to get in 'ere."

"But somebody – I couldn't find my watch this morning, and I wondered whether anybody could have got in here last night."

"Well," said Marleen warmly, "all I can say is, if they did, they must of flown down the chimney."

Mrs. Hilford looked at the chimney.

"No," she said vaguely. "It's too small."

Marleen stared at her.

"You all right, dear?" she asked anxiously. "You look quite queer."

"Yes," said Mrs. Hilford. "I feel fine. Mr. Beesum, would you mind taking your arsenic home with you tonight? I know it's silly, but it makes me nervous. It might fall open or spill or something – and if anything happened to Croydon, Mrs. Berko would never get over it."

Mr. Beesum looked at her. He decided that she was either feverish or she had been drinking. She twirled the hat on her finger and blushed.

"I mey remind you, miss," he said kindly, "thet, quite epart from my small supply, there is a fair modicum of arsenic in this and most other normal households. There's insecticide, ent paste, flypapers, Rough on Rets, weedkiller, distemper, end meny other commodities. I knew of en ox once who committed suicide by licking the distemper off his stall. Just stood there lick, lick, lick until he hed succumbed. It took some time of course, the poison content in distemper being slight, but he persisted end he passed away."

Mrs. Hilford cleared her throat.

"How terrible," she said. "But with strong arsenic, neat I mean, like yours, it wouldn't take nearly so long, would it?"

Mr. Beesum smiled. He placed the tips of his fingers together and leaned back in his chair. If she wanted information, she had come to the right place. "Meny people," he began, throwing back his head and gazing at the ceiling, "think thet arsenic is a cumulative poison. This, however, is not the case. One large dose will do the necessary equally well. The lethal draught is 0.1 to 0.5 grams. The symptoms should then set in an hour after consumption et the latest. Teken in solid form, the ecids found in the stomach ..."

"Enough to burn an 'ole in the carpet, they do say," volunteered Marleen, eager to please.

Mr. Beesum resented this interruption. "Of course, if people are going to chip in incessantly," he said. He examined his nails, frowning.

Marleen blushed. She felt Mrs. Hilford's eyes upon her and sniffed defiantly. "Well," she said, "if people can't even open their mouth without people gettin' 'uffy an' jumpin' down their throat, I must say I don't know what!"

"I hev found," said Mr. Beesum, closing his eyes, "thet when lecturing, some hecklers love the sound of their own voices so much" – he opened his eyes at Mrs. Hilford, inviting her to share his amazement – "thet they feel encumbered to make statements which their intellectual superiors think are – if you'll pardon my French – *pure cock*!"

Marleen went red with anger. "Some people," she snapped, "love theirselves so ruddy much that they will end up in 'Ell Fire – which certain other people 'ope will 'urt!"

"Go on, Mr. Beesum," said Mrs. Hilford quickly.

Mr. Beesum spread his hands flat on the table, palms down. "Well," he said, "if we are not going to be interrupted ..." He glowered at the stove.

Marleen pursed her lips. "Some people," she said to herself quietly, stroking the smaller captive rat, "think that they are God Almighty, an' one day they are goin' to find out different."

"The acids," prompted Mrs. Hilford.

"Taken in solid form," said Mr. Beesum, snatching up the threads, "the symptoms tek longer to become epparent. The ecids found in the stomach ect es a solvent, which teks time." He was getting back into his stride. He shot an uneasy glance at Marleen. She was sulkily sweeping cake crumbs into a pile in front of the *rattus rattus fugivorus*. The rat watched her closely, but did not eat the crumbs. Mr. Beesum was comforted by this gesture of allegiance. He rejoined his fingers. "When, however," he said with renewed enthusiasm, "in a solution, the ebsorbtion into the blood is much faster end death mey result in es little es a half-hour. Right. We now come to the symptoms themselves. We start with a burning sensation in the throat." He smacked his lips ghoulishly. He saw that Mrs. Hilford was watching him and determined not to disappoint her. He lowered his voice to a horrid murmur. "This is followed by pain in the stomach, pallor, nausea, and vomiting. Terrible! We now come to the second phase. Slow, shallow breathing; repid, thready pulse; cold, moist skin. We are nearing the end." His voice sank to a whisper. "*We enter the final stage.*" He paused, sucking his teeth. "*Coma!*" he barked suddenly. Both Mrs. Hilford and Marleen jumped. Mr. Beesum narrowed his eyes. He leaned forward, fixing Mrs. Hilford with a watery stare. "Convulsions," he mouthed. "And co-*llapse.*"

"Now," he added in his normal voice, "I shell partek of a cup of tea." He was well pleased with the results of his little lecture. Mrs. Hilford had put her hat on the dresser and sat on it. Marleen was pouring milk into an already overflowing cup and it was running out of the saucer on to the table. Both were pale and visibly shaken. Mr. Beesum rose. He knew when to make an exit. "I shell now resume my offensive," he said grandly. "Boiled wheat end cake, I gev them this morning end they et it all. Pre-bait, thet was. They took it very nicely. We are now ready for the knockout. Tonight we ley the arsenic. We must hope thet the enemy enjoy their supper end eat their full. Arsenic is colorless end testeless, so they will not realize for fully half an hour they they hev been duped. We must hope for a *real carnage*. What's the matter, miss? You look quite seedy."

Mrs. Hilford ran out of the room. She left the squashed hat behind on the dresser. Marleen picked it up and punched it into shape. She crammed it over her curlers and went to look at herself in the mirror behind the door.

"I look nice in green," she said complacently. The Rodent Officer took no notice. "*Don't I?*" she said.

"All rets are colorblind," said Mr. Beesum. "They like green. They think it's red."

CHAPTER 16

IT was exactly seven-thirty when Beecher entered the drawing room at the Asterisk Club. The grandfather clock in the hall did not chime because the Colonel's experiments of the morning had fouled its mechanism, but it clicked and made a faint, whirring noise.

Beecher carried a Benares tray and was not altogether in his element. While he anticipated the night's business with pleasure, he was more nervous than he cared to admit. It was the first time he had worked for Flush in an unofficial capacity. He knew that if the plan were to misfire he would suffer far more at the hands of his employer than, under other circumstances, he would from the police. Working alone was one thing; working as one of a team, the haul and the responsibility divided equally, was another; and working for Flush and his coterie of dilapidated killers was something else again. He decided, in order to cheer himself, that he would knock off a trinket or two from No. 15 in the course of his duty. Apart from this, he intended to obey his instructions to the letter.

It was now seven-thirty. All right, they stopped drinking, like the Boss had said. He stood behind the chair in which the Colonel was reclining and sipping whisky and soda.

"Ting-a-ling-a-ling!" he hissed. "Last bell."

"Double scotch, sir," said the Colonel automatically.

Beecher took his empty glass and put it on the tray. He approached Mrs. Barratt, who had a glass of pale sherry beside her. She drank virtuously, her little finger genteelly crooked. Flush glanced at his watch, putting his tumbler on the tray without looking up. The Creaker buried his face in his mug of Guinness, watching Beecher through his half-obliterated eyes. Tom was sitting on his knee. He looked at Beecher thoughtfully, jumped down, and squatted within reach of his left boot. Although he knew that Beecher itched to kick him, he knew that he would not do it if anybody were watching. The Creaker was watching and, although neither Beecher nor Tom so much as glanced in his direction, both knew it.

Flush took off the horn-rimmed spectacles which he affected for reading, folded his newspaper, and smoothed it across his knees.

"Well, Beecher," he said. "You have made your itinerary?" He realized that Beecher would not be able to concentrate until he had kicked Tom. "Take that animal outside," he said quietly.

"Don't you!" said the Creaker hoarsely. "Tom! Come 'ere, Tom!" He jumped to his foot and tried to snatch the cat. Beecher was too quick for him. He left the room, carrying Tom by the scruff of the neck like a briefcase. After a moment's silence, during which all except the Creaker looked diffident, he returned. There was a tuft of fur on his trousers, and he was slightly flushed. The Creaker glared at Flush, limped over to the mantelpiece, and put five shillings into the Benevolent Fund.

Flush pretended that he had not seen. He turned to Beecher. There was a glint of approval in his eye, but his voice gave no hint of his feelings.

"I want no broken glass," he said shortly. "You will effect entry by one of the doors."

Beecher produced a hairy scrap of paper from his pocket and unfolded it. He followed his own strange writing with a calloused finger.

"I leaves 'ere," he read slowly, "at eleven-thirty. Preliminary recce, see. I uses the side door an' goes over the wall by the lilac tree. I shall effect entry through the back door."

He looked up for approval.

"Excellent," said Flush, nodding. "What lock do they sport?"

"Bolt, Yale Night Latch xlymp, four-lever mortise. Pity it's not a rimlock – but there it is! Might of been a Chubb." Beecher smiled. "It is a crummy old 'ouse, an' there is plenty o' play between the door an' the stop bead. I shall take the bolt with me chain-wrench, the mortise with a mica, an' the Yale with a strip o' 620 Brownie film."

"Creaker!" said Flush sharply. "If you are unable to control your mirth, you may leave the room."

"I didn't say nothing," growled the Creaker. He looked at Flush with animosity.

"You guffawed."

"Was gas," said the Creaker, and heaved again.

"Well, kindly subdue it. Beecher, you will return from your reconnaissance at eleven-thirty-five. The lights downstairs will be off and you will not ignite them. I have no doubt that you have a comprehensive selection of torches."

"Yus," said Beecher. He loved torches. He had seventeen.

"Very well. At eleven-thirty-eight, Naomi, you will put out your bedroom light. At eleven-forty, Colonel, you will do the same. At eleven-forty-two, Creaker, you will follow suit, and at eleven-forty-five I shall extinguish mine, leaving the house in total darkness. At eleven-fifty, Beecher, you will leave the house."

Beecher wrote laboriously upon his piece of paper.

"You are then your own master. Take as long as you require. I want no bungling. I absolutely forbid you to strike, threaten, or tie anybody up, whatever the provocation."

"I should avoid the dark young man, especially," said Mrs. Barratt anxiously. "You never know with these writers."

Flush raised one eyebrow at her and she blushed.

"He looks so strong," she said defensively. "I don't want Beecher to get hurt."

"Nobody is going to get hurt," said Flush. "Beecher will leave the house as unsuspected as he came. I do not have to tell him that if he is discovered he need expect no help from any of us, do I, Beecher?"

"No, Boss."

"If, however, you are undetected and some slight, technical hitch arises for which you need assistance, you will whistle once, quietly. I shall be on the alert inside the back door. Naturally, you will not whistle unless it is absolutely necessary."

"Yus, Boss."

"When you have both bodies on the premises, you will place them in the coal cellar and report to me. Do you know where our impetuous neighbors have hidden them?"

Beecher looked crafty.

"I see the beefy dame up in the attics," he said. "She was bendin' down."

"Good. Try the attics first. And no pilfering, Beecher. Keep your hands to yourself."

Beecher shifted his feet.

"We depend upon you," said Flush. He produced a gold half-hunter from his waistcoat pocket. "And now, ladies and gentlemen, will you please synchronize your watches. The time is seven-fifty-three ... *now*."

CHAPTER 17

AT eight o'clock Peter returned from the Ten Bells with two bottles of gin under his arm. Rather than think about the night's work ahead of him, he was gloating about Carstairs. Less than two hours ago he had settled at his typewriter and, with savage enjoyment, killed the detective with the shrewd blue eyes. He had made him die a humiliating death, shot by one of his own ricocheting bullets in the house of a false suspect.

As he passed the Asterisk Club he saw the huge ginger cat flicking a dead bird across the pavement. It was pushing the bird along with each of its front feet in turn. When it saw him it crouched over its prey and stared at him with odalisque eyes. Peter stepped over it. The bird smelled terrible.

He let himself into his own house and hung up his coat. Marleen put her head out of the studio. When she saw that it was Peter she smiled.

"I'm lockin' up really thorough 'fore I go," she said. "May be daft, but I got a predilection 'bout tonight. Mum's psychic, see, so when it comes over me I don't take no chances." She jerked her head upwards and lowered her voice. "They asked me to make more sandwiches, but I didn't do it, like I said. You got to draw the line somewhere, I always say."

"Yes," said Peter. He was not listening. "Yes, I know you do."

"Mr. Rex 'ad to open a tin," said Marleen triumphantly. "'E cut 'imself. I couldn't 'elp bein' tickled."

On the stairs Peter passed Mr. Beesum, who was descending with a wooden spoon and a pie-dish of poisoned cake.

"That ought to disappoint them," said Peter pleasantly. He did not like the Rodent Officer, but he had not slept properly since the rats took over.

"Yes," said Mr. Beesum. His mustache twitched. "They like cake."

Peter went on upstairs. The other four were gathered around the fire in the drawing room. They were so engrossed in their discussion that they did not hear him enter. They all looked up guiltily as he shut the door. Croydon sprang off Bertha's knee and barked at him.

"Well?" said Peter. "Anything settled?"

"Absolutely," said Rex. His face was pink with excitement. "Hand around the nectar, dear, and we'll tell you all."

Hugo lit a small cheroot.

"Must you?" asked his wife automatically.

"The basic idea," he said, ignoring her, "is that if these thugs next door persist in piling up casualties they can damn well provide their own stretcher parties. We propose that I, being the one most accustomed to this sort of thing, should be the operative agent. I intend to deposit the bodies one after another on the side doorstep of the Asterisk Club. I shall chain them together and attach them to the footscraper, which will prevent any unauthorized person from carrying them away in the night. I shall put the key of the padlock into a plain envelope and push it under the door. I shall then return home, we will lock up the house, arrange certain booby-traps in case of retaliations, and go to bed with clear consciences."

"Suppose someone sees them from the road?"

"They can't. And, anyway, if they do, it's not our headache."

"I suppose it's all right in theory," said Peter doubtfully.

"It has everything," said Hugo complacently. "It has audacity, cunning, and the simplicity of all great plans."

"Hugo thought of it," said Bertha. She smiled at Fan.

"No, he didn't," said Fan quickly. "Rex did." She resented the way Hugo had taken charge.

"What will you *wear*?" asked Rex.

Hugo considered.

"Dark sweater, rubber-soled shoes, and an anonymous sort of macintosh in case I'm spotted."

"Macintoshes rustle."

"Mine stopped rustling in 1944, when I had to swim out of Casablanca."

"Hugo's done some extraordinary things," said Bertha. She looked at her husband with pride. She had been much nicer to him lately. She had a plate of sliced Spam on her knee. She broke off pieces of it and gave them to Croydon, but she did not offer it to anybody else.

"I shall want two lookouts," said Hugo. The cheroot suited his beard. He knew that he looked keen and daring. "Peter, you take the front of the house. Stand in the shadow of the monkey-puzzle tree and if you see anything unusual, whistle twice, softly. Fan, you'll be in the back garden. Stand on the far side by the lilac tree. If anything arouses your suspicions, whistle three times. Bertha will bring Lilli downstairs, and Rex will take Mr. Cann."

"Miss Cluj to you," said Bertha, her mouth full of Spam.

"All right, all right. Miss Cluj. In the meanwhile, I shall be in the kitchen conserving my strength and soundlessly undoing the back door. You and Rex report there with the bodies and then leave it all to me."

"Thank God we've got Hugo," said Bertha.

"He couldn't do it alone," said Fan. She looked at Peter. She wanted him to assert himself, but he was pouring himself a drink.

"What time do we start?" he asked.

"Some time around midnight."

"I'll make some nice hot cocoa for you when you come back," said Bertha. She was enjoying herself. She was the leader's wife.

"Thanks," said Hugo. "But, under the circumstances, I'd rather have coffee."

"I shall make Peter some Horlicks," said Fan. She was not enjoying herself at all. She was the lookout's wife.

"I'm going to ring up Bunny and insult him again," said Rex. "If I don't, how will he know that I hate him?"

"Bertha," said Peter. "Is that nice Spam?"

"Delicious. I put just a touch of horseradish on it. It makes all the difference."

"Does it? Could you spare that piece of parsley?"

"Certainly. Here you are. It may be a bit gritty. Now, if you'll all excuse me, I shall go and fix up the Loved Ones. I do feel that if they come out of my house at least they ought to look neat and tidy." She left the room. The buckle on one of her shoes was broken and in order to keep the shoe on she had to slide her foot along the carpet.

*

At eight-twenty-four Marleen left the house with half a loaf, four rashers of bacon, and the remains of the Sunday joint wrapped up in the *Sunday Pictorial*.

*

At eight-twenty-four Mr. Beesum found a dead *rattus norvegicus* in the middle of the hall, put it into a paper bag, labeled and dated it, collected his attaché case, and went home.

*

At nine-forty-one Hugo tried on Peter's Guernsey sweater and found it much too big on the shoulders.

*

At ten-two Rex rang up Bunny, found him in, made a disgusting, bubbly noise with his lips, and rang off. At ten-four and ten-seven he repeated the treatment.

*

At ten-twelve a *rattus rattus fugivorus* discovered a heap of poisoned cake under the bath and, having eaten his fill, went back to his nest behind the linen cupboard, doomed.

*

At ten-forty-one, in the house next door, Tom, the Creaker's cat, dragged his dead and stinking bird into the house through the larder window and left it on the floor in Beecher's pantry.

*

At ten-fifty-four the Colonel retired to his room, locked the door, and retrieved a bottle of one-star brandy from the bottom of his golf bag.

*

Half a minute after eleven o'clock Beecher met the new maid on her way to bed and pressed into her hand an old safety razor.

*

A minute and a half later the Creaker stumped upstairs to the bathroom and, without turning on the light, looked curiously at the house next door.

*

At eleven-eight Clifford Flush made a note in his memorandum pad to remind himself to order a sack of quicklime and two hundredweight of quick-drying cement from a contact of his on the following morning.

*

At the same time Bertha Berko leaned out of the bathroom window in No. 15 and peered down into the dark corridor between the two houses along which, later in the evening, her husband was to carry the first two corpses she had ever seen. A few seconds later she had an uncanny feeling that she was being watched. She looked nervously at the house opposite and thought she saw a large white face pressed against the corresponding bathroom window. She retreated hastily and ran downstairs to the landing window directly under the bathroom. Protected by the darkness, she stealthily parted the curtains and saw that the face was there again, watching her from a window on the same level.

*

At eleven-thirty precisely Beecher left the Asterisk Club by the side door, ducked into the shadow of the lilac tree, and cautiously raised himself so that his eyes were an inch above the wall.

*

At eleven-thirty-eight, according to plan, Mrs. Barratt turned off her bedroom lights and, in the darkness, bent her hair into butterfly clips.

*

At eleven-forty-six the Creaker's light went off, and two minutes later the Colonel, sober as a judge, put the empty bottle of brandy back into his golf bag, turned off his light, and slunk downstairs in search of the confiscated bottle of Cockburn '08. Seven minutes later, with a foul oath in Hindustani, he sat back on his heels, baffled by the diabolical mechanism of the cellar door. He was wondering whether to go upstairs and fetch his pliers, when Beecher, passing in rubber shoes, leaned contemptuously over his shoulder and opened the cellar door with a strip of panchromatic film.

*

At eleven-fifty-four Flush's bedroom light and all the lights next door were turned off almost simultaneously.

*

At eleven-fifty-five Squires, who, respecting the curfew, was reading *Beau*

Ideal under his bedclothes with the aid of a candle, set fire to his sheet.

*

For the next five minutes, nothing happened at all.

CHAPTER 18

IT was exactly midnight when Beecher pinched out his cigarette and put the stub into his pocket. In the darkness of the Club kitchen he tied the bows of his navy-blue pimsolls into a double knot. He dragged his cap over his eyes, pulled on his cotton gloves, and tested his favorite torch. It was built on the lines of a propelling pencil, and its almost invisible ray, at ten feet, made a bead of light on a target no bigger than a halfpenny.

Flush put his head around the door, his hand shading a small night-light. He had the gold hunter watch in his palm.

"Twelve o'clock ... *now!*" he said quietly. He liked his plans to go to schedule.

Beecher nodded and eased himself through the side door and out into the night.

He crept across the path in the special manner he had perfected of walking soundlessly on gravel. He squatted into the shelter of a privet bush. Slowly he raised himself until he could just see over the wall through the leaves.

There was no light, no sound from next door, but Beecher was taking no chances. His eyes already well attuned to the shadows, he cased the joint again. It was during this second scrutiny that he noticed Hugo Berko, his face half-hidden behind a jar of parsley in the larder window. Beecher waited. Hugo took a final comprehensive glance at the Asterisk territory, then, not having seen the watcher in the privet, disappeared into the body of his house.

Well, I dunno, thought Beecher. *What is it this time?* So they were up and about, were they? Beecher smiled. He had complete confidence in himself, and he welcomed conflict with amateurs. He remembered with affection the old woman whom he had once allowed to lock him into a cupboard. He had even let her dial 999 before he walked out and trussed her up. But these birds next door were a different kettle of fish. Even though they clearly lacked the professional touch, they were no ordinary first offenders. It would pay him to watch his step. Satisfied that nobody was aware of his movements, he sprang over the wall with anthropoid agility and walked silently along the gravel to the back door.

He listened until he was certain that there was nobody inside, then tested the door with the flat of his hand. He felt by the resistance that the bolt was at the bottom. He produced a wafer-thin chain wrench, inserted it between door and stop bead and jiggled the bolt experimentally. It had been recently oiled. *Thanks, suckers*, thought Beecher, persuading it home into its casing. It was almost too easy. He had hoped to be able to use his new silent saw. He opened the mortise lock with a piece of mica and the Yale with the 620 negative. He gently pushed open the door and slipped into the kitchen. Relocking the door and sliding home the bolt, he cautiously turned on his torch, and looked around him. He was always interested in other people's houses.

It was a neat little kitchen, blue tiled and with a yellow cooker. There was a tray on the table with cups and a coffeepot on it. There was a plate of bread and butter and a dish of sliced meat. Beecher took two slices and crammed them into his mouth. Chewing, he found that it was Spam and horseradish. He spat it into the sink. He did not like horseradish. "Just for that," he muttered, and with his silent saw sliced the element off the electric kettle. He tiptoed through the swing doors. He shone his torch for an instant on a large canvas of Fan's, showing a group of angular people in top-hats sitting in a tree. He shook his head irritably and started up the stairs. He was nearly halfway up the first flight when he heard a thud from the top of the house followed by a muffled oath. He sprang up the remaining steps and concealed himself behind the inadequate drapes of the landing curtains.

A door closed softly and Hugo Berko crept down the stairs. His eyes were also well trained to darkness. He saw the man partially concealed by the curtains and nudged him as he passed.

"It's only me," he whispered. "For God's sake do go and cope with Bertha. She keeps dropping them."

The man behind the curtain made a noncommittal noise, and Hugo went on downstairs. As he went, he had a moment's doubt. He looked back at the curtains and saw that the man had gone. He crept into the kitchen and helped himself to a slice of Spam. With his mouth full, he opened the back door without a sound, congratulating himself that he had had the foresight to oil the bolt. When he turned round he knew that there was somebody in the room with him. A soft, sibilant whisper told him that it was Rex with Mr. Cann.

Fan came quietly through the green baize door and across the kitchen. She touched Hugo's hand.

"Here I go," she whispered. "Out into the snow. I'm scared stiff."

Indistinctly, they saw her slip through the back door. They heard a slight rustle as she crawled under a bush.

Peter went through the kitchen without a word. His rubber soles squeaked once on the tiles, then he disappeared around the side of the house. Hugo swallowed a mouthful of Spam and hauled Mr. Cann on to his back.

"Go it, Hugo!" breathed Rex excitedly.

Hugo heaved Mr. Cann a little higher and turned nimbly on the balls of his feet. He had learned to do this when supporting wounded Social Democrats across a forbidden frontier. Then, there had been plenty of room for such acrobatics – now, in a small modern kitchen, there was not. Mr. Cann's limp hand swung out and contacted a cut-glass vase full of unpaid bills. The vase hurtled to the tiled floor. The crash echoed through the silent house.

In the Asterisk Club Flush heard the report and swore.

The Creaker heard it and thought with glee that Beecher was at last losing his grip.

The Colonel, creeping upstairs with his bottle of port, thought for one second that he had dropped it, and turned pale.

Mrs. Barratt stirred in her sleep and one of the butterfly clips fell out of her hair.

Upstairs in the attic in No. 15 Bertha heard it and dropped Lilli for the third time.

In the gloom of the first floor, Beecher heard it, assessed it, and went on upstairs. He was confused. Four people had passed him in the darkness, and one of them had been carrying the Old Tin Cann. He realized that his plans were going overboard, but he was determined to salvage as much of them as possible. He realized that there was only Epstein's wife left upstairs. With her, presumably, was La Cluj. Very well – if the amateurs were playing hide-and-seek with the Old Tin Cann, at least he would retrieve Lilli.

As he had suspected, the faint scuffling noises were coming from the attic opposite his lookout post in the Asterisk Club. He crept up the last flight of stairs. The door of the attic was ajar, and against the window he saw Epstein's wife bending over and struggling with something on the floor. This told Beecher all he wanted to know. He slipped into the room and pressed himself against a stack of trunks. He trod on something – it felt like shavings – and the girl stood upright and listened.

"Rex?" she whispered.

Beecher was silent. There were rats running about in the walls. They were squeaking and dragging something along behind the skirtings. For a moment they were still, and he heard the girl breathing quickly. She swallowed and whispered to herself. Then she ran out on to the landing. Beecher was across the room, had Lilli in his arms, and was back in his corner before she returned. He decided that if she turned on the light, in the split second before she could scream, he would hit her behind the ear. He did not want to do it. The Boss had forbidden him to strike anybody, but there were occasions when might was right.

The girl did not turn on the lights. She ran to the window and leaned out, peering downwards. By the time she was reassured, Beecher was on the ground floor and, with Lilli under his arm, was stealing into the kitchen. As soon as he was through the swing door he heard somebody eating. Without hesitation and without a sound he backed against the wall and slid behind the door, adjusting Lilli as well as he was able.

"Bertha?" came a nervous whisper.

Beecher waited. He heard a rat run across the hall. There was a soft plop as if it had jumped off something. Beecher drew in his breath slowly through his nostrils. Straining his ears, he heard the other occupant of the room do the same. *Oh ho!* he thought, and arched his chest for a test of endurance. With bulging lungs he strained his eyes at the shadow by the cooker. He was amused. He knew that nobody in London could hold his breath for as long as himself.

Ninety seconds later, just as Beecher heard his companion cautiously draw a breath, the back door was pushed open and a man walked quietly into the room.

"Thank God you've come, dear," hissed a voice from behind the cooker. "I think we're not alone." There was a scraping sound as if a saucepan had moved. "Come out, whoever you are! You're surrounded!"

"Where's Lilli?" murmured the man by the door. It was Epstein.

"Don't you understand," said the other voice, "that we are *harboring* somebody?"

Epstein made an impatient noise with his tongue.

"I can see quite clearly," he whispered angrily, "that I was insane to expect any cooperation from you. I shall have to do it myself, that's all." He pushed open the green baize door, and Beecher felt the cool draught as it flapped to behind him.

The other man ran after him, snorting with some violent emotion. "You don't care what happens to me!" he said aloud. "You undertaker, *you!*"

Beecher heard them going upstairs. The second one – it must be the dancing man – was running without any pretense of stealth. Beecher let out his breath gently through his mouth. These people, he mused, were not normal. The sooner he was out of this madhouse the better. He tiptoed across the kitchen, peered around the open door, and sidled along the wall. He looked around quickly and was about to throw Lilli over the wall when he thought he heard a movement in the arbutus. He ducked immediately and merged into the hedge. As he laid Lilli down beside him he felt a piece of paper. He picked it up and, shading his torch with his hand, examined it. It was a piece of newspaper, crudely twisted into the shape of a dart. He smoothed it out and settled down to read the news.

Fan, three bushes away, crouched on the damp earth frozen with horror. She had, for a paralyzing second, seen Beecher's crumpled profile against the pink glow of the London sky. One moment it had been there, the next, before she was even certain that she had actually seen it, it had vanished, leaving only a tiny eye of light floating a few yards away, swinging and jerking like a will o' the wisp. Mr. Cann lay beside her, waiting to be lifted over the wall. Drawing a deep breath, she tried to whistle. She failed. She wet her lips desperately and tried again. This time she managed one small, shrill blast.

Behind the library curtains in the Asterisk Club, Flush heard it and prepared to go to the assistance of his steward.

The Creaker heard it and was delighted that Beecher was in difficulties.

Mrs. Barratt was asleep and the Colonel, awash with Cockburn '08, thought it was an owl.

Hugo Berko, who was in the attic of No. 15 with Rex and Bertha, frantically searching for Lilli, heard it and rushed downstairs, sensing trouble.

Peter Hilford, who was concealed in the shadow of the monkey-puzzle tree, heard it, considered it, and decided to ignore it, knowing Fan's signal to be three whistles.

Beecher, embedded in a bush with Lilli's icy face pressed into the small of his neck, heard it and stiffened. He snapped off his torch and was rearranging Lilli for a quick retreat over the wall when an answering whistle came from inside No. 15. *That's torn it!* he thought. He pressed himself farther back into the bush. He was reasonably sure that he had not been detected, and was therefore prepared to let the amateurs tire themselves out running around in circles. When they finally retired into their house, then, and not until then, he would retreat over the wall with Lilli and nobody would be any the wiser. He sat back comfortably, awaiting developments.

Epstein appeared in the back door. Beecher saw him against the sky, one hand in his coat pocket, and for the first time during the evening felt a twinge of alarm. He knew only one reason for having a hand in one's own coat pocket on a dark night, and if there were going to be gunplay he preferred to be safely at home. He had once been shot in the heel by an accomplice named Finger Solomons, and he had never forgotten it.

Epstein ran around the side of the house. He passed within a foot of the bush in which Beecher was concealed. His wife stumbled out of the back door and ran after him. Beecher resisted an overwhelming impulse to stretch out his foot and trip her up. She hesitated by the bush as if deliberately to tantalize him further. He put the end of the lapel of his jacket into his mouth and bit on it, watching her. Somebody in the hedge, quite near to him whistled twice …

Flush, rapidly changing into a pair of rubber-soled brogues, heard and ground his teeth. He resolved to frame Beecher on some minor charge within the next few days.

Peter and Hugo, having a quick conference under the monkey-puzzle tree, heard; Peter whistled reassuringly back, and both doubled around the house. They passed Bertha halfway down the gravel path, running in the opposite direction.

The Creaker, who was leaning out of the Asterisk bathroom window, watching the events beneath with considerable interest, whistled twice, just for the hell of it. He had the satisfaction of seeing Peter and Hugo pause, hesitate, and scuttle back the way they had come.

Flush, creeping along the wall to the aid of his steward, heard the whistle and also stealthy, running footsteps, not of one person but several. He cautiously parted the privet and peered through. He blinked once, then slid back on to the path and began to think furiously.

Inside the bush over the wall was stretched Benjamin Cann. Beside him was the nice little blonde. She was sitting with her knees drawn up to her chin. Her eyes were closed and her lips were moving spasmodically. She was apparently praying.

Flush moved away and whistled one low trill. A soft answering whistle came from a bush a few feet away. Flush was behind the bush in a silent bound.

"Beecher!" he hissed. He ducked as somebody raced around the house and into the kitchen. He stretched his hand through the bush. He contacted Beecher's face and, with a spasm of irritation, pinched it.

Almost simultaneously, Beecher sprang over the wall and the girl in the privet bush stood upright and opened her mouth to scream.

Diagonally above, the Creaker leaned yet farther out of the bathroom window. He eased his paunch an inch too far and lost his balance. He was saved by his false leg, whose rigid foot by pure chance hooked under the bracket of the washbasin. The Creaker scrambled back to safety, but in his agitation he jolted the potted begonia on the window-ledge. He snatched at it, but he was too late. It spun on its base, rolled over, and fell. It exploded on the gravel beneath with a noise like a rocket …

Flush, thinking for a wild second that it had been a gunshot, threw himself flat on the ground to present a smaller target. Beecher leapt inside the back door. Fan sprang out of the privet bush, shouting for her husband. Peter raced around the house with Hugo at his heels. Rex ran out of the kitchen. Fan fell into Peter's arms. Hugo started to search the bushes for Mr. Cann.

"Be quiet! Be quiet!" he whispered frantically. "Get into the house!"

On the other side of the wall, Flush inched himself on his stomach inside his own back door. Once in the kitchen, he stood up and looked for Beecher. There was no sign of him, but Squires was standing in the hall with a candle. His feet were bare and he was shaking with fear.

"Where's Beecher?" snapped Flush.

"Upupupupstairs," whispered Squires. He swayed. "Sir," he added.

"Had he – was he alone? Answer me, you moron!"

"Alone," whispered Squires and fainted. The tallow from the candle dripped slowly into the palm of his hand.

Flush callously left him. He dashed into the dark library, parted the curtains, and saw two of his insufferable neighbors carry the sagging body of one of his ex-members into their kitchen. Two others were scrambling in the hedge. They stood upright and they were struggling with the other body. They hurried into the house and slammed the door.

For the first time in his life Flush was at a loss. Swearing impotently, he paced the library, gnawing his thumbnail. At twelve-thirty-three he accidentally bit himself.

CHAPTER 19

"BUT my *kettle!*" wailed Bertha.

"Oh, *damn* the kettle!" said Hugo.

"Somebody threw something at me," said Fan. "It burst just over the wall. For an awful moment I thought it was a bomb."

"Leaving me all alone like that!" said Rex hysterically. "I tell you that there was somebody or something in the kitchen. I distinctly heard it not breathing."

"Be quiet!" said Peter. "Do you want to wake the whole of Chelsea?"

"It was there, I tell you. I think it had wings. *Vile!*"

"I left her lying on the floor. I was only gone for a second and when I came back she'd *gone!*"

"You must have had a brainstorm and thrown her out of the window. Otherwise how did she get into the hedge?"

"I tell you I did *not!*"

"Well, how did she get downstairs? Nobody else brought her, and she certainly didn't walk."

"I don't know and I'm past caring. Who cut up my kettle with the door locked?"

"There I was," said Fan dramatically, "sitting in the privet bush and I saw it against the sky – all misshapen and awful."

"There was absolutely no need for all that whistling. Everything would have been all right if you hadn't gone on and on whistling."

"I only whistled twice."

"You did not. You were trilling away like a bloody aviary."

"I say I was not."

"You were."

"I loved that kettle. It was nearly new."

"Oh, shut up! I was *not!* Twice, I whistled. *Twice.*"

"I tell you freely, dear," said Rex, "that there came a time when I'd had enough. I couldn't go on. I slipped into the house and had a quick noggin. I couldn't help it."

"It got over the wall," said Fan. "I saw it."

Peter took her hand and stroked it gently. "What did, love?" he asked kindly.

"That humped thing."

"Think, darling. Think carefully."

"It was awfully dark. I couldn't see much. It was in the bush a little way away. I whistled, but nobody came. I heard you all pounding about, but I was so scared that I couldn't move. I just *couldn't*! Then there was a rustling and somebody whispered some word like 'peach'!"

"Peach?"

"Yes. Then the whole bush seemed to move and it sort of flew over the wall."

"The bush?"

"No. The thing."

"There you are, dear!" said Rex triumphantly. "I *said* it had wings!"

"Be quiet, Rex. Was it a man?"

"I suppose it must have been. It didn't look like one. It was all lop-sided."

"And it went into the Asterisk Club?"

"Yes. It was in that bush where Hugo found Lilli."

"Did you see it actually go into the house?"

"No. It flew over the wall and a moment later there was that explosion."

"*Ruined!*" said Bertha angrily. "The element was just lying there. I can't understand it. Who would *do* that to a kettle?"

"Oh, for God's sake!" said Hugo furiously. "There's no point in having an endless post-mortem. If you'd all followed your instructions we might have got rid of these two and be getting some sleep. But you didn't and we haven't and we aren't, so we've got to think of something else."

At this moment there was a loud, staccato hammering on the front door. Hugo's mouth snapped shut. He was still sitting on his heels over the two corpses. He had been picking arbutus and privet out of their hair. He had a dead leaf between his fingers.

"The police," he said quietly. "I've been expecting this. All right, chums, let's give them a run for their money! They may not have a warrant."

He seized Lilli by the legs and towed her across to a large sandalwood chest. Her head dragged along the carpet, and Croydon ran after it, barking. Hugo pushed her away with his foot, but she ran back, growling. Hugo lost his temper. He dropped Lilli and slapped Croydon. The little dog took the blow on the chest. She stood for a moment staring at Hugo, quivering with fury, then ran screaming to Bertha. Bertha picked her up, clicking her tongue.

"Do try to control yourself, dear," she said. "There's no point in losing your temper."

Hugo hit himself on the forehead, shut his eyes, and spoke softly in an Aryan language. Peter took over. He and Fan between them lifted Mr. Cann. Rex swept a vase of flowers and two photographs on to the floor and opened the chest. Fan dropped Mr. Cann's head.

"That's right," said Hugo bitterly. "Break his skull. It makes no difference. He's already been poisoned and shot."

Peter heaved the body into the chest and tucked in a limp arm. Turning, he collided with Rex, who had Lilli on his hands. The body slipped and they were juggling it between them when a voice from the door said, "For goodness sake, what are you up to *now*?"

Rex and Peter turned slowly. Peter held Lilli by one ankle, Rex held his hands laced under her chin.

It was the insufferable Bunny. He stood just inside the door, swaying. He had on a moth-eaten dinner-jacket with food smears on the lapels. His face was shiny and his small eyes bloodshot. He was slightly drunk.

"I knocked and knocked," he said. His projecting teeth made him lisp slightly. "But you never came because you hate me. So I went around to the back and walked in just like Swan and Edgar's. What's the matter with that woman? Has she passed out?"

Peter moved forward and took Bunny's arm. He led him into the middle of the room, disengaged himself, quietly locked the door, and put the key into his pocket.

"Sit down, you little tick," he said savagely. "You may be here for some time."

Bunny sat down and removed his shoes. He wore no socks, and his feet were grimy. His eyes flickered inquisitively around the room and came to rest on the gin. He licked his lips.

"Nobody asked you to come here," said Rex loudly, "Don't you know when you're extra?"

Bunny rubbed the soles of his feet together. "I don't like you either," he said sullenly. "I don't like it when people ring me up and blow raspberries. It's rude."

"Do lots of people do it?" asked Fan with interest.

"No. Only a few. I don't know many people. And then I got ginned up and I thought I'd damn well come around and push his silly face in."

"How did you know I was here?" asked Rex suspiciously.

"I rang up your flat and you were out, and the pubs are shut hours ago and the honky-tonks haven't really warmed up so I thought – *what's the matter with that man in the chest?*"

Hugo stepped in front of Mr. Cann. "He's passed out," he said. "They both have. We've been having a party."

Bunny stood up, squinting. He steadied himself on the back of the chair. "Oh, no, you haven't," he said. His sharp tongue flicked over his lips. "His eyes are open. I saw them." He pushed drunkenly past Hugo and stood staring down at Mr. Cann.

"He's dead," he said triumphantly. "You've shot him." Then he put his hands over his ears and opened his mouth to scream.

Peter sprang forward and clapped a hand over the open mouth. In the other hand he had the back of Bunny's long, scented hair. "Listen, you," he said tersely, "one cheep out of you and I'll bang you down and bury you along with the other clients, do you understand? It would be a pleasure. One corpse more or less makes little difference at this stage. Get it?"

Bunny's pink eyes rolled. His pointed teeth nibbled frantically at Peter's hand. Peter was annoyed with himself. He knew that he was behaving like Carstairs. He saw that Fan was watching him with pride. She looked at Bertha to see whether Bertha was missing anything. Peter did not quite know what to do next. He could not go on holding Bunny's face in his hand indefinitely.

Hugo evidently sensed his friend's predicament. He took charge. He tapped Bunny on the shoulder.

"When you're under control and you've had enough, nod," he said briskly. "But don't make any silly mistakes, because if you do, I swear you'll be sorry."

Peter was relieved. Hugo was overdoing it too. He fixed Bunny with his dark eyes. "We've run into a spot of trouble," he said, "and until it's cleared up you're not going to leave this house. Now do we let you go and give you a drink, or do we keep this up some more? If you're under control, nod."

Bunny closed his eyes and writhed. He nodded. Peter released him and he staggered to a chair.

"You're not going to get away with this," he squeaked. "I'll escape and go straight to the police. You're murderers!"

Peter handed him a glass half-full of gin. Hugo bundled Lilli unceremoniously on top of Mr. Cann, pushed them down, and shut the chest.

"I never liked you," said Bunny. "This is just what I would have expected from you."

"Can I kick him?" asked Rex. "Just once?"

"All right," sneered Bunny. "Kick me. Kick me hard. Break your instep. It might improve your *fouettés*."

Rex took him by the ears and banged his head on the back of the chair. Bunny screamed.

"Shut up!" shouted Peter. He pulled Rex away. "Bunny," he said, "we'd better explain."

"I won't listen," said Bunny. "I'll hear it in the Old Bailey."

"No, you won't. You'll hear it now. It will never reach the Old Bailey, I hope."

"Oh, yes, it will," said Bunny. "I'll see to that. You can't keep me here forever." He reached out to pinch Rex and half fell off his chair. He was very drunk.

Peter looked at Hugo. "Give him a drink," he said. "A large one."

Hugo poured an outsize gin and handed it to Bunny. "Go on," he said, "drink it up and pass out. You're boring us."

Bunny drank it greedily. He did not pass out, but after four more gins, the last of which he poured with great abandon down his jacket, he lost his voice. Hugo took this as a good omen and gave him a fifth. Then he jerked him roughly to his feet.

"Come on, louse," he said.

"Not in there!" said Bertha, hanging over the banisters. "Hugo, you *can't!* You know what happens in that room!"

Hugo took no notice. He pushed Bunny ahead of him into the spare room. He turned on the light and glanced once at the rumpled bed where, less than twenty-four hours ago, Lilli Cluj had lain.

"I'm going to lock you in," he said. "I'll leave the key on the outside of the door, and if you want anything, thump on the wall and one of us will be down, if any of us happens to feel like waiting on you, which I personally don't."

Bunny took a wild swing at him and fell over.

Hugo shut and locked the door. The other four were on the landing. They looked dubiously at him.

"What are we going to do now?" asked Fan.

"Get some sleep," said Hugo.

"What about the Loved Ones?"

"We'll pop them back in their trunks in the attics." He put a cheroot into his mouth but did not light it. It immediately made him daring and important. "I'll see to that. I suggest you all go to bed and get some rest. We shall need all our wits about us tomorrow. You'd better lock your doors. I don't think we shall have visitors. The only Asterisks on the premises are already dead, and I can't think of any reason why they should pick on us. But I'm not going to take chances. I'm going to rout out the Colt. We don't want gunplay, obviously, but we've got to show these types that we're not going to take it lying down. If you hear anything suspicious, give a shout and I'll be there hotfoot." He wheeled on his toes, ran upstairs, and disappeared into the drawing room. He reappeared a moment later with Lilli Cluj under his arm and darted upstairs looking resourceful.

"Thank God we've got Hugo!" said Bertha proudly. "Where we'd be without him I do not know."

Peter saw Fan's expression and patted her hand.

Hugo came downstairs three at a time and vanished into the drawing room. Fan stared after him resentfully. She was about to say something when Peter gently pinched her arm. Hugo came out of the drawing room towing Mr. Cann by the collar of his jacket. He trudged upstairs, whistling. Mr. Cann's trailing feet bumped after him.

The Hilfords went up to their room in silence. Peter undressed and got into bed. Fan sat at the dressing table brushing her hair in a dissatisfied way.

"Darling?" she said at last.

"Mm?"

"Haven't *we* got any gun?"

"Yes. We've got Hugo's Colt."

Fan threw her hairbrush into the air and caught it. "Hooray!" she said. "I *am* so glad. He was dreadfully bossy."

"He doesn't often get a chance to be with Bertha around."

"That's no excuse. He shouldn't have swanked. I'm sick and tired of hearing about his dangerous exploits." She stood up and pulled off her sweater. "Shout for Hugo indeed!" she said angrily through its folds. "I'd sooner shout for Croydon! Who does he think he is? He doesn't even come up to your shoulder!" She hurled her sweater at a chair, marched over to the door, and locked it. "That's not because I'm scared, either. I'm locking Hugo out."

Peter said nothing. He pushed the Colt farther under his pillow. He did not want Fan to know that it was there. It would only frighten her.

"It's cold tonight, isn't it?" she asked airily. "I think I'll shut the window." She did so, humming brightly to herself. Peter was not deceived.

"Perhaps we ought to lock it," he suggested. "It may rattle."

She did not look at him. "Perhaps you're right," she said. She locked the window and further secured it with two wedges. She took off her clothes slowly. There was clearly something on her mind. "Darling," she said, playing with the sash of her nightdress.

"What?"

"Would you think I was an absolute donkey if I made a sort of booby trap just inside the door? I mean I might, for instance, put that vase of flowers on a chair or something, so that if – if the door should blow open or anything the vase would fall down and we should hear it. Would you think that was terribly silly?"

"Not at all," said Peter. "But, don't you think, while we're about it, we might do the thing properly?" He got out of bed, took hold of the chest of drawers, and dragged it across the room. Fan ran to help him. Together they pushed it against the door.

"There!" said Fan. "Now we're safe as houses." She broke off and looked unhappily at the homemade rampart. "It's a silly simile, isn't it? Some houses aren't safe at all."

"This one is," said Peter firmly. "A veritable fortress."

"Aren't we asses?" said Fan. "Anybody would think we were scared!"

Humming casually to herself, she took the vase of flowers and arranged it on the chest of drawers so that the slightest tremor would hurl it to the ground.

CHAPTER 20

"*Oh, wouldn't it be nice,*" sang Marleen, hurrying down Flood Walk. "*If we two were in love?* De de de diddly dee, de dar!" She had forgotten the words of the next stanza, so she buzzed tunelessly to herself until she turned in at the gate of No. 15. "*A streamlined bungalow for two,*" she sang at the monkey-puzzle tree.

It was a nice morning. A pale sun was trying to poke through the branches of the plane trees along the Embankment. The fat cat from the

Asterisk Club was stretched out on the wall, basking. To Marleen the day was full of promise.

She let herself into the house thinking about Alfred Beesum. Difficult, he was sometimes, but then no man was perfect. You might as well face it, there was something nasty about each one of them, bless their hearts. But she did wish he wasn't so shy. Perhaps today …

There were two strange coats thrown over a chair in the hall. She sniffed. She did not approve of the Hilfords' habit of asking their dinner guests to spend the night. They were as nice a young couple as you would find, but she could not say the same about some of their friends.

She went through to the kitchen. Hanging up her baggy coat, she saw the sunlight slanting into the scullery. *"Eel of France with all the gulls around it,"* she sang, taking off her hat.

She peered into the shaving mirror which she had nailed on to the wall for her own use and began to remove her curlers. The first one was not too bad. The main bulk of hair snapped back against her head – it was the back ones which were the trouble. She undid them slowly, not looking, filled with foreboding. As she had expected, they uncoiled limply and, except for one unexplainable piece of frizz, hung dejectedly in strange arcs. *I won't never do them again*, she thought angrily.

She moored the offending strands with two pink slides made in the shape of Aberdeen terriers sitting down, and decided to make herself a cup of tea.

She had filled the kettle before she noticed that the element was missing. For a second she stared incredulously, then she banged the kettle on to the draining-board with such violence that a jet of water shot from the spout and caught her squarely in the chest. She screwed her lips together and mopped herself down, speaking to the kettle. "I am not goin' to get angry," she said clearly, "'cause I know that's just what you want. I shall use the old one an' put it on the gas. You 'adn't thought o' that, 'ad you?"

At eight-fifteen the front doorbell rang and she let in Mr. Beesum. Like herself, he refused to use the back door. He was in a jolly mood and greeted her with the faint twitch of the upper lip which was the nearest he ever achieved to a smile. Marleen's heart soared like a bird. She led the way to the kitchen and offered him a breakfast of her employers' rations. Mr. Beesum, unattracted by the idea of a tête-à-tête, declined. He took a handful of paper bags from his attaché case and announced that he was off on a tour of the attics and bathrooms to collect his dead.

Half an hour later he returned, looking depressed. The casualties had been slight. Five dead and two walking wounded. He placed seven bulging bags on the table and sat down heavily. One of the bags rolled over and fell on to the floor. It burst open and a mouse staggered out and lurched slowly from the room. Marleen threw a dishcloth at it.

"Let it go," said Mr. Beesum apathetically. "*Mus Musculus* – house mouse. Let it go."

"Don't take on," said Marleen, yearning towards him. "You'll get some more tomorrow for sure."

Mr. Beesum shook his head gloomily. "No," he said, "I shall have to start enother campaign. The rets are onto arsenic. Those who hev teken a sublethal dose will now decline the bait and alert the others. I shell now be obliged to ley pre-bait for another two deys et a minimum before I can epproach them again. I shell then try them with zinc phosphide."

"That mean you'll 'ave to stay longer?" asked Marleen, carefully noncommittal.

Mr. Beesum nodded unhappily. Marleen's eyes gleamed. She, too, had a campaign. She had read many serials and she knew well that it frequently took six installments to land your man. During the last three engagements she had been Getting Under His Guard. She had anticipated having to use shock tactics, which she knew as well as anyone else were chancy, at her age. Now she had two more days' grace … She laid her hand tentatively on his shoulder. To her amazement he took it. Admittedly, he took it absentmindedly and as impersonally as if it had been a lost glove, but it was better than nothing. He pulled her down into a chair beside him and looked at her with a worried frown. Marleen's heart beat faster. He patted her hand and began to explain the disadvantages of poison, the necessity of the pre-bait – that was, the regular laying of undoctored victuals to lull the rats into a sense of false security. Sometimes, he said, rats would not touch the pre-bait for several days. It was useless to lay poison until one was reasonably certain that every one of the pests in the neighborhood was partaking of the pre-bait at least once daily. One had to make a clean sweep.

Marleen nodded, an expression of incredulous interest glazed on to her face. Mr. Beesum looked at her and wriggled impatiently. Marleen turned off Incredulous Interest and turned on Scientific Appreciation.

"'Course, they breed something chronic," she murmured, making it into a question, trying to recover her lost status.

"Average litter of eight," said Mr. Beesum automatically. "Gestation period of twenty-two days. The pests mature et a mere three months."

"Cor!" said Marleen. "D'you mean they … Cor! Three months! You mean …?"

Mr. Beesum inclined his head.

"Well!" said Marleen, at a loss.

"I hev blundered," said Mr. Beesum morosely. "For the first time in all my years of experience, I hev mistimed the baiting. Calamity!"

Marleen studied his sagging shoulders and was tactfully silent. She cut a large slice of the Hilfords' fruitcake and set it in front of him. Mr. Beesum looked at it vaguely.

"Fruit," he said thoughtfully. "Might try them on fruit. They will now associate madeira with arsenious oxide – but suppose we try them with fruit and zinc phosphide, *what then*?" He brightened. So did Marleen. He had acknowledged her as an ally. "It will take time," he said cautiously. "Rets automatically avoid the unfamiliar." He broke off a piece of cake and put it into his mouth. "Tasty. Nice texture. They'd like this."

There was a heavy thump on the door, and Hugo slopped into the room in dressing gown and slippers. One slipper was his own and the other was Bertha's. His face was gray and there were deep circles under his eyes. He put two empty gin bottles on the dresser.

"Coffee," he said hoarsely. "Good morning. Quarts of it." He went out with his eyes closed, pinching the bridge of his nose, leaving the baize door flapping behind him.

"Foreigner!" muttered Marleen. "Another orgy, I shouldn't wonder! Two boutays of gin! Price of them would of kept me for a week before the ear! I am going to wait ten minutes 'fore I makes his coffee – just to show!"

Mr. Beesum began to inject his dead rat with embalming fluid. He sold them to a biological research depot for sevenpence a dozen, post-paid.

*

"Mr. 'Ilford?"

"That's right."

Peter took the telegram and gave the boy a disappointing tip. He was in no mood for telegrams. He opened it. "No contact," it read. "Please instruct further stop hope you are better Sylvia." It had been sent from Edinburgh. Peter read it again. He wished that he had drunk less gin the night before. He folded the telegram carefully and put it into his pocket. He knew that he would not be able to think about it properly until he had had some coffee.

Rex ran downstairs and gripped his arm. "Quick," he hissed. "Where do you hide the Fernet Branca?"

"Sylvia's gone to Edinburgh," said Peter, rubbing his eyes.

"*Has* she?"

Marleen came out of the kitchen with a tray of coffee. She looked at Peter closely. "You 'ung over, too?" she asked suspiciously. "Aren't you never goin' to work again?"

"I'm beginning to doubt it."

Marleen sniffed and marched into the dining room. Hugo sat at the refectory table with his head in his hands, staring at a tube of aspirins. Fan sat on the floor in a gray housecoat, gazing into the empty grate. She had combed her hair, but she wore no makeup and she looked almost transparent.

Marleen banged the tray on to the table and was delighted to see Hugo wince. "A real 'appy 'ouse this mornin' and no mistake!" she said sourly.

Nobody answered her. She pursed her lips and left the room, comforting herself that she had made indifferent coffee.

Rex slumped down at the table and poured himself a cup. Bertha hurried into the room, freshly made up and smiling.

"Now," she said briskly, relieving Rex of the percolator, "what are we going to do today?" She looked hopefully at Hugo, waiting for him to take control, but he turned away his head and ate an aspirin. "We've got to get rid of them, you know. I was reading a thing only the other day, and it said that in thundery weather it only takes a few days for freshly killed meat to go absolutely *putrid*!"

Rex put down his cup and hastily left the room.

"The arsenic will preserve them," said Hugo dully.

"*Exactly!*" said Bertha. An excited note in her voice made the others turn to look at her. "I had a brainwave last night," she said with a certain smugness. "Just before I went to sleep, it suddenly dawned on me. I can't imagine why we never thought of it before."

Croydon ran to the window, throwing back her head and barking at nothing.

"Will somebody hit that animal?" asked Hugo. "I shall regard it as a personal favor."

Peter hit Croydon, who rolled on her back and screamed. For once

Bertha took no notice of her, and after a while Croydon got up looking injured.

"Well," said Hugo. "What's this remarkable plan?"

"I know how we're going to get rid of the Loved Ones."

"How?"

Bertha sat down on a chair. She looked in turn at each one of them, then laced her hands in her lap. *"We are going to embalm them!"* she said triumphantly.

Peter turned away, his shoulders sagging. Fan stared again into the empty grate. Hugo sighed.

"Please, Bertha," he said coldly. "This is no time for playing mummies."

"Listen," said Bertha, undiscouraged. "Embalming fluid is mostly arsenic. Mr. Beesum told me. You inject it into the veins. So we fill them up, wrap them up in papyrus, and give them an ordinary decent burial under false names. Even if they're exhumed, nobody can prove anything except that they're absolutely lousy with arsenic. Once it's absorbed into the blood or the capillaries or wherever it goes, nobody can prove whether it's official or not. So we get in two sympathetic embalmers on different days, and once they're coped we can give our two a really slap-up funeral with horses and everything. It doesn't cost much, considering, and we needn't send flowers." There was a pause. Bertha looked impatiently at Hugo. "Well! Isn't that cunning?"

Hugo looked at his wife with something like respect. "It has a sort of mad logic," he said.

"You forget that Mr. Cann has also been shot," said Peter. "And anyway ..." He leapt to his feet as a piercing scream rang out from upstairs.

Before the second scream, Hugo was halfway across the room. The third came as Peter wrenched open the door. It rose, fell, and slithered away. Peter raced upstairs with Hugo at his heels. Fan and Bertha reached the door together. Fan pushed past Bertha and stood uncertainly at the foot of the stairs. There was a dead rat on the fourth step from the top and she stood looking at it, unable to take her eyes off it. She was conscious of Bertha's large, white face at her shoulder. Marleen ran out of the kitchen with the Rodent Officer behind her. She had a pudding-basin in her hand and she was still stirring something in it.

"Who did thet?" snapped Mr. Beesum.

Nobody answered him. Peter appeared at the top of the stairs.

"False alarm," he said brightly. "Rex experimenting with a rat trap. It went off in his hand."

"Why did 'e shout *three* times then?" demanded Marleen after a tiny silence. She was clearly disappointed with Peter's explanation.

"Once for fright, once for pain, once for rage," said Peter jovially. Fan knew that he was improvising.

"Rex loves screaming," said Bertha. Peter looked at her gratefully. "He was once in Grand Guignol for a whole season."

"Was 'e 'urt much?" asked Marleen hopefully.

"No," said Peter.

"He was, you know," contradicted Bertha. "He was branded in the first act, had his eyes gouged out in the second, and was burnt alive in the third."

"Who owns this trep?" asked Mr. Beesum. "I removed all mine yesterday. I cannot do justice to my campaign if people keep interfering."

"That's right," said Marleen, seizing the opportunity to let Mr. Beesum know that she was on his side against all comers. "You got to give 'im a chance. 'Sonly fair! Seven, 'e got this mornin', seven beauties!"

Mr. Beesum snorted through his nose and stalked back into the kitchen. Marleen hurried after him.

Hugo tramped downstairs. He herded the four into the dining room and shut the door.

"I wash my hands of the whole thing," he said. "I'm fed up now."

"Another?"

"Yes," said Hugo angrily. "Another. Three, we've got now. *Three!*"

"Who is it?"

"Not Rex?" said Fan. "It's not to be Rex."

"It's not. It's Bunny."

"Oh, *good!*" said Fan.

Peter frowned at her and she blushed.

CHAPTER 21

REX sat on the stairs outside the spare room.

"Now look," he said shrilly, as Peter and Hugo came upstairs. "You asked me to stay and help, but you're exaggerating. I want to go home."

"Shut up. You're suspect number one."

"I am not."

"You are."

"*Not.*"

Peter and Hugo went into the spare room and shut the door. The room was in semidarkness. The curtains were still drawn and the ceiling light was turned off. Bunny was on the floor by the dressing table. He had obviously been playing a private charade. He wore the lacy negligee in which Lilli had died, and the absurd feather hat in which she had arrived was wedged over his eyes. He had been hit on the head with something blunt.

Peter looked around the room. The bed was still rumpled, the blankets thrown aside the way they had been the night before. The wardrobe door hung open, and inside Bunny had neatly arranged his dinner-jacket on a coat hanger. It hung between Mr. Cann's macintosh and Lilli Cluj's mink coat. For a moment Peter wondered what he was going to do with the ownerless clothes. He supposed he would have to burn them. It seemed a pity to burn mink. The squat flagon of perfume which had belonged to Lilli lay broken on the dressing table. Its nostalgic smell was overpowering. There were no other signs of a struggle and no sign of anything which could possibly have been a weapon. Peter looked up and realized that Hugo was watching him in the mirror. Hugo raised an eyebrow.

"Messy," he said. "I wonder why they've given up poison."

"Who?"

Hugo did not answer. He said instead, "I've got to breathe. This smell's stifling me." He went over and opened the window.

Peter lit a cigarette and sat down on the rumpled bed.

"I'm beginning to think we may be up against *two* killers," he said slowly. "This death is right out of character."

"All right. You're the expert. What are you going to do?"

"What do you expect me to do?"

"Deduce something. Find a clue. Track down the criminal. You haven't even drawn a map."

"A map what of?"

"The scene of the crime."

"What for?"

"I never found out. According to your damn silly books, it follows like the night the day."

"Draw a map yourself. You're the wide boy of the frontiers."

"All right, I will."

"I should."

"I'm going to."

"You're beginning to annoy me."

"Mutual."

Peter got up and shut the window. He did not want to lose his temper, but he wanted to make some sort of offensive gesture which Hugo could interpret as he liked. Hugo said nothing – Peter was six inches taller than he was and standing up. He shook the ash off his cigar.

"What are you going to do now?" he asked presently.

"Check up on everybody's alibis."

"That's better! Now you're talking." Peter sat down and he added, "Except for the fact that you don't know what time he was creased, from which it follows that you don't know when people ought to have alibis, I think it's an excellent idea." He went over and opened the window. "Do you think one of the Asterisks sneaked in and did it?"

"No," said Peter. "Nor do you."

"You realize what you're implying?"

"Yes. Whatever the others were, this was an inside job."

"All right. It was you, me, one of our wives, or your wife's childhood chum. Cozy, isn't it?"

"There's no point in burying your head in the sand like a poor old ostrich."

"Ah! I've been waiting for you to say something of that type."

"Why?"

"Carstairs never buried his head. A pity, I thought, but perhaps you'll accommodate him in your next."

Peter got up. He ground out his cigarette in the potted chrysanthemum which Bertha had forgotten to take away.

"Excuse me," he said. "I don't want to have to hit you. We share the lease of this house for the next four years and there's only one dining room."

*

"ARE you crazy?" asked Bertha angrily, snapping at a sandwich. "Who do you think you are? Nobody's going to call me a murderer and get away with it. I'll do something. I'll *sue* you."

Peter had called a conference. He had taken two photographs of the body, partly because he knew that Fan wanted him to, and partly because Hugo had drawn a map. He had then locked up the spare room and herded the suspects into the dining room. Rex was still sulking. He had not contributed to the debate, but sat filing his nails with an emery board. Fan, too, was silent. She had dressed and applied a smudge of lipstick, but she still looked as if a strong east wind would blow her away. Hugo had straddled a chair and was determined, since Peter was now Master of Ceremonies, to be as obstructive as possible. Only Bertha had approved the conference. She had armed herself with pencil and paper and was prepared to take notes. As long as nobody suspected her or Hugo, she thought the idea very sensible and proper. When, however, she found that both her husband and herself were included in the list of suspects she became highly indignant.

"Hugo wouldn't hurt a fly," she said defiantly.

"Be quiet," said Hugo. He patted the ash off his cheroot and stamped it into the carpet. "Give the Maestro a chance."

Peter stared at him.

"This has got to be done," he said. "Would you care to take over?"

"No, no," said Hugo. "I only do the leg work. You're the one in the deerstalker."

"Well, let's get going," said Bertha. She was sorry that her husband was no longer controlling the operation, but she wanted to get everything cut and dried.

"All right," said Peter. "Let's take the victims in order of appearance. We'll call them A, B, and C." He looked around suspiciously, waiting for someone to recognize Carstairs' methods.

Bertha tapped her pencil against her teeth and nodded approvingly. She drew two lines down the length of her paper.

"I've made two columns," she said. "One's for Motive and the other for Opportunity. Let's do you first."

"Right," said Peter briskly. He was grateful to Bertha. He had written four books, and in each one Carstairs had held an inquiry. He had little hope that anything would emerge from the present one, but he felt that somebody ought to do something, however unpromising.

He referred to Victim A. He had admitted in the presence of Bertha and Fan that he thoroughly disliked Mr. Cann and had implied that he had no right to be alive. This, obviously, had been a declaration of Mr. Cann's undoubted guilt of the murder of a Jewish seamstress and was not a premeditation of homicide. He agreed that he had also been with Victim B on the night of her death and, except for her slayer, had probably been the last person to see her alive.

"Not necessarily," said Bertha, taking another sandwich. "Was the thermos there while you were?"

"I don't know. I think it was but I wouldn't swear to it."

"Quite," said Bertha. "I expect you had other things on your mind."

Fan hurled a lump of coal into the fire. She was needlessly violent, and a shower of embers fell on to the hearth.

"Take Victim C," said Peter doggedly. He was determined not to be sidetracked. "I can see only one possible motive for bumping off Bunny. He caught us red-handed and he was just waiting for an opportunity to hand us over to the police. He would have been a menace to the guilty party for the rest of his life. But that applies only to the murderer – and, at this stage of the inquiry, to all of us."

Hugo raised his eyes to the ceiling and said something to himself in a guttural language.

"What did you say?" said Peter aggressively.

"Nothing," said Hugo. "Nothing at all."

"You said something about Rin-Tin-Tin."

"No, no. Nothing of the sort."

Peter stood up.

"Opportunity," said Bertha loudly. "What about your Opportunity?"

"I'm fed up with Hugo," said Fan tonelessly.

"Oh, *are* you?" said Bertha. She stood up, knocking over her chair.

"Yes, I am. Tell him to shut up."

"I will not," said Bertha on a rising inflection. "Hugo's very good at these things. He's had experience."

"Hugo," said Fan angrily, "has seen a dead mule and a couple of burning trucks and he's drunk with power."

"Now wait a moment," said Hugo.

"Opportunity," shouted Peter.

Bertha picked up her chair, sat down, and licked her pencil.

"Theoretically," said Peter, "any one of us could have spiked that cocoa. Flush rang up at five-thirty to announce Cann. The thermos could have been planted any time after that."

"But," objected Bertha, "when I showed him to his room the thermos wasn't there."

"Right," said Peter. "Then somebody sneaked in and left it while Cann was having dinner next door."

Bertha wrote something on her piece of paper.

"What are you writing?" demanded Fan suspiciously.

"I'm awarding marks. One for Opportunity, one for Motive. Six is full marks. Peter gets six."

"He does *not*," said Fan. "He couldn't have killed Bunny because he was in bed with me."

"How do you know he didn't wait until you were asleep and then nip off without your noticing?"

"Because I should have felt. We always twine legs."

"A remarkable alibi!" said Hugo.

"Well," said Bertha, pulling a broken shoulder-strap out of the neck of her jersey and looking at it, "it might sound a bit odd in the Old Bailey, but I'm the umpire and I pass it." She licked her pencil again. It was an indelible one, and it was staining her teeth a strange shade of purple. "Peter gets five. Now let's do Fan."

Peter sighed. His inquiry seemed to be turning into some sort of competition, but he did not know what to do about it.

"No motive for A," he said. "For B, may possibly have been a bit …" He stopped.

"A bit *what*?" asked Fan, her eyes snapping.

"He can't mean jealous, *surely*?" said Hugo.

Fan picked up the poker. "I'm going to hit Hugo," she said. "It's the only thing he understands."

"*Be quiet!*" roared Peter. "Victim C shared common motive, but doubtful whether she had the strength to deliver such savage blows." He frowned heavily at his wife, who laid the poker gently back in the fireplace and opened her eyes widely at him. "Anyway no opportunity," he said in a more normal voice.

"The legs again?" asked Hugo pleasantly.

"Shut up, Hugo," said Bertha, writing. "Fan gets four. Now we'll do Hugo."

"Admits," said Peter, "once enamored of Victim B. Might have been suffering from amatory hangover, resenting possible rival such as Victim A."

"Very dramatic," said Hugo indifferently. "Just what I would have expected from anyone connected with Carstairs. Right up to standard."

"Look," said Peter. "Will you please lay off Carstairs? You once made perspex Scotch terriers, but I don't keep harping on it."

"All right. Get on with it."

"Death C. You had both M and O."

"No. No O."

"Why?"

"In bed with Bertha. Bed squeaks. She'd have heard."

"That won't do."

"It's as good as the legs."

"Pass," said Bertha. "Hugo gets five. Now do me."

"No M for A. Allowing that you resented Hugo's association with B …" Peter looked at her. He decided that if she were going to make a scene he would give up and go out and have a drink.

"Agree," said Bertha. "In fact, understatement."

"Well, you score the same as Fan – that is, if one allows this business of the squeaky bed, which, personally, I don't."

"I do," said Bertha placidly.

"That leaves Rex," said Peter. He was tired of the discussion. He was getting nowhere, but he did not intend to give up with Hugo present. "As far as we know, was not in the house for death A. But has a latch-key and cannot be entirely eliminated. No apparent M for A and B, but M for C is really something. Slept alone, so O for C good."

There was a pause in which Rex was given the O to defend himself. He merely stared back sulkily, refusing to be drawn. Bertha wrote busily. She had smears of indelible pencil all around her mouth and on one cheek.

"Now," she said importantly. "Here are the final scores. Peter and Hugo tie with 3M+2O. Fan and I get 2M+2O, and Rex gets M^2+3O^2."

There was a slight pause.

"There you are," said Hugo. "Go on. Arrest somebody."

Peter breathed heavily through his nose.

"Has it occurred to you," said Bertha, "that we may be harboring *two* killers?"

"Yes, dear," said Hugo patiently. "Considering that, if you count Mr. Beesum, who is a professional harbinger of doom, we've got at least five in the immediate vicinity, I can't see that two more are either here or there."

"It seems to me," said Peter, "that the three deaths must be connected in some way because of the M for killing C. Unless it was Rex making hay while the sun shone …"

"It was *not*," said Fan indignantly. "I've known Rex since I was five."

"Exclude Rex," said Hugo. "Fan knew him when she was five."

"Hugo," said Fan. "Honestly, I swear I'll hit you."

Peter stood up and pushed back his chair.

"Don't bother, love," he said. "I've been looking forward to this for some time."

"You can't hit me," said Hugo. "I'm sitting down."

"I frankly wouldn't care if you were lying down."

Hugo stood up and clasped his hands behind his back.

"No hands," he said.

"Go on!" said Rex shrilly. "Kill each other. I don't care."

"I'm tired of this talk," said Hugo. "You've had your idiotic post-mortem and we've played a little game of algebra. Isn't it possible that you're all trying to be too bloody clever? If somebody will persuade Peter to sit down, I shall go down to the Ten Bells and hope to meet some honest cretins."

Peter sat down.

"Nobody's stopping you," he said. "You're as free as air – as long as you get out."

"Thank you," said Hugo. "You're too kind."

He went out, banging the door.

CHAPTER 22

At the Asterisk Club, in his attic room and his disreputable dressing gown, Beecher was preparing to do his most elaborate exercise. He did this only twice a week, Tuesdays and Fridays, and it was the only one in which he took any real pleasure.

He hung his trenchcoat on the back of the door and placed in one pocket a handful of small change, in the other a wallet stuffed with toilet paper. He backed to the far side of the room, already imagining himself to be on a crowded racetrack.

He wandered around the room, smiling and looking inconspicuous. He checked up on how many of his plainclothes acquaintances and mild-faced rivals were present. The former he greeted with a broad smile, the latter, by mutual consent, he ignored. He selected his victim and edged slowly nearer to him. When he was within reach of him he looked around idly to see whether he was observed. Satisfied that he was not, he brushed against the trenchcoat on the back of the door.

"Excuse me, sir," he said, and strolled away. The wallet was in his dressing gown pocket. He replaced it and prepared to try Routine Number Two. This time he allowed the crowds to jostle him. He was slightly inebriated and clutching a bookie's card for an expensive loser in the previous race. He was pushed against the trenchcoat. He grabbed at it to prevent himself falling. The coat turned around irritably, bringing the breast pocket in range of Beecher's agile fingers. Sometimes this gambit was so successful that the coat, touched by a face puckered with distress, would give him a commiserating pat on the back. This gave Beecher just enough time to go through the waistcoat pockets. Once, it had been almost too felicitous. The coat, itself slightly inebriated, had been so deeply moved by Beecher's performance that it had reached for the wallet to reimburse him a split second after it had been wafted away.

He replaced the wallet, shaking his head. *Nah*, he thought. *I'd of felt meself.* He faced it. He was not in the mood. Just like any other artist, when dissatisfied, he preferred to give up. Unlike any other artist, a sloppy job would probably earn him six months hard.

He dressed himself dispiritedly and went downstairs. Squires was polishing a Ming umbrella stand in the hall. He looked up and smiled unpleasantly.

"Yore goin' to catch it," he said.

"Go spit on yer foot," said Beecher.

He picked up the end of the rug on which Squires was standing and gave it a lightning jerk. Squires sat down heavily and the umbrella stand fell on top of him. Beecher grinned and went through into the kitchen. The new maid gave him Flush's tray. He did not notice that she had shaved off her mustache. He carried the tray upstairs, knocked discreetly, and, before he had time to panic, plunged in.

Flush was sitting up in bed wearing a quilted dressing jacket. He had brushed his hair, and his manicured hands lay loosely in his lap. He was waiting. Beecher did not look at him. He laid the tray on Flush's knees and turned to go.

"Just a minute, Beecher," said Flush evenly.

Beecher stood at the foot of the bed. He moved his toes inside his boots.

"I have already seen the Creaker," said Flush, pouring tea. "He tells me that he witnessed last night's exhibition in its entirety." He held up a teaspoon and looked at it critically. "Now we all admit without prejudice that you were operating under difficulties. I want to be quite fair."

Beecher's heart sank. He licked his lips.

"Nobody," said Flush, "could have foreseen that those astonishing individuals next door would be putting on a performance of their own. But I maintain, Beecher, that such confusion can, on occasion, provide a diversion behind which a good agent can carry out his orders unmolested." He sipped his tea and looked blandly at Beecher.

Beecher shifted his feet. He said nothing.

"I think you'll agree," said Flush, frowning at his nails, "that the failure of our little scheme was entirely due to the fall of the potted plant."

Beecher waited.

"I had the situation well in hand. If somebody had not dropped this plant – a begonia, I believe – at the crucial moment, our mission would have been accomplished." He laid the teaspoon upon the slice of lemon floating in his cup and dunked it thoughtfully. "Now our problem is to prove the identity of this clumsy botanist. Can you help me, Beecher? Will you hazard a guess?"

Beecher shook his head mutely.

"No? Well, no matter. As it happens, our problem is already solved." He looked out of the window with apparent interest. "You were seen," he added.

Beecher's mouth fell open.

"I was seen?" he repeated feebly.

"Yes. The Creaker saw you. He was reluctant to expose a lieutenant, but he felt it to be his duty. Have you anything to say, Beecher? A denial, of course, under the circumstances, would be superfluous."

Beecher was confused. His training had indoctrinated him, when in doubt, to say nothing. He bowed his head.

"Thank you," said Flush. "I appreciate your frankness. You realize, of course, that you have now considerably complicated the issue? Naturally, the amateurs will now be on their guard. Nevertheless, you will have the two bodies on these premises by dawn tomorrow. If this venture is more difficult, you have only yourself to blame. Do we understand each other?"

"Yus, Boss."

"Good. You may go. Inform Squires that I prefer him to wait at table single-handed today. I do not wish to see you until you have rectified your failure of last night. Kindly avoid me. If I lay eyes upon you before then we may both have occasion to regret it." He shut his eyes and without visible effort bent his teaspoon into a loop. *"Now get out!"* he screamed. *"Get out, before I forget myself!"*

*

The Colonel rose at twelve-thirty. He sat on the edge of his bed and groaned. His head hurt. His eyes refused to focus. He had an extraordinary thirst. His neck felt strangely weak. It was just like the good old days in the Punjab.

He cut himself twice shaving and, with two tufts of bloody cotton wool sprouting from his wounds, he dressed and went straight out to the Ten Bells for a hair of the dog which had bitten him.

Beecher, who was darting around the house trying to avoid Flush, watched him go and, hurrying downstairs, followed him. As he went through the courtyard he saw that Tom had fished the carp out of its pool again. He had it by the tail and was dragging it towards the hedge. When he saw Beecher he dropped it and sprang into the lilac tree. Beecher picked up the carp and threw it back into its pool. It swam away quickly, flicking its tail.

As Beecher entered the saloon bar, the Colonel was paying for his first glass of port.

"I'll 'ave a Guinness," said Beecher, behind him.

The Colonel jumped.

"You buy your own liquor, sir," he said irritably.

"*You* don't," said Beecher. He sucked his teeth and gazed up at the ceiling.

"By God, that's blackmail!"

Beecher nodded amiably.

"'Sright, cock."

"Guinness," said the Colonel to the barmaid. "Draught."

"Bottled," corrected Beecher.

When Hugo Berko arrived at one-forty-five in search of an honest cretin, the Colonel was downing his fourth port in a mellow mood. The Colonel, who had never before spoken to Hugo, now did so, with a view to sharing the financial responsibility of Beecher's thirst.

"Morning, sir," he said. "Believe we are neighbors. What will you take for it?"

Hugo was intrigued. He had never before, as far as he knew, been bought a drink by a murderer. He accepted a pint of bitter and watched the Colonel pay for it.

"Here's to crime," he said, raising his tankard.

"May I know your name, sir?" asked the Colonel. "Old custom of mine. Never drink with strangers."

"Carstairs," said Hugo for no particular reason.

Beecher stiffened.

"Your face seems familiar," Hugo lied. "Could I have met you during the war?"

"No, sir," said the Colonel thickly. "Court-martialed in Delhi, '16. Most unjust. Framed by a tribesman." He slopped a little port down his waistcoat and made no attempt to mop it up. "All have troubles," he mumbled. "You have troubles, I have troubles. *Cherchez la femme!*" he roared suddenly. He sat down heavily on a stool. "Take Lilli," he muttered, tapping Hugo's sweater with his index finger. "Flighty. No discipline. Like 'em with spirit, but not as much as she's got now, what? Good, eh? See the joke?"

"I'm afraid not," said Hugo calmly.

"Mine's a port," said the Colonel, banging his glass on the counter.

"Don't you think you've 'ad enough, dear?" asked the barmaid without real interest.

"Eh?" said the Colonel. He nudged Hugo. "Instruct that officer to bring me a drink."

"'E's your responsibility," said the barmaid to Hugo. "I won't 'ave 'im pass out in 'ere." She slapped down the Colonel's drink.

"Nobody's going to pass out in here," barked the Colonel. He waved a hand wildly in the direction of the Asterisk Club. "*There!*"

Hugo edged his stool a little farther away. He was conscious of Beecher's small, dull eyes on him.

The Colonel stabbed himself in the chest with his thumb. "Fearless!" he said. "Absolutely fear. Going to arrange a simple accident."

Hugo felt the hair rise on the back of his neck.

"Really?" he said. "And who will be on the receiving end?"

"Sssssssh!" hissed the Colonel. "Walls, sir. Got ears. Discretion is better part. Go home, siesta, make up my mind. Slow to anger but now roused." He lurched to his feet and aimed himself at the door. "Excuse me, sir. Tiffin time. Delighted to meet." He walked unsteadily away, holding himself with great dignity.

Good God! thought Hugo. *The old boy's broken out!* He looked at Beecher for some echo of his own horror. The monolithic butler was still watching him. There was a cigarette hanging off his lower lip and he was sucking his teeth. Hugo swallowed.

"Easiest thing in the ..." said the Colonel, supporting himself on a potted plant. "Simple as this. Watch! Nothing up sleeves, gulla, gulla! Open the door!" He did so with a flourish. He went through and it swung to behind him. "And *shut the door!*" he bellowed through the glass panels. He turned right with military precision and disappeared.

Beecher rose and followed him. As he passed Hugo, he contrived to lunge against his stool, nearly upsetting him.

"You're for it, Epstein," he remarked pleasantly.

CHAPTER 23

HUGO ran all the way home from the Ten Bells. As he passed the Asterisk Club he glanced at the ground-floor windows and saw that the old cripple was in one of them, his face squashed hideously against the glass. Whether by accident or design, the fingers of his right hand were arranged in an offensive gesture. He moved them slightly, and Hugo knew that it was no accident.

He hurried into the courtyard of No. 15 and saw that Mrs. Barratt was clipping the hedge between the two houses with an enormous pair of shears. The sun flashed on the wicked blades and Mrs. Barratt looked up and smiled. She was wearing an organdy sunbonnet, and the way she smiled made Hugo's blood run cold.

"What lovely weather for the birds," she said. She leaned across the hedge and snipped off a plant from the Berko's rock garden.

Hugo rushed into his house. As he slammed the door he saw that the mighty cat from the Club was sitting in an elm tree watching him with half-shut eyes, swinging its tail like a metronome. Marleen looked through the swing door.

"Oh, it's you," she said, disappointed. "Anything wrong? White as a sheet, you are."

Hugo did not answer her. He burst into the dining room and found his wife, Rex, and the Hilfords sitting despondently around the table. Peter was drawing something on a piece of paper, and Bertha was eating chocolate blancmange out of a cup with a fork. Croydon leapt off a chair and barked.

"The Asterisk Club have run amok," said Hugo hoarsely. "We're in danger. The old man is looking for victims, and I gather he's not fussy who he picks on. *Barricade the house!*"

*

"You are inebriated," said Flush.

He took the Colonel by the shoulder and shook him.

"Correct," said the Colonel. "Thank God, sir!"

"Where have you been?" barked Flush.

"Hundreds, thousands, brigades of men have followed me," said the Colonel. "Afghanistan, Nepal, Northwest Frontier."

Beecher stole into the hall, saw Flush, and stole out again.

"Simple accident," said the Colonel. He sat down on the umbrella stand.

"I demand to know where you have been," grated Flush.

"He was in the public house, sir," said Squires from the top of the stairs. "So was that man next door what carves with a beard, sir."

"Arrest that sepoy!" said the Colonel.

"You have been talking." Flush stood over the Colonel, white with rage.

"To the flag!" shouted the Colonel.

*

"What you doin'?" asked Marleen.

Hugo and Peter pushed the sideboard from the dining room against the front door. Croydon ran from the studio, trod on a fallen peach, and fell down. Rex rushed after her carrying a bust of Haile Selassie. He put it on the sideboard and darted into the dining room.

"What you *doin'*?" said Marleen.

Bertha hurried out of the studio unraveling a coil of rope. She shut the dining room door and tied the rope on to the handle. The other end she tied tightly on to the foot of the banisters.

"What's that for?" asked Marleen. "What you *doin'*, Mrs. Berko? I got a right to know."

"Let me out!" shouted Rex from inside the dining room. He hammered on the panels. "Open the door, you pig!"

Mr. Beesum came out of the kitchen holding a dead rat by the tail. He stood beside Marleen, staring, his mouth ajar.

Hugo and Peter between them carried a boulder of basalt from the studio and rolled it against the sideboard.

"*Let me out!*" screamed Rex.

Fan raced downstairs, pushed past Marleen, and disappeared into the kitchen. Croydon stood in the middle of the hall and barked hysterically.

"What are they doing?" asked Mr. Beesum.

"I dunno," said Marleen. "I keep askin', but they won't say."

*

Flush slapped the Colonel with the back of his hand.

"You besotted fool!" he hissed. "You have been conferring with the opposition."

The Colonel fell off the umbrella stand. It toppled against the wall and split in half. Squires made an inarticulate noise and ran downstairs to inspect the damage.

"Ming!" he whispered. "Was Ming! A beautiful thing!"

"*Clifford!*" said Mrs. Barratt, bursting from the kitchen. "Oh! You struck him! An old man! You viper!"

The Colonel lay on his back on the floor, playing possum.

"Corpse," he remarked.

Mrs. Barratt scuttled to his assistance. She snatched an umbrella and hit Flush weakly on the back of the knee.

*

"Is it a siege, Mr. Rex?" asked Marleen. She disliked having to ask Rex, but she had to know.

"What do *you* think?" said Rex. He picked up the large-leafed plant he had found in the woods and scurried upstairs.

"But 'oo *against*?" said Marleen.

Nobody answered her.

"Why don't you send for the pleece?" she insisted loudly.

Hugo was pushing Bertha's loom against the studio door. He hit himself in the forehead and pointed a finger at her.

"Go home!" he ordered. "You're fired!"

"All right," said Marleen. "But just tell me what you're *doin'*!"

*

"Go on, Boss," encouraged the Creaker from the door of the drawing room. "Snatch off 'is arm!"

"Go to your rooms," snapped Flush. "Nobody is to leave the house."

Tom raised his tail in the air and stalked back to the kitchen. Finding the new maid too engrossed in eavesdropping to be aware of his intentions, he jumped on to the table and ate four raw, filleted soles. A windfall.

*

"Get upstairs," said Peter to Fan. "Go into the bedroom and lock yourself in."

"What are you doin', Mr. 'Ilford?" asked Marleen. "Oh, *do* tell me!"

Hugo came out of the kitchen with a pail of water. He saw Marleen, put down the pail, and rolled up his cuffs.

"*Will* you go home?" he shouted. "I fired you half an hour ago. You're trespassing!"

"Mad," said Marleen. "Absolutely mental."

She had no intention of accepting her notice. She flounced into the kitchen, clapped on her hat, stole a bottle of chutney, and went home. As she passed the Asterisk Club she saw Flush pacing up and down the drawing room. His usually immaculate hair was ruffled and he was biting his nails.

*

Fan sat on the floor in her bedroom warming her back at the gas fire and waiting for Peter. She was not at all frightened. She was beyond that. But events seemed to have got out of control, and she was not sure what to expect next.

Peter banged on the door.

"Hist!" he said. "It's me."

Fan let him in.

"I never heard anyone actually say Hist before," she said.

"Wait!" said Peter abruptly. He laid his hand silently on the handle and jerked open the door. Fan looked over his shoulder at the empty landing. Peter closed and locked the door. "As it happens," he said, "there's nobody there."

Fan watched him with interest but without surprise.

"Now listen," said Peter. "This is terribly important. We're in quite a spot. If Hugo's right, and the old chap next door really has gone nuts, he'll probably have a stab at one of us. For the moment, we're all right, because I defy anyone to get in downstairs. But what poor old Hugo has forgotten is that it cuts both ways. We may have locked a homicidal maniac out, but we've also locked one in. I'm pretty certain that Bunny was killed by somebody in this house."

"Do you still think Rex did it?"

"I don't know. I think one of those three did. Rex is the most likely. He might have done it in a moment of manic elation. I've often suspected he's that type."

"Well, he's not. I like Rex."

Peter sighed. He produced a small automatic from his pocket.

"Take this," he said. "You're not to move without it, do you understand? You're not to be alone with any member of the household except me. You are not to eat anything you haven't prepared yourself. You are to eat only canned food. You are not to use tea, sugar, milk, or any other thing which could have been tampered with. Keep away from the windows. If anybody comes nearer to you than eight feet, challenge him or her immediately. Don't hesitate to use that gun, but shoot below the knee if you can."

Fan weighed the little gun in her hand.

"I feel like Bulldog Drummond," she said. "What a pity it's only a Colt. I'd much rather have a Mauser."

"This isn't a game, Fan."

"I know, darling. But I do feel that this sort of thing may never happen to us again, so we might as well get the goodness. Where's Rex?"

"I've locked him in the drawing room. He's suspect."

"Is he armed?"

"He said something about a piece of coal in the toe of a sock."

"Oh. What have you got?"

"The airgun."

"I see. I wonder whether the Berkos have got anything. Hugo's been looking very shifty lately. Have you noticed?"

"Imagination."

"I don't think so. Bossy and shifty, he's been."

"Keep away from the window!"

"I've never fired a revolver before. Is this the safety catch?"

"Yes. For God's sake be careful!"

"Is it loaded?"

"No. But you can't be too careful with firearms."

*

Four-ten.

Hugo sat on the bottom stair in the hall with his head in his hands.

The rats came out from the skirtings and skittered in and out of the barricade around the front door. A large white one suddenly skidded and fell down. Hugo watched it. It was dead.

He took a Verey pistol out of his pocket, broke the barrel, and slipped a green rocket into the breech.

*

Five-three.

Flush stopped trying to concentrate upon *The Times* crossword puzzle and, bored by the long hours of inaction, went into the kitchen to fire the new maid. He found her in the larder, dipping a piece of bread into a tureen of congealed gravy.

"Leave," he said. "I dislike you."

*

Five-twenty.

Bertha lifted Croydon into the house through the downstairs lavatory window, then climbed in herself. She listened for a moment to make sure that there was nobody in the hall, then stole along the passage with the dog under one arm and a heavy, leather-bound volume under the other. Hugo was sitting on the bottom step, but he was asleep. He was grinding his teeth. Bertha struggled out of Lilli Cluj's mink coat and hung it up in the hall. She had enjoyed wearing it, although she knew that it was unwise. She crept past Hugo and was stopped on the half-landing by Fan.

"Challenge!" said Fan excitedly. "I've got a gun!"

Bertha put Croydon down and fumbled in her capacious pocket. "So have I," she said, producing it. "I've got the Biretta."

"Mine's a Colt."

"It's not yours. It's Hugo's."

"So's yours."

"Is yours loaded?"

"I won't say. Is yours?"

"I shouldn't dream of telling you."

"Where are you going?"

"To study the bodies, if you must know."

"Don't move! Why?"

"I'll swap guns if you like. This one keeps tearing my pocket."

"Well, I don't like. I expect mine shoots bigger bullets."

"I bet it doesn't. I do wish you'd stop waving it around. I know perfectly well it's not loaded."

"You don't know any such thing. Anyway, nor's yours."

"I never said it was."

"*Why* are you going to study the bodies?"

"Because I happen to have taken the trouble to go all the way to the Public Library to get a book on embalming, and before I can do another thing I've got to find out where their veins are. Now will you please stop playing games and let me pass?"

Fan stood reluctantly aside, and Bertha went on up to the attics, followed by Croydon. The little dog seemed subdued. She turned at the bend in the stairs and gave Fan a reproachful look from under her silver eyebrows.

Bertha shut herself into the attic and wedged a chair under the door handle. She rolled up her sleeves and removed Mr. Cann from his trunk. She laid him flat on his back, opened her book, and compared him with the diagram on page one.

*

Five-forty-seven.

Beecher, bored with waiting for darkness to fall, sat behind the curtains in his little attic room and watched Bertha in the corresponding room opposite. He could not see what she was doing, but he knew that she was up to no good. She was bending over something on the floor with a pencil in her mouth. Once, he saw her lift a limp hand and study the wrist closely. It was not her own hand because there were three of them. Beecher probed a back tooth with his tongue. "Soppy," he said aloud. He leaned out of the window and, with exquisite precision, spat on Tom, who was prowling along the path beneath.

*

Six-ten.

Peter stopped walking around the spare room in search of inspiration and went up to the drawing room in search of a drink. As he unlocked the door, Rex sprang up from the sofa and faced him, trembling with indignation.

"About time, too, you drain!" he said stridently. He saw the airgun and goggled. "What are you doing with that cannon?"

"Preparing for any eventuality."

"It's not fair! I've only got this."

He held up an elongated purple silk sock with a large bulge in the toe.

"Idiotic!" said Peter. "You'd never get within range."

"No, I suppose not. I rather like it, though." He giggled. "Madly rude. Do you want some gin?"

"Very generous, considering that it's mine. I'll pour it myself, thank you."

"It's perfectly all right, Uncle. I left my sack of arsenic in the Palm Court."

Rex did a casual *entrechat*.

"What happened about Sylvia?" he asked.

"I don't know. Do you suppose she can have had a brainstorm?"

"I wouldn't be a bit surprised. She's not normal, that one."

"I suppose I ought to send a telegram."

"I'll do it."

Peter looked at him, surprised.

"That's very nice of you," he said suspiciously.

"It's nothing," said Rex, smiling sympathetically. "You look worn to a sliver."

He went down to the hall and phoned a telegram sending Sylvia to Grimsby.

Hugo came out of the studio and looked at him.

"So that's it?" he said. "A troublemaker."

Rex rattled some coins in his pocket.

"Do *you* like Sylvia?" he asked. "She once said that your head was too big."

"Oh, did she? Send her to Guernsey. She always gets seasick and that's a good long crossing." He went upstairs, hitting the banisters angrily with the Verey pistol.

In the drawing room Peter was pouring himself a drink.

"I'll have some, too," said Hugo. He rubbed his eyes. "Is there any Vermouth?"

"There is, but I notice that Rex isn't drinking it, and he's been alone with it all the afternoon."

Rex came in. He was eating spaghetti out of a tin with a pair of nail scissors.

"Do you suppose," he asked, "that the mad old goblin next door has thought better of it? Or do you imagine that this is the lull before the showdown?" He arranged his feet in the fourth position and looked down at them.

"They'll probably wait until it's dark," said Hugo. He stared moodily out of the window at the thickening twilight. "It won't be long now."

CHAPTER 24

AT seven o'clock it was quite dark. Half an hour later, Beecher, who had been sitting in his attic room closely watching the house next door, was at last satisfied that he knew the whereabouts of each of its occupants.

Mrs. Epstein was still in the attic opposite to his. She had drawn the blinds and turned on the lights. Several times Beecher had seen her distorted, stooping shadow. She was still fooling around with the bodies. Beecher sucked his teeth and flexed his hands. He had slightly strained his toes in not tripping her up last night, and it was only reasonable that she should suffer for it.

There was also a light in the front room on the first floor which he knew to be the drawing room. The ground floor, except for the kitchen quarters, was in darkness. It was reasonable to suppose that the loonies, with the exception of Mrs. Epstein, were in the front room. If one or more were lurking in the darkened parts of the house, then he would meet them under ideal conditions and deal with them according to his degree of dislike. On the last trip he had been hamstrung by the Boss's No Violence order, but this time he had a free hand. The Boss had not actually said so, but Beecher chose to think that he had implied it by omission.

He went downstairs slowly, walking his fingers down the stair rail. *I'm goin' to 'it one of them*, he thought, patting his cosh. *I'd prefer Sunny Jim, but any one will do. I'll it 'em regardless.*

He met Flush in the hall. His master looked at him with hatred and turned away.

"I shall be waiting in the library," he said over his shoulder. "I advise you against further grotesqueries."

Beecher prudently did not reply.

He pulled on his cotton gloves and let himself out of the back door. Then he eased along the wall until he was opposite to the kitchen window next door. The curtains were undrawn and inside there was a little man with a bedraggled mustache and gold-rimmed spectacles dissecting a rat. The dresser had been pushed against the back door and a crude booby-trap with a pail of water hung above the window. Beecher moved back out of sight and ran a professional eye over the drainpipes. One led up the side of the house to the cornice but gave access only to the lighted drawing room. Another disappeared into the wall beneath a small, frosted window. Beecher dismissed it. He had once before been wedged in a window of the same type.

He got silently over the wall and inspected the dining room window. An overturned table stood against it with an armchair on top of it, the whole structure waiting to fall at a touch. Beecher put a hairy hand over his mouth and pushed a laugh back into his throat. So it was a barricade, was it? He crept down the gravel path on the far side of the house and cautiously played his torch over the brickwork. The tiny circle of light found the snout of a drainpipe. He followed it upwards and smiled happily. It was an ideal drain, broad, strong, with numerous tributaries, and freshly painted green, his favorite color.

He brushed the gravel from the soles of his plimsolls and spat on his gloves. A moment later he was standing on the window-ledge of a first-floor room. He eased back the window clasp with a tool like a flexible palette knife and stepped swiftly into the dark room. He carefully closed the window behind him, drew the curtains, and turned on his torch. He was in a double bedroom. From the roll of cartridge paper and the T-square on the dressing table he guessed that the room belonged to Epstein and his wife. There was a string of pearls on the bedside table. He picked it up and bit the large center one experimentally. It broke at once. It had the consistency of melba toast. Beecher threw it on the floor and slid out of the room. He found himself on the landing, facing the drawing-room door.

He moved quietly over to it and turned the key in the lock. For a second he wondered why all the keys in this madhouse seemed to be on the outside of the doors. He supposed that they locked each other in when they became dangerous. He was turning to make his way up to the attics when he heard a slight sound on the half-landing below him. He trained his turreted eyes into the well of the stairs. For a moment he saw nothing. Then a red bead appeared and hung in the air. It was the glowing end of a cigarette. It moved, paused, and glowed brighter just long enough for Beecher to see the rosy outline of a brooding face. *'Ullo-'ullo-'ullo!* he thought. *If it isn't me old chum Epstein!* He slid the cosh out of his pocket; drew his breath and prepared to hold it indefinitely; and then started downstairs.

Walking on the outsides of his plimsolls, rolling his weight from heel to toe, he tested each stair for a creak before he trusted it with his full weight. His eyes never left the bright bead of the cigarette. It rose to the face, glowed, fell, and rose again before he was near enough to hear Epstein breathing. Another two steps down and he was within striking distance. A supersensitive, exploring foot told him that he was on the small landing. The cigarette was still below him, so Epstein must be sitting down. A step forward and Beecher was standing over him. The cigarette rose and stopped abruptly. Beecher felt rather than saw Epstein turn towards him. He reached out and in one movement seized the sculptor's beard and tapped him neatly on the back of the skull.

Hugo fell forward without a sound. Beecher caught him and lifted him over his shoulder. He retrieved the fallen cigarette and took an experimental puff at it. It was a cheroot. He smeared it down the wall until it was extinguished. As he had anticipated, he found that the key of the door Epstein had been guarding was on the outside, so he carried Hugo into the spare room and laid him on the floor. Finding a table-cloth, he cut it into strips with his knife and bound his captive into the most uncomfortable position he could devise. He then turned his atten-tion to the room. He had to know what Epstein had been guarding. He could hear the rats squeaking in the walls.

His pencil torch roved. It struck an overturned lamp on the floor and a humped eiderdown. Beecher moved forward to investigate. From under the yellow silk protruded an ankle. The torch moved upwards, and its tiny circle of light found a ruche of coffee-colored lace. Beecher smiled. He recognized that negligee. For the past three months he had handed it regularly to Lilli Cluj with her morning tea. Snapping off the torch, he picked up the light body, slung it over his shoulder, and stole down-stairs. The hall was in complete darkness. There was a thread of light under the kitchen door, so Beecher made for the dining room. Some simian instinct made him stop a foot from Bertha's loom and turn on his torch. The handle of the dining room door had been tied with a length of rope to that of the room opposite. A pail of water stood just outside each, with a tripwire stretched between them. Beecher shook his head. He cut the rope and removed the bucket of water. He laid the body on the sideboard which formed part of the barricade and stealthily eased the loom away from the door. He removed the bulb from the light on the wall, reasoning that if anybody wished to inspect the slight alter-ations he was making to their defenses it would take longer in total darkness. Then he picked up the body and carried it into the dining room. It took him five minutes to move the fortifications from the side window, then, with the body in his arms, he climbed out into the dark passage between the two houses. He left the window open, thinking, with pride at his forethought, that it would greatly facilitate his return trip for the Old Tin Cann.

As he went into the Asterisk kitchen, Squires looked up from polish-ing a large brass elephant and clicked his tongue.

"Oh, you are *orful!*" he said. "I don't know 'ow you dare, I don't really."

Beecher stepped up to him and dragged his hand down Squires' face.

Neither said anything. Squires did not move, but he paled. Beecher took hold of Squires' nose and twisted it. Squires' eyes began to water, but he still sat holding the brass elephant. Beecher stepped back and looked at him thoughtfully.

"Any time," he said. "No trouble at all."

He made his way unhurriedly to the library and knocked quietly.

"Come in," called Flush.

They sat in a circle around the fire. Mrs. Barratt laid aside her knitting and looked up with interest. The Creaker was brushing Tom with a blue hairbrush. The Colonel was sitting sulkily by the window playing with a horsewhip. Flush took off his spectacles and folded up his newspaper. Beecher laid the body at his feet. Flush glanced downwards. He scratched the side of his nose.

"You have surpassed yourself, Beecher," he said quietly. "May I take this opportunity to retract everything I have formerly said about your mental equipment?" He leaned forward and stared into Beecher's eyes. "You are not a cretin, Beecher. You are a dangerous lunatic." He put one hand over his eyes. "You have fetched the wrong body," he said softly.

*

"Well, 'ow was I to *know*?" Beecher protested ten minutes later. "*Nobody* would of known! It's got no 'air on its legs."

"Oh, be *quiet*!" said Flush, unable to restrain himself.

Beecher opened his mouth and closed it again. He clenched his fists and glared at Flush. He felt that in some complicated way he had been tricked into making this shameful mistake. It was not his fault. It was somebody else's, but he did not quite know whose.

Flush gave the body an irritable push with his foot.

"Who *is* this man?" he demanded. There was a pulse throbbing visibly in his throat.

"I'm sure *I* don't know, Clifford," said Mrs. Barratt quickly. "What a *clumsy* way to kill anybody!"

Clumsy. For Beecher, the word rang a half-forgotten bell. Ah, yes! He had it. That was the word the newspapers had applied to the Creaker's job. "A clumsy, brutish killing ..." He glanced involuntarily at the old cripple. The Creaker was in his usual place on the sofa, eating wine gums out of a paper bag. He dipped in his hand and brought out a square red one. He looked at it, dropped it back, and chose another, a round yellow one, which he popped into his mouth.

"Creaker," said Flush. "Have you seen this man before?"

"Nah," said the Creaker. "Don't get around much any more."

"Can he be one of our country members?" Flush stood up and shot his cuffs.

Beecher apprehensively took a step backwards and trod on Tom, who had climbed off his master's knee and was tearing a hole in the back of a chair. Tom gave a strange, hoarse shout. Flush looked at Beecher with a gleam of approval. He went to the tray of drinks and poured himself a whisky. The Creaker, behind Flush's back, leaned forward, his face puckered with rage, and struck Beecher across the shins with his stick. Beecher's face twitched. He snatched the cosh from his pocket and seized the Creaker by the lapel. He was not quick enough. Flush turned round, holding a siphon of soda water. He looked at Beecher with raised eyebrows. Beecher bit his lip and let go of the Creaker. There had been something sticky on the man's jacket, something treacly. Blood? wondered Beecher. Or merely drool from the wine gums? He looked thoughtfully at the Creaker's unusual cranium.

Flush bent to look more closely at Bunny. "At a very rough estimate," he said, "this man has been dead for between twenty-four and thirty hours." He stood up and sipped his drink. "I intend to know which of you is responsible for his death," he added casually.

What a crew! thought Beecher. *He didn't ask no questions about the first two – didn't seem to mind them. Go on, Boss! Ask 'em about the first ones 'fore they start askin' you!*

"Naomi," said Flush, "where were you after midnight last night?"

"Playing bridge with Auntie Mollie at 24c Monmouth Crescent, W. 11," said Mrs. Barratt at once in a singsong voice.

Flush massaged the bridge of his nose. "Please. I am not asking for your official alibi. We all know perfectly well that you were in this house. What I want to know is *what you were doing.*"

Mrs. Barratt's eyes flickered. She stroked her dress over her knees. "I was with the Colonel," she murmured. "All night long," she added firmly.

Flush studied her. He knew that she expected him to disbelieve her but this did not necessarily mean that she was lying.

"Is this true, Colonel?" he asked, wondering why he did so, knowing that it would only lead him deeper into doubt.

"Sir," said the Colonel, looking gratified, "must refuse answer. Honor of a lady."

Flush suppressed a sigh. "Creaker," he asked, discouraged, knowing that unless the formalities were observed, his members would feel that they had scored a minor victory. "Where were you? What were you doing?" He knew well that the Creaker would give his standard answer and he braced himself in advance against losing his temper.

"Was with you, Boss," said the Creaker automatically. "'Cause if I wasn't, where was *you*?"

Flush clenched his teeth until he could again trust his voice. He turned to his steward. "Beecher, can you prove that you did not return to No. 15 last night?"

"Was with the boys in Lupus Street," said Beecher. "An' if you are tryin' to pin anythin', I still am an' I can prove it."

Flush twisted his signet ring on his finger. For a moment he wondered why he had never killed Beecher. On the heels of this thought came another. Why had none of his members ever attempted to kill *him*?

"Go to your rooms," he barked. "Dress for the street. Go in order of seniority to the armory and each provide yourself with an automatic of not larger than .38 caliber. Nobody is to take more than one, and you are to sign for them in the ledger. Colonel, we shall require none of your homemade machinery. Nobody is to take the Luger – I believe the Dorset police have recently had occasion to note its rifling. I shall probably take the Steyr. You will see that your weapons are fully loaded and fitted with silencers. You will conceal them adequately. I want no theatrical bulges in your clothing. Now go! Report here within ten minutes."

His members were staring at him. The Colonel cracked the horse-whip and spoke softly to himself in Hindustani. The Creaker's eyes gleamed. Mrs. Barratt looked alarmed.

"Clifford," she whispered. "Where are we going?"

Flush's lips twitched into an unpleasant smile. "We are going," he said slowly, "to pay a friendly call on our neighbors. Beecher, replace this body where you found it."

CHAPTER 25

AT eight o'clock, somewhere in the darkness of the ground floor of No. 15, an alarm clock began to clamor. Mr. Beesum, who had just finished with his dissected rats and had their more interesting organs safely in test-tubes of alcohol, jumped. He bustled nervously out of the kitchen into the hall. The swing door flapped behind him. He fumbled his way along the wall and turned on the light. Nothing happened. The alarm clock stopped. In the sudden silence, Mr. Beesum heard his own heart beating heavily. From upstairs there was not a sound. Even the rats were still. The whole house seemed to be waiting. Mr. Beesum did not like it at all. He turned and ran back to the lighted kitchen. He was confused and unhappy. Since Mr. Berko had dashed into the house and started pushing the furniture around, he had felt uneasy. There was something going on which he did not understand.

He scratched his chin apprehensively. He still had to take a sticky board up to the main run in the attic. He dreaded going again into the brooding silence of the hall, but he did not want to admit to himself that he was afraid. He picked up the board and marched into the hall. He forced himself to walk upstairs slowly. As he passed the spare room on the half-landing he thought he heard a groan. He stood listening for a second, but it was not repeated. It was probably a dying rat. He shook his head and went on upstairs. There was a line of light under the attic door. He knocked politely and turned the handle. The door resisted him and he gave it a slight push. There was a crack of splintering wood and a chair fell over. A voice inside called, "You can't come in." The door opened slowly inwards. Mr. Beesum stopped in his tracks, unable to move. His mouth dropped open and his eyes bulged. He clutched the sticky board convulsively to his breast.

Mrs. Berko was crouching on the floor over a dead man. She had rolled up his trousers and was marking the veins of his legs in variously colored chinographs. A dead woman was stretched on the floor beside her clad only in a brassiere and brief panties and decorated all over with multicolored tracery. The small white dog was lying with its head on one of her feet.

Mrs. Berko looked up over her shoulder and saw him.

"Oh!" she said helplessly.

She pulled down the legs of the dead man's trousers.

Mr. Beesum suddenly found the strength to move. He made a small inarticulate noise, turned and stumbled downstairs as fast as his legs would carry him. The sticky board was now firmly stuck to his jacket and it got in his way. He kept banging his knees and twice he nearly fell. The dog ran on to the landing above him and began to bark shrilly. Mrs. Berko ran after it.

"Stop!" she shouted. "Stop or I'll shoot you! I've got a gun."

Mr. Beesum could not stop. With his breath whistling through his teeth, he fell down the last three stairs. Somebody was trying to get out of the drawing room in front of him. The handle turned, but the door was locked. Mr. Beesum was trying to pick himself up when somebody hurled himself against the door and the lock snapped. The door burst open and a rectangle of light leaped across the dark landing. A man was in the doorway and he had a rifle in his hand.

"Halt!" he said, leveling it.

"You just stop!" said another voice. Its owner appeared behind the first man. He had what looked like a club in his hand. A woman – it was Mrs. Hilford – ducked under their arms and came out on to the landing.

"Challenge!" she said, standing over him with an automatic. "Put up your hands! *Reach!"*

Mr. Beesum, chattering with terror, raised his hands into the air. He tried to stand up. He banged his knee on the sticky board on his jacket. His foot slipped on the top step, and with a thin scream he rolled headlong downstairs.

He hit the wall of the half-landing with a crash. For a moment he lay there, his face pressed into the carpet, then he tried to scramble to his feet. He was on all fours when the door behind him was flung open and a man sprang from it on to his back. Mr. Beesum was flattened. He was seized by the shoulders and shaken. The man picked him up, hit him on the head, flung him back on to the carpet, and knelt heavily between his shoulderblades.

Mr. Beesum lay still. He was dizzy and he could not breathe. He made two weak attempts to spit out a strand of carpet and gave it up. The man took him by the neck and banged his head against the banisters.

"So!" he said. "You'd knock me down, would you?" It was Mr. Berko. He was very angry indeed.

Mr. Beesum lay quietly, watching a spectacular display of green stars. He was convinced that his tormentor intended to kill him. He relaxed and pretended to be dead already. It worked. Mr. Berko stood up and gave him a push with his foot.

"Get up!" he ordered. "Get up or I'll knock you down!"

Mr. Beesum compromised. He rolled over, aching in every bone, and sat up with his hands in the air. The overhead light flicked on.

"Oh, my God!" said Mr. Berko. "It's you! Mr. Beesum! Oh, God! Good evening."

Mr. Beesum turned his head away. He found himself looking down the barrel of an automatic. He focused slowly and saw Mrs. Hilford kneeling beside him holding the gun with both hands. Behind her was the dancing man holding a loaded sock. At the top of the stairs was Mr. Hilford pointing an airgun. Halfway up the flight of stairs above was Mrs. Berko. She was leaning over the banisters and waving a revolver. Mr. Beesum shut his eyes and groaned.

"Corks!" said Mrs. Hilford. "It's Mr. Beesum!"

"I wonder whether I broke anything," said Mr. Berko. "I jumped on him as hard as I could – and you know, of course, that Bunny's gone?"

"*What?*"

"What do you mean, he's *gone*?"

"*Where's* he gone? How can he have gone?"

"That thug from the Asterisk slugged me in the dark, and when I came to, he'd gone."

"Don't be silly. How did he get in? What about the barricade?"

"I don't know. But it was him. It was that horrible bruiser who wears the cloth cap."

"But why should he want Bunny?"

"Well, well, well!" said Mr. Hilford. "So somebody has at last pulled a quick one on old Pimpernel Berko!"

"One more cheap crack out of you and I swear I'll smear you all over the landing."

Mr. Beesum opened his eyes and squinted along the pile of the carpet. The light shone on to it, and he could see each thread separately, like the hairs on a rat's back. He sat up slowly and shook his head. Somebody took him by the arm and pulled him to his feet. His knees buckled. Mr. Berko supported him. Mr. Beesum relaxed and made himself heavy. They carried him upstairs and into the drawing room. They laid him in a chair and went on talking in whispers. He leaned back gratefully and closed his eyes. Somebody pushed the cold rim of a glass against his gums. He swallowed a tasteless liquid which burnt the back of his throat. It scalded its way down to his stomach and exploded there warmly. He began to feel better. He drank some more of the liquid, and this time it tasted like gin. He saw, without surprise, Mrs. Berko and the dancer carry into the room one of the bodies he had seen upstairs. It was the man. He wore a woolen vest and a pair of gray flannel trousers and he had been shot in the left shoulder. They laid him on the floor by the window and went away again. A few minutes later they returned with the dead woman. They laid her on the floor beside the man and covered both with a fur rug. It was not quite long enough and their heads stuck out at one end, their feet at the other. Neither wore shoes.

Mr. Beesum belched and remembered to raise his fingers to his lips. "Pardon," he murmured.

Nobody seemed to hear him. They were whispering among themselves again.

"We've got to be terribly nice to him," he heard Mrs. Hilford say in a low voice. "If he goes away, we'll have the rats forever."

"To hell with the rats!" said Mr. Hilford. "We've got *him* forever. He's a material witness."

Mr. Beesum cleared his throat ostentatiously and they all looked at him.

"I hev seen what I hev seen," he said.

"Yes," said Mr. Berko. He said it briskly and seemed about to plunge into a long explanation, then he changed his mind. "I know," he said feebly, scowling. He looked at Mr. Hilford. "You cope. This is your department."

Mr. Hilford sat down beside Mr. Beesum and lit a cigarette.

"We've found – er – some bodies," he said. He pointed to the dead on the floor. "Those. They've apparently been poisoned." He stopped and pulled the lobe of his ear.

"Ar," said Mr. Beesum.

"Yes. We've decided that, for various reasons, they are not suicides. We think that they were probably poisoned by your arsenic." Mr. Beesum opened his mouth to protest, and Peter rushed on. "I'm afraid it's murder. It's our first experience, and we rather, well, lost our heads. We've had them for nearly three days, and we can't very well send for the police now because …"

"Because," said the dancing man quickly, "they'd only be stuffy and difficult, and if they sent us to jail, I'd *die*."

Mrs. Berko looked at him sharply.

"Do you mean that literally?" she asked. "Are you trying to confess?"

The dancing man looked at her with dislike.

"No, dear," he said. "If I confess I shall do it in Trafalgar Square in my green tights."

"I do not approve of homicide," said Mr. Beesum stiffly.

"Agree," said Mrs. Hilford. "You wouldn't believe what a nuisance they've been." She looked at him with an ingenuous smile. "How do you get rid of your dead rats?"

"Ar," said Mr. Beesum. He leaned back in his chair and screwed up his lips. "Thet depends." The gin was warming him and he felt quite sorry for them. "It depends upon the poison chosen," he said more amiably. "There is a large demand for dead rets, either whole or dissected."

Mrs. Hilford nodded.

"Yes," she said. "There must be."

"*But*," said Mr. Beesum, examining her serious face without suspicion, "the rets must be in *prime condition*. There is, for instance, little or no market for rets who have parteken of corrosive poisons. The organs must not be demaged. I hev known a fine large *rattus alexandrinus* to be thrown useless away if even slightly corroded, whereas the smallest *mus musculus*, if in mint condition, will fetch a penny-three."

"Cheap at half the price," said the dancer.

"What happens to the corroded ones?" asked Mrs. Berko with a winning smile.

"Egain," said Mr. Beesum, "I em unable to give you en unqualified answer. *Officially*, I seal each victim into one of the paper begs you heve doubtless noticed end deposit them at the Waste Section of the Town Hall."

"I see. And what about off the record?"

"Unofficially," said Mr. Beesum with an expression of mild cunning, "end hoping thet the metter will go no further, I *heve* been known, when confronted with a case of severe deterioration, to slip it into a sewer."

"Quite," said Mrs. Hilford.

She gave her husband a slight nudge and opened her eyes at Mr. Beesum. Mr. Hilford nodded casually.

"There's a manhole right outside the front door, oddly enough," he remarked.

"I'm told that the flow is remarkably fast," said Mr. Berko. He looked half-asleep. "If one should have the misfortune to drop anything into it ..."

"My dear, you might never see it again," said the dancer. He was executing a series of rather sloppy *pliés*. "Just wafted away with the other ghastlies to some deserving swamp at Friar's Crutch."

"I'd just love to see down our manhole!" said Mrs. Hilford. "Perhaps Mr. Beesum would arrange an instructive tour?" Her hair was braided into two small plaits tied with green ribbons and she looked at him hopefully under her eyelashes.

"Oh, no you don't!" said Mr. Beesum quickly. "If you are thinking what I em thinking, you are barking up the wrong wall. Anyway," he added, after a brief pause, "they would not get past the screen."

"What screen?"

Mr. Beesum coughed.

"No," he said apologetically, "it won't do. They would be swept along with the – ar – crude sewage to the Grit Pit. End there they would stop. The screens are designed to catch end remove regs, vegetables, end papers."

"Suppose these screens should become accidentally damaged?"

Mr. Beesum clicked his tongue.

"Thet would be tempering with Council Property."

"Of course. Only theorizing."

"Well," said Mr. Beesum obligingly, "they would pass with the screened sewage into the Sedimentation Tenk. There – if they did not sink with the sludge – they would pass through the Tenk Effluent to the Sprinkler. Now, no matter how you look et it, they would not be sprinkled."

At this moment there was a strange noise from downstairs. It was as if somebody had dragged a finger down a pane of glass. Then several pairs of feet clattered across the tiled hall without any pretense of stealth. Peter stood up, staring towards the door. Something metallic clanged against the banisters on the first flight of stairs. Several pairs of feet began to walk upwards without haste.

Hugo was on his feet. He had put down the Verey pistol and, without looking, he snatched the Colt. Peter had the Biretta. They advanced quietly until they were within six feet of the closed door.

Rex's hand closed around the Verey pistol. He took cover behind Bertha, who was fumbling with the airgun. Fan picked up the loaded sock, looked at it and threw it down. She darted forward and stood beside her husband.

"Get back!" said Peter.

Mr. Beesum, without knowing what he was doing, drank a glass of gin in one loud swallow. He sat holding the empty glass as if it were a grenade.

The feet had reached the half-landing. Somebody brushed against the curtain and the wooden rings rattled on their rod. Croydon sat up in an armchair and the hair on her back rose. Peter took Fan roughly by the arm.

"*Will* you get back?" he said furiously.

The first pair of feet were outside the door. There was a soft click as

Hugo slipped the safety catch on the Colt. Croydon sensed that something was wrong and tried to struggle behind a cushion. Peter took Fan by the shoulders and gave her a push. She staggered against a small table. She picked up a photograph of Bertha's father and prepared to throw it.

The door handle turned. It was made of glass and as it twisted, its facets caught the light and flashed on the ceiling.

The door opened a few inches. It rucked up the small mat on the inside. An enormous ginger cat walked into the room with its tail in the air.

Peter staring at it, amazed by its size, felt a draught of cool air. When he looked up, there was a man standing in the doorway with his hands in his pockets. It was the President of the Asterisk Club. He wore a soft black hat and his expression was unfriendly.

"Good evening," he said. "I advise you to drop those toys. You are covered from the rear."

Fan, from sheer fright, was the only member of the party who did not instinctively glance over her shoulder to verify this. It was thus that she witnessed a phenomenon on which, as an avid reader of the more virile type of detective fiction, she had previously reserved judgment.

An automatic sprang into Flush's hand. It was large and exotic. One moment it was not there, the next, although Flush had not appeared to move, it was. It was one of the species she had read about. She recognized it immediately. It was wicked, blue-black, snub-nosed. It was a high velocity police special, and it was fitted with a silencer.

Rex held his nose and pulled the trigger of the Verey pistol. A green rocket hit the wall with a shower of sparks and a deafening roar, shot through the window and sailed over the house opposite. Rex stood stupefied, staring at the hole in the window. The ginger cat had forced itself under the sofa. It was grunting, trying to tuck its tail in.

"That was not necessary," said Flush, frowning.

Croydon barked softly from behind her cushion.

"How did you get in?" asked Peter, eyeing the Steyr with respect.

The cat backed out from under the sofa and looked at Croydon appraisingly.

"I took the liberty of making entry through your dining room window. I shall, of course, compensate you for any slight damage we may have caused to your paintwork."

Flush stepped into the room. Behind him were Mrs. Barratt, the Creaker, and the Colonel, drawn up in echelon. The Colonel's eyes caught the light. They were the color of boiled sweets. Mrs. Barratt wore a cloche hat and a stole made from the skins of many small animals.

"How do you do?" she said sociably. As the arms of her hosts were raised above their heads, she decided against shaking hands. She advanced into the room, selected a chair next to Mr. Beesum, and sat down.

Mr. Beesum passed a hand across his eyes. The gin was beginning to confuse him. He stared at Mrs. Barratt's stole.

"*Rattus concolor*," he said listlessly. "You got thet in Pakistan, I shouldn't wonder."

"Yes," said Mrs. Barratt vivaciously. "Stone martins. How do you do?" She shook hands with obvious relief that the proprieties had been anyway partially observed.

The Colonel had gravitated to the table on which stood the drinks. He stood with his head bent forward as if he were listening, staring at Hugo. There was a horsewhip dangling out of his pocket beneath his coat.

Flush, without lowering the Steyr, glanced down at the two bodies on the floor.

"I see that you are already entertaining two of our members," he said with quiet anger. "My steward will join us shortly. He will return the third victim whom he appropriated under a misapprehension." He paused and glanced around him with hard, blue eyes.

"What do you want?" asked Hugo shortly.

He was edging closer to Rex, who still clutched the Verey pistol.

"I have come to inform you that I have certain principles. One is that I have never yet allowed a policeman on duty to cross my threshold in anger. You evidently share my feelings. You have not sought the assistance of Scotland Yard. I am not interested in your motives for this. I merely assume that they exist. As indeed do mine."

"I bet they do," said Peter rudely. "You looked better with a beard, Mr. Flush."

A muscle in Flush's cheek twitched. He trained the Steyr on to Peter's stomach. His finger tightened on the trigger.

Mrs. Barratt prodded him gently in the back with the Schmeisser. "Now, Clifford," she said, "we don't want any unpleasantness."

Flush lowered the gun. Peter swallowed and ran a finger around inside his collar. Flush was white with rage.

"I am tired of your horseplay," he said with cold fury. "This fiesta is to cease. In future, if you persist in flaunting our dead, I shall personally retaliate in kind. Do you understand me?"

Beecher elbowed his way into the room, holding the stiffened body of Bunny as if it were a spear. Hugo, recognizing his attacker, snarled and prepared to spring at him. Beecher noticed with pleasure the ugly bruise behind his ear. He dropped Bunny and snatched the cosh from his pocket. Flush gave him a backhand blow on the elbow with the Steyr. Beecher yelped and turned the raised cosh on to his master. The situation was saved by Mr. Beesum, who rose, tottered a few steps towards Bunny, then fell on his knees making an odd humming noise. Beecher's attention was distracted. Flush noticed the Rodent Officer for the first time.

"Who is this individual?" he demanded.

"He's the rat man," said Bertha faintly.

"Is he sufficiently intelligent to realize that he can blackmail us all indefinitely?"

"I'm afraid so. He's one of our main problems."

Flush looked thoughtfully at Mr. Beesum, who was on hands and knees, crawling around Bunny and moaning softly. "I will attend to him," he said shortly. "Beecher, gag this gentleman and remove him."

Mr. Beesum rose to his feet. His splintered spectacles hung drunkenly from one ear. One end of his mustache was tucked into his mouth. Regardless of the battery of automatics trained on him, he staggered across the room and struck Flush weakly in the chest.

"Rodent!" he squeaked. "Filthy dirty *rodent!*"

"Should I cosh 'im, Boss?" asked Beecher hopefully.

"Perisite!" panted Mr. Beesum. "Perisite end harbinger of death!" He hung round Flush's gun arm, breathing heavily. "Death end disaster!" he hissed. "You are a *ret*! I do not approve of homicide and *I hete rets!*"

Flush wrenched his arm free and hit him on the head with the Steyr. Mr. Beesum banged his chin on the sticky board, clapped a hand to his pointed skull and fell down.

Hugo had taken the Verey pistol from Rex and slipped a rocket into the breach. He stepped behind the Colonel.

"Drop that gun, Flush," he said. "Or I blow the Colonel all over the carpet!"

"Hugo!" said Bertha. "I forbid you to shoot that man."

"Rockets are extremely noisy," said Flush contemptuously. "You will merely summon the police. If you insist upon shooting him, kindly do so with a silenced gun."

Mr. Beesum, sitting on the floor, shook his head in a drunken manner, picked up a spindly chair, and threw it at Flush. Flush was caught off balance. He fell on one knee. The Steyr went off. It made little more noise than an exploding paper bag. A neat hole appeared in the ceiling and the overhead electric bulb fell in a fine shower of glass.

Beecher put an arm around Mr. Beesum's neck from behind and lifted him off the floor. The Rodent Officer fought feebly. His legs threshed. Flush stood up and straightened his collar. He took a threatening step towards Mr. Beesum, then thought better of it.

"Remove him!" he snarled at Beecher.

Beecher carried his captive towards the door by the neck, taking pleasure in half-strangling him.

"Ret!" choked Mr. Beesum. "Ret, ret, *ret*!"

"Release him, Beecher," said Flush suddenly.

Beecher tightened his hold on Mr. Beesum's throat. "'Sall right, Boss. I know 'ow. Bombardier Frisbee …"

"Release him!"

"But, Boss, that girl they found at Cooden … Bombardier Frisbee …"

"You're fired!" said Flush.

Beecher reluctantly put down Mr. Beesum. The little man adjusted his broken spectacles. He was a dirty shade of gray and he breathed in long, painful gasps.

Flush walked over to him. He bent and looked into the myopic eyes.

Mr. Beesum, nodding like a mandarin, indicated the other Asterisk members with quick, guillotine movements of his spectacles. "Them too! Rets!"

Flush tore his eyes from Mr. Beesum. "This man is not normal. I believe him to be a paranoiac."

"A what?"

"Paranoiac. One of the milder forms of schizophrenia."

"Cleptrep!" said Mr. Beesum angrily. "I em the last sane man." He reached out a twitching hand and took hold of Flush's lower lip.

Flush slapped the hand down. "So I am a rat?" he asked gently. Mr. Beesum nodded. "And my friends too, I think you said? What about Mr. Cann and Miss Cluj?"

"All rets," said Mr. Beesum. He delicately touched the lobe of Flush's ear. Then, before Flush could forestall him, he gave it a vicious flick with his thumb.

Flush seized his wrist and gave it a savage twist. "Murderer!" he said. "You have accounted for three!" Forgetting himself in the heat of the moment, he sounded genuinely shocked.

"Opposite!" said Mr. Beesum. "E and O E," he added, shooting a furtive glance at Bunny.

"E and oh, E?"

"Errors and Omissions Excepted," translated Mr. Beesum. "En expression much used in the profession." He jerked his head at Bunny. "Error."

"You killed him."

"Error."

"And the others?" breathed Fan.

Mr. Beesum turned to peer at her. He made a testy gesture with his bony hands. He seemed amazed by her stupidity. "Rets do not count," he said kindly.

"Three!" said Mrs. Barratt. "What a *pity* he's mad!"

CHAPTER 26

SOMEBODY in the room sighed. Flush stepped back and mopped his forehead with a silk handkerchief. Tom sat down on a photograph of Hugo lounging in a very small aeroplane. The glass broke and everybody jumped. Fan moved closer to Peter and took his hand.

"Silence!" shouted Mr. Beesum. "You are all under arrest!" He seized an armchair and dragged it into the center of the room. "The bench," he said, patting it.

"What's he up to now?" hissed Rex.

"*I* don't know," said Bertha.

"Contempt!" said Mr. Beesum over his shoulder. "Three days." He arranged three vases of flowers in a row on the table by the window. "The jury." He pulled a bookshelf away from the wall and placed it a few feet from the door. "The dock," he explained. Uninvited, he poured himself a stiff gin. "This will be quite en ordeal," he said. "I require a stimulant." He drank it, grimacing.

"Darling," said Fan to Peter in a despairing whisper, "what are all these people doing in our dear little house? They're *murderers*!"

Mr. Beesum sat down in the armchair in the center of the room. "*Quiet!*" he shouted. "The prisoner pleads not guilty on all three counts."

"Clifford," said Mrs. Barratt, "ought we to allow this exhibition?"

"Yes," said Flush, staring fascinated at Mr. Beesum. "Most interesting."

The Rodent Officer rose and began to pace up and down between his audience. He held the lapels of his coat and watched his feet. "Sir Alfred Beesum, K.C., Milord," he said, looking up briefly. "For the defense."

As he passed Fan, she cringed against Peter. The Rodent Officer looked at her and smiled broadly. It was the first time she had seen his teeth. Instead of six in front, he had only four.

"My client," he said deliberately, staring up at the bullet hole in the ceiling, "was a citizen of unsullied repute … until he was overcome by Nemesis. Then …" He paused dramatically and glared at the three vases of flowers.

"Darling?" murmured Fan.

"Be quiet," said Peter. "He's addressing the jury."

"… end then," said Mr. Beesum slowly, "his affianced, to whom he was deeply attached, fell into the clutches of a ret!" He resumed his pacing then came to a halt with his back to the wall. He lowered his head as if about to charge. *"On the twenty-eighth dey of June in the year nineteen thirty-seven, she was pushed to her death off a train outside Bournemouth by one Mr. Clifford Flush!"*

"Pure fabrication," said Flush. He glanced uneasily around at his fellow members. "A common symptom of paranoia."

The members said nothing. Their faces were expressionless.

"Fect," insisted Mr. Beesum. "Now! How does my client react to this scurvy ect? He is a prudent man end he wants to meke no snep decisions. He turns to history. He learns thet in Ancient Egypt, 1500 B.C.., one worshipped the Ket. He learns thet Zoroaster heted rets end considered their messecre a personal service. He notes thet Saint Gertrude protested against rets and ret fleas. He marks thet Apollo Smintheus sleys rets in their thousands. History! My client is supported by history. On the fifth of July of the year nineteen-thirty-seven, he has reached en irrevocable decision. Ledies end gentlemen, he hes decided, for better or worse, *to become a ket!*"

Fan giggled wildly.

Mr. Beesum did not appear to hear her. "For the next eleven years," he went on, drumming his fingers on the sticky board on his jacket, "my client studied rets of all types. He ettended the hearing of every notorious murder case in the London area. He was present et the trials

of Mrs. Berrett, Colonel Quincey, Bud Bond alias the Creaker, Benjamin Cenn, end meny others. All the equitted, he notices, are always
welcome et the establishment known es the Esterisk Club. He hes, in
fect, *discovered a nest*! Well, what now? He knows what Apollo
Smintheus would do end he determines to do likewise. Exactly one
week ago, he *ects*!"

Fan shuddered. She leaned against Peter and shut her eyes. As she
listened to the flat, staccato voice droning on, a series of horrid tab-
leaux reared. Mr. Beesum, inconspicuous, mild-eyed, almost invisible,
prowling in the dead of night round the Asterisk Club, an attaché-case
in his hand full of panic-stricken rats. Mr. Beesum, crouched in the
shadow of the creepers, posting rats through the letterbox and the larder
window, an excuse to call the next day and play pied piper. Mr. Beesum
snarling with rage in his frayed Burberry as Tom's stale, unholy presence drove away the rats one by one. Mr. Beesum brooding in a bed-
sitting room redolent of formaldehyde, surrounded by the corpses of
embalmed rats. Finally, most unnerving of all, Mr. Beesum stalking
around her own house while she slept, starting all over again, releasing
the rats, waiting under the monkey-puzzle tree to see whether they had
taken this time, fanatically planning an attack upon the Asterisk Club
from the flank ... She opened her eyes.

"On the third day," he was saying, "my client presents himself to
Mrs. Berko end offers his services es Rodent Officer. Fortune smiles!
Mrs. Berko mentions thet she hes a room to let. Better end better! He
immediately passes this information to the Esterisk Club, anonymously."
He nodded several times, defying them not to appreciate his acumen.
"On the first dey of his duties, a lodger errives. My client hurries to his
room – ostensibly to ley a sticky board – end is gratified to recognize
Benjamin Cenn, whose trial he hes ettended the dey before." He rubbed
his hands together. "Kismet!" he said, smacking his lips. "My client
returns to the kitchen end brews up his cocoa. He decides, regretfully,
egainst the use of arsenic. Being tasteless end odorless, it is easy to
edminister end it is a slow, painful death – but it tekes too long. The
patient is ept to complain in time for medical aid to reach him. No. My
client decides in favor of oxalic acid which has a slightly bitter teste
end is not so punishing but which produces prompt collapse."

He noticed that Mrs. Barratt was taking notes.

"Easily obtainable," he dictated. "Soluble in water, resembling Ep-
som salts. Industrially used to bleach straw hets. Entidote – a solution
of scrapings from eny whitewashed ceiling." He waited for Mrs. Barratt

to catch up. "Ret Cenn tekes one dram, ten grains. Result – positive. The following morning there is no sign of the body but a cupboard in the execution chamber is locked. Heigh ho! thinks my client, end goes about his business. He overhears Mrs. Berko meking arrangements to eccommodate Ret Cluj. *Double Kismet!* He buys enother thermos. It cost twenty-two end sixpence, but Apollo Smintheus spared no expense end nor does my client. He gives Ret Cluj forty-five grains."

Mrs. Barratt wrote busily. Then she looked up eagerly and Mr. Beesum inclined his head.

"The following dey," he went on, "Ret Cluj hes also disappeared. One of the ettics is locked end my client forms his conclusions. On this dey, he leys the poisoned bait for the furred enemy. It is, of course, several deys too early, but it will delay his campaign considerably end he needs time. He still hopes to come to grips with Ret Flush, his sovereign enemy." He looked over his spectacles at Flush and licked his lips.

"We come to the morning of the fourth dey. My client collects his dead. Two *norvegici*, four *fugivori*, one *mus musculus*. He is returning downstairs when he hears a sound from the room on the half-lending. Consternation! He epplies his ear to the keyhole. There is somebody in thet room! Who? Enother ret from the Esterisk Club? He opens the door quietly end looks in. Stupefaction! Thunderclep! Sitting et the dressing-teble is Ret Cluj!" He looked around, inviting his listeners to share his amazement. "She hes her beck to him. She is wearing the neglijay in which he hoped she hed died end a feather het. My client is aghast! Ret Cluj has declined the bait! She mey even suspect a trep. If so, she will alert the others. No time to lose! He hits her with the iron prong he uses for sewer work. He lights the bedside lemp end leys it beside the body. A simple dodge, but he hopes thet it will presuppose thet the execution hes been carried out the previous evening in his ebsence."

"So!" said Hugo quietly to Peter. "Carstairs fell for a crummy little trick like that! Well, well!"

"What about you, Batwing?" demanded Peter angrily.

"Don't tek on!" Mr. Beesum reproved him. "We all meke mistakes. Even my client hes done so! He hes not killed Ret Cluj for the second time, es he imagines – he hes brained this chep! A sorry blunder! Set a trep for the ret, *beng goes the ket!*"

He sighed deeply. He went behind the armchair which was his improvised bench and became the judge. "The jury will now retire to consider their verdict," he boomed.

He marched across the room to the three vases of flowers by the window. "I em now en usher," he explained in a stage whisper.

He carried the flowers ceremoniously to the door, opened it and placed the vases on the landing. Then, before any of his astounded audience could move, he leaped out of the room and slammed the door. The key turned in the lock with a click.

Almost instantaneously, there was a stutter of muffled explosions. A half-inch group of bullet holes in the door testified that the Asterisk Club was quick on the draw.

"Hold your fire!" shouted Flush.

He was across the room in a single bound. He stood back, took aim, and shot the lock off the door. He heard Mr. Beesum running across the hall below. The Colonel seized Flush by the shoulder, pushed him roughly out of the way. Flush was about to strike his Treasurer with the Steyr when he saw the man's expression. He fell back before the glaring eyes, and the Colonel darted downstairs.

Hugo sprang on to the balcony, cocking the Verey pistol. Mr. Beesum, with a shattering of plate glass, fell out of the hall window and ran across the courtyard below. Hugo, quite unable to contain himself, fired the Verey pistol. He missed. A red rocket bounced on the pavement and shot thirty feet into the air. The report echoed down the street.

Mr. Beesum bolted down Flood Walk, heading for the Embankment. He was bent close to the ground and running like the wind.

The Colonel burst from the hall window in hot pursuit. He raced across the courtyard and hurled himself into his Bugatti. The engine whined, belched, and broke into a full-blooded roar. The Colonel wrenched at the wheel and forced the car into a tight turn. The front mudguard smashed a paling outside the house where Ford Maddox Brown had once lived. A man put his head out of a window in the eaves and shouted.

As the Colonel flashed past, Hugo saw that he was smiling. His white mustache was flattened against his cheeks and his hair fluttered in the wind. With a screech of tires, he turned the corner after Mr. Beesum. Hugo heard the car clamoring down Cheyne Walk.

"What's 'appening?" called a woman on the far side of the road. "What's up over there?"

Hugo did not answer. He went inside and shut the window.

"What a noise!" said the woman. "People runnin' an' shoutin' an' a red light, bomb or somethin', come out o' the window!"

"Green one there was too!" said the man in the eaves. "Look at my fence! Just *look* at it! Talk about fireworks! Amount of din there was over there, anybody'd think there'd been a murder!"

CHAPTER 27

"MR. 'ILFORD?"

"Yes."

Peter took the telegram and slit it open. *Have located man with flat package*, it read. *He will not give it to me Sylvia.* It had been sent from Grimsby. Peter ground his teeth. He tipped the boy and tramped upstairs. Marleen was in the spare room on her hands and knees, disinfecting the carpet. She had evidently, as usual, not taken her dismissal seriously. There was a paper carrier beside her half-full of dead rats.

"Where's Mr. Beesum?" she called, pushing back her hair with her wrists.

Peter paused in the doorway. He felt oddly let down now that the only corpses in the house were those of *fugivori* and *norvegici*. "He won't be coming any more," he said.

"Why?" demanded Marleen. "He never finished! With me own eyes I saw an *alexandrinus* in the larder only 'smornin'."

"We're being lent a cat," said Peter. "The cat next door. He's apparently a great rat killer."

Marleen sat back on her heels. "Mr. Beesum never said good-bye to me even," she remarked gloomily.

"He didn't say good-bye to anybody."

Peter wandered across to the window and stared into the road. It was a nice morning. The plane trees were trembling in a soft breeze. Outside the Asterisk Club there was a smart black-painted removal truck. It had *Flush Inc., Bournemouth, Folkestone, and Bath* painted on the sides in a Gothic script. A young man in a dyed battle-dress was leaning against it, picking his teeth with a match. He stood up and spat out a splinter as Beecher and Squires between them carried a large wardrobe out of the Club. They heaved it into the truck and the young man in the battledress lashed a tarpaulin over it. Beecher looked up and saw Peter. He turned his back and behind it raised two fingers in the victory sign.

The telephone jangled in the hall, and Peter went down to answer it.

He went slowly, wondering why, now that all his problems were solved, he felt so depressed. It was a feeling that, as a small boy, he associated with the end of the holidays. Fan and Bertha, on the other hand, had recovered their spirits as soon as the corpses had been removed from the house. This morning they had slid back into their normal routine as if nothing had happened. He lifted the receiver and growled into the telephone.

"Good morning." It was Flush. "Your – er – guests are just leaving."

"The truck?"

"Yes. The young man in the battledress is one of my country members, a Bombardier Frisbee."

"I see. Um – how did the Colonel get on last night?"

"He had quite an alarming experience. His car apparently went into an uncontrollable skid and forced a man on the Embankment to leap into the river."

"How terrible," said Peter without conviction.

"Yes. The Colonel was obliged to dive in after him in a gallant attempt to save his life."

"This man couldn't swim?"

"Oh, yes! Quite well, I believe."

"So the Colonel succeeded?"

Flush coughed. "No," he said. "He failed – but only after a considerable struggle."

"Too bad." Peter cleared his throat. "Well. Good-bye, Mr. Flush, and thanks for everything."

"A pleasure, I assure you, my friend."

Peter rang off and went to the front door to watch his ex-lodgers leave. Beecher was standing in the road beside the truck, kicking at the tires. As it drove off, he suddenly hit the side of it as hard as he could and went back into the Club with his hands in his pockets.

*

"Give us a pint o' bitter, gorgeous," said Mr. Crick.

"You just wait, impatient!" said the barmaid. She stroked her hips and regarded Mr. Crick fondly.

"I'll take a large rum, madam," said the Colonel.

"I hear you had a ducking last night," said Hugo tentatively.

"Yes, sir. Slight chill today. Nothing like rum for a chill."

"Nothing. And – congratulations!"

"Pish, sir!" said the Colonel. "Handed in my resignation this morning," he added with satisfaction. "Bad type, that Flush! Would have allowed you to shoot me like a dog last night."

"Oh come!" said Hugo, at a loss.

"Pukka." The Colonel nodded sagely. He seemed to bear no animosity. "Bad blood will out. Great-grandfather hung for stealing sheep. Shocking business!" He took a crumpled aster out of his pocket and put it into his buttonhole. "Consented to be my wife," he remarked.

Hugo spilled his bitter. "Who?"

"Naomi. Good little memsahib, worth her weight. Going out to Singapore. Wogs, of course, but can't have everything."

My God! thought Hugo. He looked at the old man, stupefied. *Your number's up! You'll be her third!* The Colonel's baby-blue eyes met his. *Or will you? Will she be your third?*

"But you see," Rex was saying to Mr. Crick, "why monkey-*puzzle?*"

"Ho," said Mr. Crick. "You 'ave come to the right chap! Me uncle on me mother's side once climbed one o' them in 'is birthday suit. 'E won 'is bet all right, but the spikes goin' upward like they do, the puzzle was to get 'im *down!*" He roared with laughter, slapping the counter.

Rex was slightly shocked. "Out of this world," he said, and wandered away.

Fan and Bertha were sitting in a corner under an aspidistra.

"Really, my dear," said Bertha, "I'm determined to take a course in embalming. I'm fed up with my loom, formaldehyde's dirt cheap, and I'd like to rake in a few shekels. I've got a proposition to make to Peter."

"Like what?"

"Hugo and I are thinking of starting a small funeral parlor. I mean, now that we've had all this experience, it seems such a waste not to capitalize it somehow, doesn't it? And after that nightmare business, imagine what heaven it would be to do everything quite openly and above board! Look at this." She produced a small magazine from her pocket. It was the *Embalmer's Journal* and it had Chelsea Public Library stamped on the front of it in mauve ink.

Fan took the magazine. It fell open at the small advertisements. One of them was heavily ringed in red chalk. Peter wandered over with a tankard of bitter. He sat down and read the passage over Fan's shoulder. *Sale*, it said. *Upstairs, downstairs, along the narrow corridor – our patent flexible stretcher solves this awkward problem. Also raffia grave sets, tassels, robes, ruffles, angelskin shrouds much reduced. Nickel-plated chin rests, phantom equipages, a few horses still available. Apply Box 0848.*

"Now that's quite a coincidence," said Peter. He looked at Bertha. "Where do I come in?"

"We wondered whether you'd like to drive the phantoms and handle the publicity."

Peter's spirits unaccountably rose. "I might at that," he said. "Now that Sylvia's disrupted my business and I've bumped off Carstairs, I shall be wanting a few dees. What about Hugo?"

"He'll do the monumental masonry."

"What about me?" said Fan.

"You can do the *maquillages.*"

"Thanks."

"And look after the horse."

"What horse?"

"Black. They wear rubber shoes and the most wonderful plumes."

"Where do we get the planks for the coffins?"

"*Please,*" said Bertha. She looked pained. "You've got to learn the jargon. The *longboards* for the *wooden overcoats.*"

"Is that official?"

"Slang. You must know the slang or it gives the whole show away."

Fan and Peter exchanged glances.

"It all sounds rather – gay," said Fan.

Bertha smiled. "Haven't you noticed that undertakers always look quite indecently jolly?"

"We might be able to fix some sort of hookup with the Asterisk Club."

"*Really* Fan!" said Bertha, but she looked thoughtful.

Rex and Hugo came over. Rex stood fingering the aspidistra and Hugo sat down by Bertha.

"Well?" he said. "What do you think? Personally, I can't help feeling that there's a really solid future in death."

"That reminds me," said Bertha. "I suppose we'll have to find another lodger."

"No thank you," said Fan and Rex simultaneously. "I couldn't eat the last one."

The door opened cautiously and Squires crept in. He was carrying a small tin suitcase and wearing a hat several sizes too large for him. He looked around nervously. It was obvious that he had never before been in a public house and wanted to get out of it as quickly as possible before he was contaminated. He sidled over to the Colonel and touched his arm.

"The Master said you was to give me two weeks' wages," he whispered. "I'm leavin', I am. I don't fancy it there. I'm a *good* boy."

THE END

If you enjoyed *The Wooden Overcoat* (who wouldn't?), you'll be glad to know that the Rue Morgue Press will be publishing the other three books in this series: *Lion in the Cellar* (0-915230-89-5, $14.95, February 2006), *Murder Every Monday* (0-915230-91-7, $14.95, April 2006), and *Murder's Little Sister* (0-915230-93-3, $14.95, June 2006). Ask for them from the bookseller who sold you *The Wooden Overcoat*. For more information on The Rue Morgue Press turn to the following page.

About the Rue Morgue Press

Since 1997, the Rue Morgue Press has reprinted scores of traditional mysteries, the kind of books that were the hallmark of the Golden Age of detective fiction. Authors reprinted or to be reprinted by the Rue Morgue include Dorothy Bowers, Pamela Branch, Joanna Cannan, Glyn Carr, Torrey Chanslor, Clyde B. Clason, Joan Coggin, Manning Coles, Lucy Cores, Frances Crane, Norbert Davis, Elizabeth Dean, Constance & Gwenyth Little, Marlys Millhiser, James Norman, Stuart Palmer, Craig Rice, Kelley Roos, Charlotte Murray Russell, Maureen Sarsfield, and Juanita Sheridan.

To suggest titles or to receive a catalog of Rue Morgue Press books write P.O. Box 4119, Boulder, CO 80306, telephone 800-699-6214, or check out our website, www.ruemorguepress.com, which lists complete descriptions of all of our titles, along with lengthy biographies of our writers.